INFIDELITY

INFIDELITY

PAT TUCKER

URBAN BOOKS
www.urbanbooks.net

Urban Books
10 Brennan Pl.
Deer Park, NY 11729

ISBN 1-59983-013-2

First Printing: January 2007
10 9 8 7 6 5 4 3 2

Printed in the United States of America

The Reunion

When Persha Townsend strutted out of the ladies' room at Razzo's Cajun restaurant in southwest Houston, she abruptly stopped cold in her tracks. She froze momentarily at the sight of Clarke Hudson. It just absolutely could not be him, she had tried to convince herself.

Unable to move, she blinked a few times to ensure her eyes weren't completely mistaken. While her eyes may have been somewhat uncertain, her heart knew instantly. It was beating so quickly, she had to place a hand over her chest to try and calm *it* and herself.

It was definitely Clarke, all sexy and debonair, real and in the flesh. The man she once wanted to marry, bear his children, and do anything that just *might* keep him happy. Back then, Clarke's spectacular body was as close to perfection as any man could come, and from where she stood, nothing much had changed about it. Her hands were quite familiar with every nook and cranny of that body. All two hundred and fifteen pounds of well-defined muscles, carefully distributed over his six-two frame. He was like sexy dessert on a stick.

His hair was gone now, he was sporting a fierce bald style and it fit him so well. His pecan-colored skin glistened; it had always been so clear and silklike. When he walked, his slightly bowed legs still had that sexy swagger she remembered.

As he stepped closer, her heart thudded, beating just a bit irregular. For a moment, she wondered if he'd even recognize, let alone remember her. It had, after all, been at least ten years since they'd seen each other last and just like Clarke's, Persha's look had changed too.

Persha had allowed her hair to grow out of that bobbed style she wore back then. Now it hung in layers, just past her shoulders in a tight flip that her friends often tried to imitate. And she had finally shed those forty persistent pounds, bringing her down to a comfortable, but curvy one twenty-five.

Her caramel-colored skin boasted its own glow, after numerous chemical treatments and specialty mud-packed facials. And the trademark glasses were a thing of the past since she traded in her rims for the new LASIK surgery that was a complete success.

Whatever doubt Persha had about Clarke's memory quickly faded when a lovely smile crept across his pretty face.

"Naah-ahh." Clarke shook his head.

"Ahh-haa." Persha quickly returned his smile. She grinned so hard her cheeks tightened a bit, but she shook it off.

"Giiiirrrl!" He extended his muscular arms, but she didn't know if she should fall into them or wait to see if he'd pull her close.

She remembered spending what seemed like endless hours in his strong embrace. Back then there was not a day she'd considered a future without him. Oh, theirs was going to last the test of time for certain.

"Now if this ain't a small world. Persha Townsend! How long have you been here in H-town? And please tell me you're not just here visiting," he all but sang.

Clarke took her by the shoulders and gazed into her eyes, penetrating straight through to her soul. Persha thought she'd melt right there in her designer stilettos. Quite surely the sudden cream between her thighs was evidence of her definite demise.

"Damn, girl, a brotha couldn't handle losing you again." He shook his head to emphasize his words. After all this time even his slight touch still said so much.

"Aaaeey Clarke." She reluctantly escaped his embrace, smiling while hiding her astonishment. Even the scent of his cologne was invigorating.

"Damn, shorty! Let me take a good look at you! Turn around," he said, all but tossing her body into a slow spin. That was the nickname he had for her back then. Only Clarke could make the description sound so sexy.

"Yup! It's all still there! You look real good girl, and after all these years too. So whassup?" Clarke's eyes smiled as he gazed at her.

He crossed his muscular arms over his well-defined chest and stood back a few feet, still shaking his head in disbelief. "Been taking care of yourself, I see." He chuckled.

"You're not looking too bad yourself." She smiled.

Leaning against the wall, she felt her shoulders relax as they eased into a comfortable conversation about the past; their past.

"After all these doggone years, I can't believe it's you!" The words escaped from his mouth as her eyes softened.

Persha struggled to keep her breathing steady, as lustful memories flashed through her mind. Oh, she remembered those sizzling steamy nights like only minutes instead of hundreds of days and weeks had passed. She had been with other men since Clarke, quite a few, but none had touched her, reached her on the level he had.

"What ever happened with us?" Clarke asked using a tone just above a whisper, like he used to do back in the day.

"Shoot girl! We had something real, real good back then."

Persha shook her head, agreeing with his skewed version of their history. She reminisced about the days when she foolishly believed they'd never be apart. Still young at heart in those days, she never thought she could love another man. No, not the way she loved and worshipped Clarke Hudson.

Trying to change the subject she quickly asked, "So what do you do here in H-town?"

Persha still couldn't believe she was standing there talking to the one and only Clarke Hudson. He was still the man who after so many years was able to make her heart turn to putty, and her panties wet.

Clarke reached into the pocket of his designer slacks, which hung perfectly off his body and pulled out a gold-plated business card-holder. She still liked the way he carried it, his style, and everything about him. Nothing had changed; it was all just updated to keep up with the times and trends.

"I'm with the ad agency here in town," he said, extending the card to her. "You gotta stay in touch girl," he teased, his voice low and inviting.

Persha felt her panties go from damp to drenched, as she took the card and quickly glanced down at it. Her eyes glazed over his VP title next to his glossy picture on the card. She held it with care and eased it into her own pocket.

"So let me guess, a fine brotha like you can't still be single, right?" she hoped, cocking her head to the side as she gazed at him longingly.

"S'cuse me?" a voice laced with attitude said.

Persha snapped out of her trance quickly.

Clarke turned and stepped aside. He smiled. "Oh, Persha, this is Menesha." The smile quickly faded from Persha's face and she straightened her body where she stood. She didn't want to hear what she was sure was coming next.

"Is this what's keeping you from our little party? Your food? It's gettin' cold you know." Menesha's icy gaze ran over Persha from head to toe, then back up again.

"Oh, sorry girl, I just ran into an old college friend and we started shooting the breeze," Clarke said. Menesha looked at Persha again and offered what seemed like a forced smile. Persha contemplated the nature of Clarke and Menesha's relationship; she couldn't tell for sure if this was the kind of jealousy she suspected.

"Emph, hi." Her thin lips curled.

"I'm sorry, it's my fault, we just started going on and on and soon we were talking about old times, old friends and that kind of stuff." Persha smiled, but regretted it when the gesture went unnoticed and wasn't returned.

"Well, you'd better get back before Kelsa comes back." She touched Clarke's shoulder and squeezed by them both, but not before looking at Persha one last time.

"It was good seeing you, girl. You take care of yourself." Clarke turned. "That's my wife's friend, we're catching a bite before our movie starts over at Loews. I'd better get back."

Just as easily as he had walked back into her life, he was gone again. But this time she vowed to not allow ten years, much less a week even to slip between them.

Back at her table Persha pulled a chair out and slouched into her seat.

"Damn, girl, we thought you fell in or something," her friend Cricket said. Cricket was a slender, masculine woman with a pretty face that was framed by a short curly Afro. She had slim features and a caramel complexion.

"I told Kori to go look after you, but our food got here, and well, you understand." Cricket looked at Kori and they started chuckling. Kori was short with skin the color of cornbread, and sandy-brown hair she wore in a ponytail. She was small and petite, but her mouth made her seem so much bigger. The three had been friends since meeting back in college. They'd even migrated south together shortly after graduation.

Persha pulled her chair up to the table.

"Glad I didn't *really* fall in. I'd drown waiting on you two heifers to rescue me!"

Kori popped another shrimp into her mouth. "What took so long anyway?" she asked.

"You'll never guess who I just bumped into!" Persha squealed with excitement.

"Who?" Cricket asked.

"She said guess, silly!" Kori quickly looked around the restaurant, then back at Persha when no one familiar caught her eye.

"Clarke Hudson!" Persha tried to gauge her friends' reaction.

Persha could tell from the look on Cricket's face that she was not the least bit amused. She often wore her no-nonsense face like armor, hard, cold, and uninviting. At the mere sound of Clarke's name, Cricket's eyes widened in alarm, and she twisted up her mouth.

"Not that low-down sewer lurking hoodrat who left you behind in Vegas!" She snickered. "Ooouch!" Cricket screamed, nearly in the same breath. "Why did you kick me, Kori?"

"Can you stop talking about folks for just a hot minute? You got your nerves talking about somebody else's man. You can't even hang on to one."

"Look you two, it's not that serious, I just ran into the man. I didn't say we were hooking up or anything like that. I just bumped into him; dang, y'all need to chill out!"

"Yeah, but I know how much he meant to you. And what's he doing here anyway?" Cricket asked, angling her head to the side.

"Girl, he lives here! He's vice president at an advertising agency!" Persha could hardly contain her enthusiasm.

"A what?" Cricket frowned. "Girl please, ain't nobody in their right mind letting him be in charge of anything, and you know I'm right," she said. "Hmmm, vice president my foot."

"I know, I know how you feel about him, Cricket, but look at his card. He always was real smart," Persha said, digging the card out of her pocket, and directing her attention back to Cricket.

"Hmm, this don't mean a thing, he could've made these on his home computer." Cricket inspected the card closely. "Besides how'd a street thug like him get a real J-O-B anyway? Much less a vice president title? I ain't buying it, we all know he was only in school 'cause he could run and dribble a ball at the same time."

Persha and Kori looked at her, rolled their eyes, then continued talking.

"So you bump into the old love of your life, the one that got away, you guys chat it up for a few minutes then walk away just like that? No lunch, dinner, happy hour, or even breakfast plans?" Kori winked.

"I was about to drop a hint, but just before I could get the words out, his *wife's* girlfriend walked up!"

Kori dropped her fork, and Cricket stopped before taking another bite. With her mouth hung open her carefully arched brows shot up.

"Yup! Good 'ole Clarke Hudson is married. I still can't believe it myself," Persha admitted in a hushed whisper. She started picking at her own food, while her friends silently watched her every move.

It was Kori who spoke first. "Gurl phuleeze, Clarke Hudson married? The Clarke Hudson we all know? Hmmm." She sucked her teeth. "Well, we all know that wife, whoever she is, is only a substitute for the real thing. I ain't even trying to believe he has a wife!"

"Well, where is he? Where are they sitting? Were they leaving when you saw him?" Cricket asked, immediately searching the busy restaurant with her eyes.

"Don't look now, but I think they're out on the patio." As soon as Persha said it, both heads quickly turned toward the patio.

"I said don't look," Persha screamed.

"Girl, I have got to see what this wife of his looks like. Was her friend nice? What did she say to you?" Kori asked, still eyeing the patio. "Shoot, what did *she* look like?"

"Not only was she *not* nice, but girlfriend wasn't too happy to find me holding up dinner by talking to her friend's hubby."

"Why didn't you tell her, you've already been there and done that?" Kori turned her attention back to her food, then looked up. "Yeah, like Toni Braxton said, he wasn't man enough for you, right?" Kori sang before filling her mouth.

Persha laughed and nodded, agreeing, but deep inside she knew the truth. And even after all these years, when it came to Clarke Hudson, unfortunately, her love for him was still all too painfully real to deny.

The Thrill Is Gone

"I just can't baby, I'm so sorry, but you know how I feel about doing *that*," Kelsa, Clarke's wife said in a whiny voice, the frown still plastered on her face.

He was fuming as he sat staring down at her pathetic ass. She was kneeling down in front of his open legs, his dick was rock hard and he needed release.

"So lemme get this straight, you don't mind when I do it to you, but you can't hook a brotha back up right?" He shrugged, disgusted and frustrated.

"Clarke, now, you know I try my best to keep you happy and satisfied. But you asking me to do something that I'm very uncomfortable with. You know I love you, but I just can't do it baby, I can't." Kelsa fell back onto her butt. She pulled her knees up to her chest and wrapped her arms around them.

"'Sides it's not like I ever ask you to go down on me, you do that because you want to." She was no longer looking at her husband. It was as if she couldn't face him.

"So you trynta' tell me that you don't like it when I do it?" Clarke felt himself getting heated. He looked at his wife. She was about five-four with a mocha complexion and light eyes, but at this very moment she was nothing more than a child who didn't want to step up to her womanly duties. And he didn't have time to play her childish game.

"That isn't even what I'm saying, let's just stop talking about it, 'cause I feel like you're just gonna start twisting my words around," she sobbed.

"I just don't understand why a man can't even get his dick sucked at home by his own fucking wife!" Clarke snapped.

He heard her sniffling but he didn't care, he was sick and tired of her shit. She wanted to sit back and reap all of the benefits of him pleasing her, but when it came down to what he wanted, she wanted to sit up there acting like a child. Clarke looked down at his fading erection. He thought about how things had gotten so heated between them in the first place.

Kelsa had walked into the bathroom just as he stepped out of the shower. One sight of him naked caused her to rush him. So he moved it into their bedroom, quickly undressing her and laying her on top of their bed.

"Oh, yes baby," she had squealed.

Clarke spread her legs and sucked her dry until she hollered. Then instead of entering her, he figured he'd try to get back some of what he had given. And Kelsa was doing pretty good at first. She started kissing his nipples, and playing with his chest. When he sat upright and she eased herself between his legs, he actually got excited, he thought she was finally going to do it. Nothing felt better to Clarke than a great blow job. Hell, any kind of blow job really.

When Kelsa started kissing his belly button and palming his balls he just knew he had finally broken her down. For years he had been trying to convince his wife that there was nothing wrong with sucking her man off, but she refused to give in. She was always talking about how nasty *it* was. At times he wanted to say he married her thinking he had gotten himself a nasty girl, shit, there was nothing wrong with being nasty when you're married, he surmised.

Things were going good at first. Kelsa started kissing his thighs, playfully biting at them and squeezing his balls with a bit of force, just the way he liked it. The shit had him all worked up and he was ready to get in her mouth. But the more he moaned and squealed with delight, the more she kissed near or around his crotch.

Finally Clarke put his hands on top of her head and tried to guide her closer to the target, but Kelsa still managed to ease away.

He let her kiss some more, one time she even allowed his member to rub against her cheek, but that's as far as she would go.

"Come on baby, just kiss it," he encouraged. "You can at least lick it a little for me."

She gazed up at him and shook her head, saying no. Soon she eased back down onto the floor and away from him completely.

"Clarke!" Kelsa snapped.

He looked at her. "Yeah?"

"So what's it gonna be? I asked you a question," she huffed.

"Oh, my bad, my mind was somewhere else, whassup?"

"I asked if you don't want to have sex with me now just because I won't, you know, go down on you."

"Nah, nah, it ain't even like that, here, why don't you come up here, I'm not into making you do anything you really don't want to do. If you don't like giving head you ain't gonna be any good at it anyway."

Kelsa wasted no time crawling back onto the bed.

When Clarke saw her lie on her back and spread her legs, he nearly wanted to bolt from the room. Their lovemaking had become so mundane. It was like the missionary position was all she knew.

First came the kissing, then sucking nipples a few times, then he'd stroke her to see if she was wet and he'd enter her. Kelsa usually just laid there, she didn't want to let him do it from the side, didn't want him to take her from behind and she sure wasn't about to ride. He was fed up, but he'd fuck her and get it over with. At least she laid there and allowed him to bust a nut.

Clarke crawled on top of his wife, entered her, closed his eyes and immediately started thinking about Persha. Because he knew, *she'd* do it all, and she'd like it too, or at least she used to. One thing he knew for sure was, he'd have to find out as soon as possible.

The Seduction

When Persha had called Clarke saying she had just been thinking about him, he suggested they meet up. It had been two days since their chance encounter at the restaurant, and although her brain knew better, her heart wouldn't allow her to pass up an opportunity to see him alone and in the privacy of her own home.

When she told herself it would be a great chance to "catch up" she shook the thought from her mind. She had stopped lying to herself years ago, she knew for sure she wanted to do a whole lot more than just catch up with Clarke. But, she did decide, she wouldn't make the first move. If and when he did, she wouldn't turn him away, but she wouldn't strike first.

The moment Clarke knocked on the door, Persha couldn't differentiate between the knock and the sound of her pounding heart. She was more than just a little excited about seeing him; although thoughts of him being married stayed on her mind, it would take more than a ring to keep her away. She justified her forbidden lust for this sexy married man by telling herself he had been hers to begin with.

Persha pulled the door open and Clarke strolled in. He was carrying a vase of flowers that he put on a table in the foyer. He wore a pair of chocolate-colored slacks and a fitted bronze-colored silk shirt. She stood still at the door, leaning against it as he walked into her living room.

"And thanks for the flowers, they're lovely," she managed.

"This is what's lovely," he said looking around. "It's nice, shorty, real nice," he added.

Persha watched him closely as he looked around her place. Just when she thought she should offer up a tour of the place, he was in her face. The way she was pinned up against the door and he was moving in, she knew they were headed to a point of no return. But she didn't care.

"Um." Persha licked her glossy lips. She silently kicked herself for not changing into a matching bra and panty set, the good stuff she wore when she knew she'd be getting busy.

"I'm so glad you like it," she cooed.

Their eyes met, and he stood so close and near, she could feel his warm mint-laced breath bearing down on her face. After all these years, she still enjoyed having him close.

"I like everything I'm seeing in here," he said. Clarke moved a step closer, taking up what little room separated them.

Before she could blink again, his lips were on top of hers. His tongue was strong, it shoved its way into her mouth, flickering along her gums and pushing toward her throat. Persha kept up, struggling to suckle his with hers. It didn't take long for the panting to start. She clawed at his bald head, rubbing it vigorously.

He pulled back, took her face into his hands and planted wet kisses all over her cheeks, nose, and lips.

As this was going on, Persha started tugging at his shirt. She managed to pull it out of his slacks, and ran her hands up and down his moist, bare chest. She inhaled his scent, filling her lungs with as much of his aroma as she could stand.

"Emmmm," she moaned.

Clarke kissed behind her ear, and sucked her earlobe. It turned her on immensely. By now his hands had wandered beneath her blouse, and into her bra. When he pulled at the lace cup and squeezed her nipple between his forefinger and thumb, the sensation brought water to her eyes, but still she liked it.

"I want, no, I need to taste you, to have you in my mouth, inside me," she cried.

Clarke ran his fingers through her hair and grabbed a fistful of it. He pulled her face into his and kissed her again, this time harder than before. When they pulled apart again, they were both struggling for air. Clarke took her by the shoulders and moved her away from the door. With his body now leaning against it, he pulled the shirt over his head.

His chest, with its magnificent muscles and ripples, was so pretty, and even better than before, she decided. Using her tongue, Persha slopped from his nipple, down the center to his belly button, then back up again.

"Take what you want, shorty . . . it's all here waiting for you," he said.

Persha dropped to her knees and used trembling fingers to unbuckle his belt. She fumbled at first, but finally gripped the leather strap and tugged at it to loosen the clasp. If he was just as eager, he masked it better.

"Hurry," he breathed.

Her eyes glanced up briefly, then she mumbled, "I am." Before she returned to his belt, she French-kissed the side of his bare hip where love handles would normally be on a thirty-four-year-old man.

Persha savored the salty taste of his skin. He yelped as she seductively worked his flesh with her tongue. With the belt undone, she glanced up again and smiled.

The room was quiet, so much so that every breath they took made sounds that filled the room. Their breathing had calmed a bit, but there was no denying the building passion that had erupted the moment Clarke stepped into the room. When his pants fell to the floor, his erection stood stiff and long.

She smiled as she greeted her old friend with a wet and wanting mouth.

"Aaah. Sssssssss," Clarke moaned.

He felt bigger than she remembered. Persha tried to deep throat him, but settled on sucking after she had to fight the desire to gag. She wanted to be better than his wife. She sucked, then raked along his shaft with her teeth.

Clarke's eyes rolled back up into his head as he clutched Persha's head to hold her in place. When she felt his body quiver she suckled the head even more and pulled herself back.

"Damn girl, that was tight," Clarke said, still struggling to breathe steady.

When Persha stood, he reached into his pocket and pulled a black-and-gold wrapper from his pocket. He used his teeth to rip the packet open, strapped the condom on and pulled up her skirt.

Persha looked down at his covered erection and smiled.

He guided her body toward the nearby sofa. He tore off her panties, bent her over the back of the couch, and rammed himself into her.

"Oooh, Clarke, Oh God, Clarke," she cried.

"Yes, Persha?" He worked his hips.

"Welcome home baby," she huffed as she looked back over her shoulder, smiled and bucked, shoving her hips to meet his thrust. "Wwel-come home."

"I don't know why I ever left," he said, as he used his thigh to spread her legs ever farther apart. Clarke dipped his legs ever so slightly and held onto her by the waist. He rotated his hips, licked her back, and moved at a wild pace.

She matched his every move. She loved him taking her from behind. His strokes were long and strong; she enjoyed his passion. She struggled to squeeze her walls around him.

Nearly an hour later, they collapsed next to each other on the floor. With her chest heaving up and down and his moving just as much, they gazed into each other's eyes.

"Damn, that shit was right on time, shorty. I see you ain't lost a damn thing over the years, huh?"

"Whew! I could say the same to you." She smiled. "You want something to drink?"

"Yup, then I wanna eat something, and I ain't talking about no food either," he said, grinning.

Persha stumbled to her feet, kicked the torn panty over to the side and made her way to the kitchen. She knew then she was hooked.

All over again.

Three days later at work, when she should've been focusing on writing out new policies, Persha was rereading the lovely e-mail Clarke had sent hours prior. It was a poem titled "My Someone Who."

My needs are small my wants are few,
All I need is someone who . . .

Someone who I can call in the wee hours of the night,
Someone who takes me for me whether I'm wrong or right . . .
Someone who can stand the laughter, despite the rain . . .
Someone who knows the heart, and yet the pain,
Someone who listens and protects my secrets,
Someone who knows imperfect love and still wants to keep it . . .
Someone who can make me laugh when I want to cry,
Someone who cares whether I live or die . . .
Someone who will take my faults and not cast blame,
Someone who will still love me all the same . . .
Someone who will catch my tears before they fall,
Someone who will answer each and every call . . .
All of these things, and so many more I have found in you . . .
My thoughtful someone who, I love you, you know I do.

She had nearly memorized the poem by the time he called. It warmed her heart to know the years had done little to diminish what they had shared in the past. When she saw his number appear on the caller ID, her heart nearly stopped.

"Hello?"

"Persha?"

"Yes baby, it's me," she whispered, glancing up at her coworkers.

Persha tried not to show off the smile that had spread from ear to ear across her face, but she couldn't help but feel giddy each time she spoke to Clarke.

"You wanna hook up later?"

"What time?" Persha asked, now fidgeting with the telephone cord.

"I think six should be good, let's meet at Schmitz and McCormick, off Post Oak," he said.

"I'll be there," she sang.

Hours before quitting time, Persha couldn't keep her eyes off the clock. She knew the hands of time were only moving slowly because she was going to meet her man after work. Theirs was turning into quite the fairy-tale romance. Years ago, she would've given her right arm and her firstborn for this type of relationship with him.

Persha was so thrilled to be in this situation. Despite his wife at home, Clarke was still able to make her feel like the one and only woman in his life.

The Secret Taboo

Clarke rolled off of Persha's moist body exhausted and fulfilled. He glanced over at her with a look of sheer satisfaction plastered across his face. She was still catching her breath. Her legs trembled as she adjusted herself and snuggled her body up next to his.

"Damn, shorty, you just get better and better," he confirmed.

She thought the words, but didn't dare ask them, although she wanted to desperately. *Better than her?* His compliment warmed her heart. She had wanted to drain him, to give him unspeakable pleasures and unparalleled bliss. Persha lifted her body up on one elbow and gazed down at him longingly.

"Are you happy?" she asked.

"Am I? Shorty, a brotha ain't had nobody break it off like that in a long-ass while. Girl, you just too much, too damn much." He sighed.

She was beaming on the insides, but struggled to maintain a sense of modesty. She intended to give him the best pussy for as long as he'd take it, and she hoped that would be for a very long time.

"Well, I've enjoyed the time we've spent together, and I'm not just talking about all the splendid sex, either."

"What?" Clarke faked concern. "You trynta say my sex ain't the bomb-diggity?" he joked.

Persha shook her head vigorously. "No, no, no, Mr. Hudson, that's not what I'm saying at all. Perish the thought!" She giggled.

"Hmmm, I didn't think so, 'cause a brotha would have to wake Mandingo back up again," he teased.

Persha's eyebrows shot up. "Is that a threat? I mean are you willing to back that up?"

Before she realized what was happening, he took her by the back of the head and lowered her down to his pelvic area. Persha didn't hesitate to open her mouth and revive his limp member.

The minute she felt him stiffen between her lips, she straddled him quickly and wiggled her hips to help offer him a better fit. He grabbed her hips, guiding her body just right.

"Emmmm, Clll-arke," she moaned. Persha reached up and rubbed her own breasts.

"Yes, Persha."

She rocked her hips, then palmed his chest, raking her fingers along its ridges. Persha squeezed her eyes shut and savored the sensation of him delving deep within the walls of her womb.

"Damn girl, I'm about to—"

Persha rocked her body even harder. She leaned forward, shoving her bare breasts into his face. He responded by palming, then squeezing them together.

"Oh, yes Clarke, that's it baby, that's exactly what I like," she cooed.

"I know, shorty, I know. Remember, I know all about you . . . this is still my pussy, baby," he responded before suckling both nipples at the same time.

Round two ended in an eruption of physical euphoria for them both. As she struggled to catch her breath, her mind tossed around his last words before she snuggled up next to his sweaty body and closed her eyes.

Remember, I know all about you . . . this is still my pussy, baby.

You damn straight it is. She smiled as his words rang out in her head, and she tried to get some rest.

The Aftermath: Persha

Two weeks after the restaurant reunion, Clarke was knocking at Persha's front door. With flowers in hand, he glanced around the darkened parking lot, and rang the doorbell when she didn't answer right away.

"Aeey Boo," he greeted, the moment she opened the door.

She smiled at the fact that he brought flowers every time he visited.

Thirty minutes after he arrived, Clarke sat across from Persha to enjoy dinner by candlelight. She had prepared T-bone steaks smothered in wild mushrooms and red onions, over rice pilaf and steamed vegetables. They were drinking Riunite with the meal.

"Damn, a woman who can handle her business in the bedroom and the kitchen," he said before stuffing his mouth with the last of his steak.

"I'm so glad you're enjoying dinner," she said.

Music played softly through the surround sound

system. Persha had carefully selected a series of instrumental jazz pieces so that words wouldn't interrupt their conversation. With rose petals scattered all over the room, a sweet lingering scent filled the air.

Persha had been a little concerned about an odor that seemed to linger all over the house. She was praying he didn't notice it. If he did, she couldn't tell, the way he was constantly smiling at her over dinner.

"Shorty, what ever happened to us? We used to be so good together, you remember?" he asked.

She remembered all right, remembered everything about the devastating heartache she struggled with for months when he finally walked out for good. They were students at UNLV, the University of Nevada Las Vegas back then. Clarke was a runnin' Rebel.

He had always told her how his father Clarke Sr. was such a die-hard Rebel fan. He often talked about how they were there for the most memorable day in sports at the Sam Boyd Stadium on campus.

Persha still couldn't forget the sheer delight in his eyes when he described being there when former Los Angeles Lakers superstar Kareem Abdul-Jabbar passed Wilt Chamberlain as leading scorer in the NBA.

He told her how on that April day in 1984 he knew at the age of thirteen he wanted nothing more than to become a Rebel, because he'd never in his life seen his father so excited. Clarke did go on to bring screaming fans and his father to their feet at that very stadium. Everyone thought that Clarke would get drafted and that the two of them would get married.

But things didn't work out that way. After two years of failing to make an NBA team, coupled with his frustrations over constant arguments with his father, Clarke dropped out of school, went overseas, and left Persha heartbroken and alone. Back then Clarke made it clear that her tagging along was not an option. But that was the past, long, long ago, she told herself, shaking off the memories.

It was close to midnight and they had moved to the couch, sipping wine and talking about their current lives. Persha was all too aware of the time, but she didn't want to bring it up.

She wondered why his cell phone or pager hadn't gone off throughout the night. Quite surely his wife had to be worried about his whereabouts. If he were *her* husband, she'd be with him, or at least know where to find him, she thought. But just like while they were on their other dates, nothing ever rang or vibrated, and she wasn't about to complain. So they continued their evening without interruption.

The next day, Persha was sluggish and slow. When she arrived at Kelly's restaurant off Broadway to meet Cricket and Kori for their usual bimonthly Saturday morning breakfast, they noticed her lethargic behavior right away.

"Y'all order yet?" she grumbled.

"Un-huh," Kori said, eyeing Persha suspiciously. Cricket just sipped her juice and glanced at her watch.

Pulling her chair closer to the table, "I know I'm late," Persha said as she released a yawn she couldn't suppress. "My mother called and insisted we prayed before I headed out this morning. She wouldn't let me off the phone until I repeated some verse her pastor said in church last week." She reached for the menu, muffling another yawn.

"Well," Cricket looked at her. "What was it?"

"What was what?" Persha looked up from the menu.

"The verse, the one you had to recite?"

"Oh, what's to come is better than what has been when the Lord is the captain of your destiny."

"Hmm," Cricket said. "Okay, but what's the Saturday-morning sermon got to do with you being all worn out? You all didn't do *that* much praying," she persisted.

"Thought you were calling it an early night. Isn't that why you couldn't meet us at Cabos for drinks?" Kori asked, her voice laced with sarcasm.

Persha struggled with another yawn. She moved the menu in front of her face, but Kori quickly snatched it down.

"Okay, who is he?" Kori said as she started giggling. It didn't take long for the three of them to start carrying on like schoolgirls until the waitress interrupted them.

After the waitress walked away with Persha's order, Kori leaned forward.

"Okay, dish the dirt, girlfriend, and don't you dare leave a single thing out. I want all of the juicy dirty details," Kori insisted.

By now, Persha had Cricket's attention too. Knowing there was no way she'd get away without telling her friends something, she braced herself and started.

"Well, remember a while back when we were at Razoo's and I ran into Clarke? You guys asked why we didn't make plans to hook up?"

The skeptical look on Cricket's face slowed the story, but Persha knew there was no turning back.

"Yeah?" Kori asked eagerly.

"Well, keep in mind he did give me his business card, and—uh, I was bored one day, so—um I called him, and well—um, one thing sort of led to another, and—"

The waitress came back with two Texas-sized plates. She gracefully eased them onto the table and looked at Persha.

"Yours will be here in a few minutes, 'kay?" she stated as she walked away.

Persha looked on as steam rose from Kori and Cricket's

plates. "Ummm, sure smells good," she said as the two dug in.

After swallowing her first bite, Kori looked up at Persha and said, "Okay, bring it!"

"O-kaay, well, um—I agreed to cook dinner and he came over last night."

"Alone?" Cricket pressed.

"Of course alone," Persha snapped.

"What's dinner got to do with you being late meeting us and tired this morning. Looks like you could hardly keep your eyes open," Cricket retorted.

"Unless dinner turned into breakfast." Kori grinned.

"Let's just say at about three in the morning, I had to all but push him out the door."

"OHMIGOD! What about his wife?" Cricket asked, wearing a worried look all over her face.

Persha shrugged and nodded toward the waitress, who was finally bringing her plate. Once the waitress left, Cricket leaned closer to the center of the table.

"What about Clarke's wife?" Cricket whispered.

"Oh, girl, he says things aren't going too good at home. Besides, every time we're together, she never calls or pages him. Most times we hang out for hours." Persha shrugged one shoulder and turned to her food.

Kori stopped chewing and Cricket placed her fork down on the plate. "Every time?" they asked in unison.

Realizing her slip way too late, Persha rolled her eyes and sucked her teeth.

"I can't believe you've been holding out on us," Kori stated as she started giggling again. But Cricket didn't crack a smile or utter a word. She looked at Persha and started shaking her head.

"See, that's why I didn't tell y'all I was kicking it with Clarke again. I don't need you judging me," Persha said, snatching her food off the fork with her teeth like she had an attitude.

"Ain't nobody judging you, Persha. It's just you've been down that road, why put yourself through his crap *again?* It's like falling into a ditch, finally struggling to pull yourself out, only to walk over there and deliberately fall right back in again," Cricket said, snickering. "Nothing good can come from such a fall, especially the second time around."

"Oh, stop being so damn melodramatic, Cricket," Kori hissed. "I want to hear all the juicy little details." She started squirming in her chair. "Gurrl, how long y'all been kickin' it with each other again?" Persha closed her eyes. "Nuh-uh, don't even try to get all emotional on us now. You might as well spill it," Kori insisted. "The cat is out, bay-bee, so start dishing, girlfriend!"

"Talking about what? He's a married man!" Cricket snapped. "What would your mother say? You know better, Persha."

Persha slowly looked up and released her next words with a heavy breath. "You didn't even have to go there, Cricket."

Paula, Persha's Bible-quoting holier-than-thou mother was the very last person she wanted to think about. She didn't want to think about what Paula would really say.

"Besides, you just don't understand," Persha softly insisted.

"Don't understand? Huh, let me guess: Clarke is just some downtrodden husband, stuck in a lousy marriage and life would be so much better if only she'd agree to a divorce. Then he'd be all yours, right?" Cricket said sarcastically.

"Awwh, Cricket, you always hating," Kori said. "So he's married. If he says he ain't happy that's not Persha's fault. Girlfriend shouldn't be blamed because *his* wife didn't learn how to keep her man at home. And Persha's mama ain't got nothing to do with this!"

Persha didn't want to talk about it anymore, but she knew Kori was just getting started. She knew this would happen once her secret got out, that's why she wanted to avoid telling them for as long as possible. She and Clarke had been seeing each other on the down low ever since that chance encounter.

"I'm not some little dumb mistress who's being told to give it more time," Persha said in her defense. "Clarke and I go way back and I know him better than any woman ever could. I know he's not happy with her, and I know how to make him happy. Besides, like he said, we were so good together."

"*Were,* Persha? Were, as in past tense? I mean where's this going? What's gonna happen with you two?" Cricket said.

"Well, if you really must know, he really is going to leave Kelsa, and eventually we're gonna get a place together and go from there," Persha said with authority.

"Work it, gurl!" Kori said as she snapped her fingers a few times and reached over to give Persha a high five.

Cricket cocked her head to the side and looked at Persha through narrowed eyes. "Didn't you learn anything from what you went through with him before? Why put yourself through something like that again?" she reasoned.

"It's gonna be different this time around. I have a strong feeling. Since we've had this time apart I think we'll actually be better for each other now. Sometimes it takes someone else for two people to realize how much they really mean to each other," Persha insisted. She had already decided she was going to keep seeing Clarke, and nothing would change that.

"And, gurl, he has always looked so damn delicious!" Kori said, licking her lips for effect. "You bet' not let him get away again," she warned.

But Cricket took a deep breath and with a pained expression on her face said, "I don't want to see him hurt you again. Know when something's no good for you and know when to walk away and stay away." She shook her head and added, "Persha, how could you possibly forgive and forget? Don't you remember? Loving that dog nearly destroyed you."

Persha took in her friend's words. Back then, it was safe to say that Clarke was a dog who had trampled on her like a frightened little kitty. But now she was grown, and even more so at the age of twenty-nine ready to prove for sure that every cat has nine lives.

Clarke

Turning over for the third time, Clarke struggled to shield his eyes against the sun's penetrating rays. He had stopped hitting the snooze button a good twenty minutes ago and knew he'd be late, but his job came with some perks.

On Fridays he had the option of not going to the office at all if he really didn't want to, but he'd already decided to go in for a few hours. Afterward he'd head out to his weekend sleepover.

His bag was already packed for his getaway with his lovely companion. And both were excited about spending two entire nights together. It had been years since they were able to be alone for days with no one else around.

Clarke never really considered himself a ladies' man. In fact, he remembered the days when girls wouldn't give him a second look, much less thought. That was before he crafted his skills on the basketball court.

Back then he witnessed how smooth his father was with the ladies, but considered himself the complete opposite. After his mother passed away and he was alone with his old man, they never wanted for anything.

Most of the women in the working-class neighborhood he grew up in looked out for them with well-cooked meals and anything else his father needed. Clarke didn't hang around much after his mother passed away. He was two years away from college by then and well focused on his game.

In high school he had two girlfriends and both of those were during his senior year. By then he was captain of the basketball team and spent lots of time alone. His father owned a trailer rig and was constantly on the road during those years, so Clarke was independent long before most young people his age.

The more serious of his two high school girlfriends, Nancy, was devastated when he was accepted at the University of Nevada Las Vegas. She thought they'd both go to school in Arizona and get married after college, but that was the last thing on Clarke's mind. What girls didn't know back then was that his first and only true love was basketball. That was what he and his father had in common. Clarke Sr. loved basketball and Clarke knew if he wanted to win his father over, he had to be not just good, but great at the game. And his game earned him a full ride to UNLV, leaving his father awestruck. He would be the first Hudson to attend college.

Clarke met Persha within days of his arrival on campus. Over time he came to realize she loved him far more than he could possibly love her, but she was good to have around and made his time in school easier.

The main concern he had with her back then was her lack of motivation. He struggled to remember her major back then but couldn't. Yes, she was pursuing a degree, but she really had no idea of what she wanted to do with the rest of her life. She had no vision, no dreams, so she latched on to his. He seemed to be the only thing that she was passionate about.

Clarke knew Persha wanted to be his wife, and that would've been enough for her, but not him. He understood that then, and even though he never told her, he always wanted a woman who posed a challenge, a woman who was passionate about something, something other than a man and not afraid to pursue that passion.

Clarke knew when he left UNLV that he'd be leaving Persha, and he knew she'd find someone else. But even knowing that didn't make leaving her easy. He had learned something very important from her. Clarke realized back then that when a woman was passionate about a man, that man was comparable to king of the world. Everything he desired was a possibility. If Persha merely thought he wanted something, she'd make it her mission to see to it that he got it. And he liked that more than anything else. So Clarke vowed back then that he'd always find women who loved him more because it was easy for women to become passionate about him. He'd leave the challenge for someone else.

When the phone rang, he snapped out of the past and caught it on the first ring.

"Hello?" he said, hoping to hear the voice of someone in particular on the other end, but instead it was his wife's.

"He-eey what're you doin' at home still?" Kelsa asked.

"Why'd you call if you didn't expect me here?" he asked, trying to mask his disappointment.

"I tried you at the office and they said you weren't in yet, so I figured I'd try you at home. So what gives, don't feel like going in today?"

He eased his massive frame back onto the bed and sighed.

"I'm going, it's just a slow start, that's all."

"Well, I have a surprise for you." Kelsa giggled.

Clarke sat up as his heart started racing. He didn't like surprises, but he didn't say anything. He just waited.

"You still there?" she asked.

"Yeah, I'm here, whassup?"

"Well, if I told you, it wouldn't be a surprise now would it?"

"Kel, I'm not in the mood for games, okay? What's going on?" He didn't attempt to hide his agitation.

Clarke started wondering why he didn't get up when the alarm first went off. He'd probably be stuck in traffic and would've been able to avoid this call altogether. He knew something bad was coming.

"Remember I was supposed to work a double? Then go to the retreat?" She giggled, but Clarke didn't see the humor in what he knew was bound to come next.

"Yeah?" he managed

"Well, looks like I'll be home a lot sooner." Clarke didn't respond. "Hheeeelllo?"

"I'm still here," he said impatiently.

"I thought this would be good news. Now you don't have to worry about spending the weekend all alone." There was a pause. "You don't even sound happy," she sobbed.

"Oh, nah, I'm cool. That is good news, I just . . ." He sighed. "I'm happy."

"Well, damn, I'd hate to hear you handling bad news."

"So what time are you coming home now?"

"I'll be there by six or seven."

"Hhmm."

"Is something wrong?" she asked.

"Nah, I'm cool."

"Clarke, I think I know you by now, you are my husband, and I know when you're not happy. What's going on?"

"I don't want to talk about it," he said.

"But I do," she persisted.

"Well, it's just that I already made plans with the fellas. You know how that is. They already talkin' about how much I've softened up since we got married. But it's okay. I'll just break the news to 'em."

"You can hang with them anytime. I thought we'd go somewhere for the weekend," Kelsa suggested.

"Yeah, but we've kinda had these plans since you said you were going to the retreat. Everyone has changed schedules and juggled a few things for me. I guess I'll just have to . . ." He heard her sigh.

"Well, um, wait," she said.

Silence hung in the air for a moment. "You know what? Why don't you go ahead and hang with the guys. I just thought we could do something real nice tonight, but you know, I'll probably be tired anyway."

"You sure, baby?"

"Yeah, I'm sure. You go ahead. We'll be able to do something some other time."

"Are you really cool with that, Kel?"

"Yes! I insist. Who're you hanging with anyway?"

"Antwone, Jay, and a few others. We're going fishing," Clarke replied, quick on his feet.

"Fishing?" Kelsa gasped.

"I know, it's something different for me. But since I haven't been hanging lately, I basically had to agree to whatever they wanted to do."

Silence blanketed them. A few seconds later he barely heard her voice when she conceded, "Maybe I will go to the retreat after all."

When he hung up the phone, he didn't hesitate to get out of the king-sized sleigh bed and make a dash for the bathroom. He wasn't about to wait around for her to call back with any more surprises.

Persha

Persha hadn't been feeling well lately, and this morning was no exception. When she tried to get out of bed, her head felt light and she was tempted to lie back down.

She couldn't quite put her finger on the true source of her problem, but she hadn't been feeling herself for at least the last two months. And there were no signs of improvement.

After naps or a full night of sleeping, she always felt weak, like her body was never fully rested. Determined to go to work and meet up with Clarke later, she forced herself into an upright position in bed.

Maybe if I take it easy, I can make it, she thought. She eased up, but even as slow as she was moving, her head started doing that floating thing she was becoming accustomed to. And that only made her stomach get that sick feeling all over again.

In addition to the sickness, the mildew odor that had seemed to have been haunting her house, reappeared despite the various plug-in air fresheners she'd bought and placed throughout the house.

Suddenly, she was making a quick dash to the bathroom for the third time that morning. The first woke her out of her sleep at about 3:45 A.M. Her stomach had roared, grumbled, then ached like she'd eaten something that didn't agree with her.

Diarrhea had become a common thing for her as well. If she didn't know better, she'd think she was pregnant. But she took her pills religiously, like an addict getting a daily fix, so she knew that simply wasn't possible. Or was it?

It was her second trip to the bathroom a couple hours after the first when she noticed blood in her stool. It shook her up a little bit at first, but then she told herself that if it happened again, she'd call somebody to take her to the emergency room.

As Persha sat in the bathroom holding her stomach, her mind wandered to Clarke. She wondered when he was going to let her know whether he was coming over tonight or not. During their dinner date on Wednesday, he alluded to the fact that Kelsa would be attending a retreat and that meant he wouldn't have to sneak off from their time together in the wee hours of the morning like he had been doing since they had rekindled their romance.

But here it was Friday, and she still hadn't heard anything else about it. He hadn't even called. The only phone messages she received were daily prayers from her mother.

Honestly, she felt so weak that she'd be lucky if she could even make it through the day, let alone have enough strength to entertain Clarke. But the mere thought of her forthcoming rendezvous with Clarke made the challenge worth what little effort she could muster.

After using the restroom that third time, Persha was relieved to find that her stool was normal and that she didn't have to rush to the doctor's office. She convinced herself that a long steamy hot shower and a large feast, maybe something from the Macaroni Grill, one of her favorite restaurants, might get her back in the groove of things. She'd make it to the office, and if Clarke didn't want to hang out tonight, if she was up to it, she'd catch up with Kori and Cricket and go from there.

By the end of the day, Persha felt like she was struggling to hang onto what little energy she had. She had felt a little better earlier throughout the day, especially when she was outdoors and breathing in the fresh air, but she didn't feel up to going back home.

Sitting at her desk, she thought back to her conversation with Clarke earlier that afternoon. First off, when she called his office, she sat on hold an uncomfortably long time before he picked up. And when he did, his voice didn't have that happy-to-hear-from-my-sweetheart-sound that it normally depicted.

"Clarke, is everything okay?" she had said as she toyed with the cord from her phone. She always fidgeted when she didn't feel quite comfortable.

"Ah, just a busy day around here, you know how that is," he said.

"Yeah, so are we hooking up tonight or what?"

"Emph," he cleared his throat. "Let me close my door; get some privacy around this camp." After a few more minutes on hold, his voice rang back in her ear. "Okay, well, I have some bad news. I told you Kelsa was going to that retreat, but she called and said she was able to get out of it."

"Really?"

Persha said kind of flat. She didn't want to come across too disappointed, because she knew he worked hard to spend time with her and she appreciated every second of the stolen moments they shared.

"Yeah, tough break, huh? So I was thinking, maybe

we could meet for a drink after work, but I can't really hang. How's that sound to you?" he asked.

"Well, let me check with my girls because I told them we'd do something if I didn't have plans."

"So you giving a brotha the boot just 'cause he can't make it for an all-nighter?" he joked.

"No, not hardly!" she answered. "But a sistah has to keep up with her situation too. It's hard trying to share yourself."

When Clarke didn't say anything at first, Persha wanted to take it back. It was a stupid joke, and she didn't mean anything by it.

"You know what I mean, Clarke. They complain about you taking up all my time. So honestly, it would be good if I could hang out with them for a few hours tonight, you know, like old times."

"Oh yeah, baby, no offense taken. So when you gonna let a brotha know whassup?"

Persha was really disappointed. She wanted nothing more than to wake up Saturday morning with Clarke in her bed, and she in his arms. But she was careful, not wanting to come across like some silly little mistress either. Hooking up with Clarke was cool, but she didn't really *need* his company.

"I was waiting to call Cricket back after I talked with you. So let me see what they're talking about then I'll call you back."

"Okay, that sounds cool. If I'm not in the office, just hit a brotha on the hip," Clarke said before hanging up the phone.

When Persha hung up the phone, she took a paper holder from her desk and threw it against the wall. Persha was already tired of this, Clarke disappointing her by canceling dates. But what she felt for Clarke wouldn't allow her to just throw in the towel and give up.

On the patio at Magnolia's on the Richmond strip, Persha, Kori, and Cricket were enjoying one of their favorite pastimes: people watching.

"OMIGOD! I can't believe she squeezed herself into that!" Kori gasped as an obese woman walked by wearing a tube-top dress.

"Of all the restaurants offering happy hour specials, you had to pick the only one in the city that thinks happy hour doesn't include half-price drinks," Cricket said to Kori.

"Girl, this is an upscale spot," Kori said. "So that means you'll meet the kind of people we want to be around."

"Yeah, this is just like your plan to hang out at Maverick's, the bar in the Hotel Derek with eighteen-dollar martinis, right?"

"Oh chill out, Cricket, will you?" Kori said as she rolled her eyes. "You always hating," she hissed before turning to Persha.

"What's wrong with you?" Kori asked Persha. "You haven't said much. You feeling okay?"

Barely able to keep her eyes open, Persha sat up at the sound of the questions directed at her. She told herself to shake it off. But that did little to help. The last thing Persha wanted to do was go home and sit up all alone, and she was so tired of being sleepy all the time.

"Oh, girl, I'm cool," Persha replied. "Just over here chillin', that's all."

"Well, you've been *chillin'* a lot lately. Anything you want to share with your very best friends in the whole world?" Kori asked.

"I'm fine. Just thinking, that's all," Persha replied as she struggled to mask a yawn.

"Something you want to share?" Cricket jumped in.

When she didn't respond right away again, Kori reached over and touched Persha's hand. "You not having problems with Clarke are you?" she asked sincerely.

"No, nothing like that. We're fine, it's just . . ." She looked around the patio, the tears had already started stinging in the corners of her eyes. "I don't know what's wrong with me lately. I never feel good anymore. I can't tell you the last time I felt like myself. I just don't feel good and I can't put my finger on it."

"Well, what's wrong? Is it your stomach? Your head? Is it your feet, your heart? What hurts?" Cricket asked, jumping into her nursing mode.

"Well, that's the strange thing really, nothing hurts so to speak. It's like I feel weak all the time, kind of like I'm on the verge of getting sick, but not quite there. And it's strange; whenever I'm inside, I feel even worse."

"Inside?" Kori said as her thinly arched brows shot up.

"Like at home?" Cricket asked.

"No. Now that I think about it, anytime I'm inside, really; at home, at the office. That's why I wanted us to sit out on the patio. It's almost like I'm making myself sick when I'm inside."

"Sounds like cabin fever to me," Kori said casually.

"Cabin what?" Persha's brows inched upward.

"Cabin fever," Kori said. "You know, like in the winter you get so sick of being in the house that you start to convince yourself you're sick, and you actually start feeling bad."

"She might be on to something," Cricket said as she licked the salt from her glass and then sipped her margarita. "Think about it, remember during tropical storm Allison when we had all that doggone rain and flooding. We just felt so stuck indoors that we spent that one Saturday on the phone all day."

"Yeah," Persha said, finally feeling encouraged.

"Well, it's almost like that. We were so eager to get outside, it felt like we'd die if we had to spend one more day inside," Cricket said.

"But I don't remember feeling like this," Persha quickly said.

"Yeah, but remember I was. It felt almost like I was pregnant, but knew I wasn't doing the do. Yeah, that was really tough," Cricket sympathized.

"I feel like that, but to the tenth degree," Persha said as she studied her friends' faces. She had a feeling the question was on the tip of their tongues, but neither wanted to ask, so she let them off the hook. "And no, I am absolutely not pregnant!"

"Whew!" Cricket released.

Kori shook her head and downed the rest of her drink.

"I know better, it would be senseless to get pregnant by a married man," Persha said.

"But it makes *sense* to be sleeping with his trifling ass? Right?" Cricket said.

"Oh, Cricket, don't even get on your soapbox!" Kori screamed.

"No, I'm serious," Cricket defended. "Persha, what kind of friends would we be if we didn't at least try to set you straight?" Cricket rolled her eyes at Kori before continuing. "It's been almost six months, girl, and this dog is still talking about he's gonna leave her? Then you stop dating, so while he gets to go home to wifey, you're sitting at home all alone and waiting on him! It's just not right. It's a bunch of foolishness!"

"Damn, Cricket, when you say it like that, it sounds all thrown off. But just think about it, when they hook up, I mean *really* hook up, that's gonna be one helluva love story," Kori said.

Cricket rolled her eyes at Kori then looked at Persha. "Who cares about a helluva love story!" She suddenly sat back. "You know what, it's all about you. I spoke my peace, so I'm just gonna have to leave it alone. If somebody's sloppy seconds makes you happy, then so be it," she snapped.

In a quick sweeping movement, with one hand over her mouth, Persha shoved her chair back and rushed toward the bathroom. Lucky for Cricket too, had she not had to run and throw up, Persha just might have had to give Cricket a piece of her mind.

Clarke

Clarke sat back in awe over the greatest blow job–filled weekend he had ever experienced. It was one great big suck fest, and he enjoyed every hot tantalizing minute of it, both giving and receiving. He told himself it only got better and better with each encounter. He considered himself a real lucky man.

As he walked around the house and made sure everything was in order for Kelsa's return, he kept thinking about the awesome night he had had. He tried, but couldn't think of anyone who could suck dick like that, not Persha and certainly not Kelsa. And that's what kept him going back time and time again.

He looked at the clock and figured he had a good thirty minutes to call and say something sweet to Persha before he'd hop in bed and try to get some rest. He was worn out, but the weariness felt good.

When Clarke dialed her number, the phone rang five times but there was no answer. His heart started racing a bit, and he wondered where the hell she could've been on an early Sunday morning.

He hung up and called right back. When he did, her sleepy voice grumbled to life after only three rings.

"Hhhhello?" Persha said.

"Persha?" Clarke stated.

"Ah, yes, it's me," she answered groggily.

"Baby, what's the matter? Sounds like you had a rough night. You okay?"

"Emm-hmm. I'm good, just tired. That's all," she managed.

"Guess you don't feel like hooking a brotha up. You know, with a little phone sex?"

"Actually, I haven't been feeling good lately; always sleepy."

"Oh, shorty, you don't have a lil' something on the way, do you?"

"Nah, nothing like that. Just a little tired." She yawned. "That's all."

"Damn, so no love for a brotha this morning, huh?"

"Sorry, babe, I'm way too tired."

Clarke rolled his eyes, then sighed. He walked to the patio and looked out. He didn't panic when he saw Kelsa's Explorer pull into the driveway. He calmly walked to the back and sat on the bed.

"Well, I'm sorry you're feeling bad, but maybe I'll check up on you a little later. Cool?"

"Yeah, that'll work."

"All right, I'll holla."

"I love yo—"

He didn't want to hear that shit so he quickly hung up the phone. He wondered why she'd been acting all funny lately. He was hoping she wasn't gonna try and pull that "I'm pregnant, so leave your wife or else." He just wasn't willing to hear it.

"Are you just getting home?" Kelsa asked. She walked in and dropped her overnight bags at the door.

"Nah, baby, I got here like around three or four this morning."

Her brows crumbled together. "Why is the bed still made if you've been here that long?"

"Girl, what is this? A Spanish inquisition? I fell out on the couch, damn, what's up? Why you gotta sweat a brotha like he stole something?"

Kelsa sashayed over to the bed and dropped her purse, then sat next to Clarke. She frowned a bit and looked into her husband's eyes.

He smiled and tilted his head, giving her his best puppy-dog look. "Whassup, baby girl?"

"I don't know. It's just, well, I called around three-forty-five this morning and you weren't here." She frowned.

"Ah damn. Is that what you up in here giving me the third degree over? Baby, why didn't you say something? Of course I didn't answer. I wasn't here. We didn't get back 'till about five."

"But you just said you got here at three."

"Nah, I must've mixed up the time. I got here about five, you know, I didn't clock in. A brotha didn't know he had to." Before she could say anything else he jumped up from the bed with his hands on his belt buckle as if he was prepared to drop his pants.

"What? Don't even tell me. Now I gotta whip out the thangie for a smell check? 'Cause I will. A brotha will do it if that's gonna make you feel better," he joked.

Kelsa frowned and simply nodded her head. "I'm sorry, Clarke. I don't know what's wrong with me lately. You're right, I guess I was just a little jealous of you spending time with the guys instead of me."

Clarke sat back down, put his arms around her and eased her close.

"Awwww baby girl, you ain't got to be jealous," he said in a comforting tone. "Did you hear anything more about your request?"

Kelsa pulled back a bit. "Oh, yeah I did. My supervisor discreetly advised me that I might want to stay on the overnight shift for another eleven to twelve months."

"Ah damn. Nah!" He did a couple of air punches to further emphasize his disappointment.

"Well, she reminded me that the head nurse slot will be opening soon, and I'm almost a shoe-in. Well, you know, if I continue to do good work and not make too much noise about my shift." She smiled.

"No shit?" His eyes lit up.

"Yup!"

"Damn, Kel, that's great news, baby! Head RN? That's got to come with a better schedule and big bucks to boot, right?"

She nodded again. This time, she shared in his enthusiasm.

"So, baby, I really need your support. Just hang in there with me and when I get that new promotion, we can go to breezy Belize to celebrate."

"Awwww, baby, that's cool. Real cool."

Now all he had to do was make it through the afternoon without any sex. He watched her intensely, hoping her actions would disclose whether she was in a romantic mood. She walked into the large closet they shared. When she emerged wearing flannel pajamas instead of a slinky nighty, he was relieved.

"Clarke, I hope you're not hungry. Baby, I'm so wiped out. If you let me take a nap now, when I get up, I'll fix you the best meal you've had in years. I'm talking fried catfish, cornbread, dirty rice and—"

Clarke eased his finger up to her lips, cutting her off. A smooth smile crawled across his face. He could hardly believe his good fortune.

"Will that meal include something ice cold?" he asked.

She frowned. "What?"

"A cold brew, a beer."

"Whatever you want, baby, whatever you want. Just let me sleep for a few hours. I'm beat."

He smiled and eased back onto the bed. She could sleep till the cows came home for all he cared.

Persha

Persha looked around the bustling restaurant. Amid the chaos, she struggled to remain patient. She'd been kept waiting for fifteen minutes already and she wasn't happy.

She thought about waiting for him before being seated, but as tired as she was, she had looked forward to getting a table and relaxing with an ice-cold drink of water.

"Ma'am, would you still like something from the bar while you wait on your guest?" the waiter asked.

Persha put the glass down and shook her head. "Nothing from the bar, but I'll take an iced tea while I wait. Thank you," Persha said.

Persha watched as the waiter walked away. From her seat, she watched the front door and finally spotted Clarke. He was talking with one of the hostesses. The young woman pointed to the rear of the restaurant and Persha smiled when she saw Clarke looking in her direction.

"Finally!" she mumbled under her breath. It didn't

take long for her anger and anxiety to begin fading. A sense of relief and sheer lust started settling in. But before Clarke could make it to her table, a well-dressed man stopped him.

Persha couldn't hear what they were talking about, but Clarke's body language told her it wasn't a conversation he wanted to have. He motioned toward her table and watched as Clarke and the man looked and smiled in her direction. Clarke motioned towards the table once again. This time, the man gave Clarke a piece of paper and let him go.

"What was that all about?" Persha asked as soon as Clarke made it to the table. He pulled his chair out and sat down. She noticed he hadn't offered a kiss, but she was too tired to fuss.

"Oh, I was supposed to get the dude's nephew an internship. I haven't done it yet, so he just asked me about the details," Clarke answered.

Persha looked at the stranger again, then back at Clarke when a lovely young woman sat at the man's table.

"Well, why don't you get on top of that? You don't need people attacking you in public places," she joked.

"Yeah, I know you're right, but I've been swamped lately. I'll get around to it though."

He picked up his menu and sighed. "It's been a rough day." Clarke looked at Persha. "Hey, whassup? You don't look too hot," he said.

She couldn't believe he had finally noticed. Lately he seemed preoccupied when they were together. She had called this lunch meeting to talk about a bad habit he had suddenly developed. The last few dates they'd made, he called and canceled at the very last minute. Sometimes it happened after she'd already been waiting.

Persha knew she had to proceed carefully with

Clarke—after all, he was married. By sleeping with him, she realized she was opening herself up for heartache.

But she understood that he was going to have a little talk with his wife about a separation. Lately, he hadn't been saying too much about that either.

"You order yet?" Clarke asked.

"No, I wanted to wait for you." She struggled to sit up straight. There was simply no explanation for her recent failing health. She had a doctor's appointment for later that afternoon. She hoped she'd walk out of the doctor's office with a pill to make her better, instantly if she could help it.

"Is it still cool for me to stop by tonight?" Clarke placed the menu down for a moment.

"Yeah, that's cool. But are you going to come or are you just going to cancel on me again?"

Persha told herself it wasn't the time for tears, she didn't want to break down like some silly little girl, but she couldn't help it.

When Clarke reached for her hands across the table, it was as if he opened the floodgate. Tears quickly rolled down her checks and she couldn't do a thing to stop them.

"Hey, hey shorty, what's wrong? Whassup?"

"I'm sorry, Clarke. I haven't been feeling well, and with work and everything else, I guess I need you and, um . . . I—ah, I just don't know," she stammered.

He immediately got up and sat in the chair next to her.

"I know this isn't easy, but don't worry about it. We'll work it through. I had a little talk with Kelsa just last weekend and she knows things just aren't working between us. She asked me to give her some time. Her mom or somebody's real sick, so she's got a lot going on."

Clarke put his hand on Persha's shoulder and rubbed her back.

"Why don't we eat and then bounce up outta here?" he said.

With a look of sheer shock on her face, Persha didn't quite know what to say. She didn't want to overreact and force him to take back his offer, but she didn't want to seem desperate either.

"You mean you'd come over like right now?" Her eyes brightened slightly.

"Yeah, if you'll have me, shorty."

"Well, we don't even have to stay. We can pick up something on the way and eat back at my place," she offered longingly.

Clarke glanced at the dude's table he had stopped to talk to earlier and hesitated before speaking.

"You want to do that?" Persha asked. Her mind had already started thinking about the great sex they could have. They'd cap it off by falling asleep in each other's arms. She'd even muster up enough energy to cook something later, once they got up.

"Clarke?" He quickly turned to face her. "I asked if you want to just pick something up on the way back to my place."

"Oh, well, since we're here, why don't we order then leave after we eat. I thought you liked Landry's."

"I do, but I'd much rather be at home with you." She waited again for his response. Clarke picked up the menu and didn't say another word until the waiter came back.

"You know what you want?" he asked Persha when the waiter appeared.

She was too embarrassed to say anything other than her selection. After the waiter gathered the menus and worked his way to his next table, Persha adjusted the linen napkin in her lap.

"So you didn't have any plans for this afternoon?" Clarke asked.

"I did, but nothing I couldn't reschedule if we're going to my place," she tossed in, hoping to refresh his memory.

"Well, I tell you what, why don't you take care of what you need to after lunch, then we'll meet back at your place." He looked at his watch then continued. "Say about five. How does that sound?"

The question lingered on the tip of her tongue. She wanted to ask so badly, but couldn't bring herself to utter the words. Instead she shook her head in agreement and fumbled with her napkin again.

Clarke's cell phone broke the silence. At that moment, Persha felt her heart sink at an unbelievable speed. She swallowed back tears as he looked down at his waist. She had a strong feeling he wasn't going to show up. She could all but feel it, despite the knowing feeling; she still refused to ask whether he would.

"Damn, what now?" he cursed as he picked up the phone and began pushing buttons.

"It's the office paging me." Clarke's eyes were still on the phone. "Shit! It's nine-one-one!" He moved his chair back to get up. "I need to call them back, excuse me for a moment. If the food comes before I get back, start without me."

Persha watched him walk toward the restrooms. A part of her felt relieved that she would still make her doctor's appointment. The last thing she needed was this sickness to turn into something worse. So she decided she'd have lunch with Clarke, go to the doctor, and then meet him back at her place.

Her heart wanted to believe he'd show up this time.

She noticed him approaching the table with a look of bewilderment on his face. All she could do was prepare herself for whatever lame excuse she was sure was about to spill from his lips.

"Damn, shorty! What the hell's wrong with you? Don't you feel that?" Clarke flapped his arms to nervously emphasize his words.

Persha sat confused by his comment. Her heart started racing. She was frowning. When the waiter came to the table, he dropped his entire tray and stood staring at her.

"Jesus, ma'am!" the waiter exclaimed. "Are you okay?" His blue eyes stretched wide in horror.

Persha had no idea why they were both staring at her in shock, and not at all the food on the floor.

"Baby, your nose, it's bleeding!" Clarke screamed with his face completely twisted.

"What?" When Persha jumped up from the table, Clarke and the waiter stumbled back.

"My nose?" Persha grabbed the napkin and held it to her face. Suddenly feeling the wetness she franticly started looking around for the restroom. Blood was all over her blouse.

"Should we call an ambulance?" the waiter yelled after her. Before she could make it to the bathroom, she felt all eyes glued to her and the bloody mess.

"I don't need anything! I'm fine," she mumbled through the blood-drenched napkin.

A few minutes later she emerged from the bathroom. Although her silk blouse was still stained with the blood that she couldn't wash out, she felt okay.

Clarke was waiting for her at the bathroom door.

"I don't know what's wrong. I have a doctor's appointment today. I'm sorry about lunch. I'm sure your appetite is gone, but I'll make it up to you later. You are still coming by this evening, right?"

"Yeah, but whassup with you. What's going on, shorty?"

Persha felt more hurt by the look of sheer disgust that was plastered across his face.

"I really don't know. I've been so sick lately. I have no idea what's wrong. When I'm home all I can do for relief is sleep. I think it'd be best if I try to head over to my doctor's office right away."

"You need me to drive you?" he asked. But his expression remained the same.

What the hell do you think? Persha thought. *Blood was just gushing out of my head like a water fountain and I have no idea why. Do you really think I need to be driving?*

"Well, I don't want to put you out," she mumbled softly. But deep down, she hoped he'd insist.

"Okay, well, I do need to get back to the office anyway. So, I tell you what, why don't you call me to let me know you made it there safely. Here, let me walk you to your car," Clarke offered, all but pushing her toward the front of the restaurant.

Persha was pissed, but what could she say? At least he did offer, even if he didn't really mean it. On their way out of the restaurant, she noticed Clarke's friend and his date were already gone. She was oddly relieved at that even though she didn't know him or the woman.

At the doctor's office, Persha felt lucky she had made it safely. As she sat in the waiting room, she couldn't wait to hear her name called. Finally, the nurse called her into the back and led her into one of the five patient rooms while she checked her heart, pulse, and everything. After that, Persha was more than ready to see the doctor.

As she sat in the room waiting, she remembered that she was supposed to call Clarke. At first she was a bit concerned by leaving him to worry about her. But then she figured that if he was all that concerned about her well-being, he would've driven her and waited to find out what was wrong with her in the first place.

Once the doctor came into the room and began questioning Persha about what had been ailing her, Persha found it hard to describe what the past few weeks had been like for her. She told the doctor how she was constantly tired and described her bouts with diarrhea, the nosebleeds and a few other flulike symptoms, even though she knew the flu was not the culprit.

"Okay, Ms. Townsend, are you allergic to anything?" Dr. Connell asked.

"No," Persha replied, shaking her head.

Dr. Connell studied her chart again. "Well, you don't have asthma. I do see signs of an upper respiratory infection, but there's more to it than that. Based on what you've told me so far, I'd have to say I think you're suffering from mold poisoning. Have you noticed any mold growing on any of your walls in your home, typically the basement?"

"Mold what?" She frowned and waited for clarification.

"Yes, mold. We've seen an increase in the number of patients falling victim to mold and it can get worse. There was a sudden rash in our area, especially after the recent rains and hurricanes along the coast." He flipped through her chart, then placed it on a nearby table.

"What? Mold? Is that what I think you're saying, or actually what is mold? And mold poisoning?" Persha cleared her throat.

"Throat a little sore?" Dr. Connell asked.

Persha answered by nodding. She was still trying to gather her composure.

"Any wheezing? Problems breathing? Dry eyes?"

"Yes, and diarrhea. At night I'm coughing so much I can hardly sleep."

"Sounds like all the usual symptoms. This can be serious, and depending on the severity, you may need to make some life changes." The doctor got up. "I'd suggest taking a good look around your house."

"Like get a test done? How do I know I have a mold problem?"

"Oh, depending on how bad it is, you can smell it; you can also find mold spores."

She wondered if her face showed any signs of just how confused she was at that very moment. The only thing she knew about mold was what happened when you let a loaf of bread go bad.

"Let me see if I can make this any clearer for you. Molds are fungi. Tiny particles of mold are present in both indoor and outdoor air. Molds produce microscopic cells called spores, which are very tiny and spread through the air. Live spores act like seeds, forming new colonies when the conditions are right."

"So it multiplies? How does it even form?" Persha asked.

"Moisture. Plain and simple. Any major plumbing leak, firewood stored indoors, failure to vent outdoors clothes-dryer exhaust, even watering plants can generate large amounts of moisture. Like I said, after the massive floods from tropical storm Allison, we saw hundreds of people suffering from it. I'm sure we'll see more cases when people start returning to their homes after the Hurricane Katrina and Rita cleanups."

"Well, now that you mention it, I did have several pipes burst during the storm, but that was repaired and I have some firewood I've been holding onto for what, two years now, I just had no idea. How come I've never heard of this?"

"Unfortunately, Ms. Townsend, you're like many people who suffer from mold-related illnesses. They don't find out about it until it actually affects them or strikes close to home."

He leaned against the counter and looked at her chart again.

"I'm, um, I'm still so confused," she said.

"And I understand that confusion, but at this point, at least until the blood work comes back, I strongly recommend that you stay at a friend's house; at least for tonight so that we can verify or count out mold poisoning."

"So I need to leave my house?"

"I'm suggesting that until we get your test results back. If it's not mold poisoning as I suspect, then you can go back home and we will keep hunting for the real culprit."

"What if it is mold poisoning?" she asked.

"I don't want to scare you, but things won't get any better."

Persha's eyes narrowed. She had no idea what she was going to do, but she knew for sure she had to consider the worse-case scenario.

"We'll work through this. If it's mold poisoning, we'll get you feeling better soon."

"Yeah, but basically you're saying my house is making me sick. So that means I'll have to leave the house for good if, in fact, it's mold."

"I've seen cases where that has happened."

"So what am I supposed to do while we wait?"

"You'll find someplace else to stay. I'll put you on antibiotics to clear up the mild infection, then we'll find out for sure about mold and move from there."

"Fair enough."

She felt better having been somewhat diagnosed. By

the time she made it to the lobby, the doctor had suggested she go on antibiotics as a precaution.

On the drive from the doctor's office, Persha tried to make sense of everything the doctor had just informed her about. But before she could even think straight, she needed to get home, grab a few things, and get out of there before she got any worse.

A few evenings later, Persha sat waiting for Clarke to show up at her hotel room. She had rented a room at the Marriott near Highway 59. When he finally knocked on the door, she was eager to spill her story.

"Did the doctor fix my baby?" Clarke asked as he strolled in, kissed her cheek, and dropped his bag on the couch.

When she closed the door, Persha leaned up against it.

"Uh-oh, shorty, is the news that bad?" He grinned.

Persha didn't feel up for his witty remarks. Finally, she sauntered into the room and turned to Clarke who already had the remote in his hand.

"Well, actually, Clarke, I was diagnosed with mold poisoning. My house and everything in it may have to be condemned."

"What the hell?" he screamed and jumped back in his seat.

"That's not even the worse part of it. Not only have I been walking around here looking like death warmed over, but now all I have to my name are the clothes on my back, two outfits that were at the cleaner's, and no place to lay my head."

Clarke's brows cocked upward as he took in the information.

"I don't have a place to live, Clarke," Persha contined as she started crying. "What the hell am I going to do?" she screamed.

"You can't go back home, like in a week? Can't you stay with Kori or Cricket?" She shook her head to answer his question. "You know Kori shares a room, and Cricket is taking care of her sick aunt."

He reached for her. "Come here. We can work this out."

In the comfort of his arms, for a flash second, she felt some kind of hope, almost like things were *really* going to be okay.

"When do you check out of this room?" he asked.

"Friday. Then I have to move, and I don't know where I'm gonna go. I haven't even told my mother. I don't want her worrying out there. Her solution is always for me to come home."

"Nah, shorty, you can't go back to Nevada. I mean, you can't just leave a brotha hanging. Don't worry about it, we'll figure something out."

"I wish I could be as confident as you." Persha blew out a breath and eased back into the sofa.

"Shorty, let your man handle this. Hey, I'm here to take care of you, right?"

Though she was reluctant, she nodded anyway. Persha wanted desperately to believe the answers to all of her problems truly lay in his eyes. A part of her was glad he even offered to help. She figured maybe things really would be okay. She was starting to feel better, and knowing Clarke would help, she was okay.

By Thursday evening, Persha had gone back to worrying again. It had been two days since she last spoke to Clarke. She had less than twenty-four hours left in the room, and her money was running out fast.

She didn't even feel like going through the motions with Kori and Cricket. She could just hear them now, sounding off about what she should and shouldn't do. So far, Clarke was the only one who knew her predica-

ment, and she wanted to keep it that way until she
knew her next move.

When her cell phone rang she silently prayed it
would be Clarke on the other end. Instead, when Kori's
voice rang out, she could no longer hold in her frustration.

"Gurrrrl, what's wrong? You need me to come
over?" Kori asked.

"No, you can't. Besides, I'm fine," Persha managed
through sobs.

"I can't? Why not? And if you're so fine, then why
are you crying? And how come you not answering your
phone? And what's up with you anyway? And where
you been?" Kori rattled off.

"I don't even want to get into it."

"Nah-uh, I'm coming over right now! You at
home?"

"Wait, Kori. You really can't come over. I'm not at
home. I've had to move out. I'm at the Marriott. My
house has to be condemned and my insurance company is trying not to pay me for it. Thank God I trans-
ferred my phone to the cell. Clarke is supposed to help
me but whenever he calls, he doesn't even mention
what we're gonna do about my problem. I don't want
to bring it up, but the truth is I don't know what I'm
gonna do."

"Chile! Hold on a minute! I can barely keep up,"
Kori said. "So where are you? And your house is being
condemned? Hold up, I need to call Cricket on three-
way."

"No! Please don't," Persha begged, sniffling.

"I don't believe this. You need your girls right now.
We can pull together to help you out."

"I appreciate that, but Clarke's supposed to be taking care of it."

"Oookay, so what's the game plan?"

"Well—um, I really don't know just yet. But what I do know is that checkout is noon tomorrow. So I need to get in touch with Clarke real fast."

"You know I'd let you crash over here if I could. But you know how these folks are acting. Gurl, did I tell you that they left me a note talking about there were four bananas on Saturday and now there's only one left? Please watch my portions!"

Persha started laughing. "What?"

"I know! They're counting the food, eggs, bread, and all. I can't wait till this lease runs out. I don't have time for this shit."

"I don't think I've ever heard such a thing."

"Tell me about it. But, Persha?" Kori said.

"Yes?"

"The next time I talk about renting a room to save money, can you please bitch-slap me back to reality and tell my cheap ass there just has to be a better way!" Persha laughed at her friend's comment. "Now, I'm for real, girl! This shit is crazy! Folks up in here counting food and shit. I don't need this," Kori threw in.

"Well, the last thing I need to do is burden you with my problems," Persha offered.

"Chile, please, one more problem ain't gonna break me down. But I tell you what, I think we should call Cricket, you know they have room over there. You can stay in one of those empty bedrooms. How many do they have?"

"Kori, you know I'm not about to go stay over there with all those damn cats! I don't see how Cricket stays there."

"Last time she counted, girl, she said there was something like nine or fifteen-million cats."

"Oh hell no! I'll wait to hear from Clarke, if not, I'll

just call Moms for a loan to hold me over. Nine cats? That's just downright nasty ain't it?"

"Gurl, all I know is that place reeks of feline. But maybe you should think about it," she said, giggling.

"Nothing to think about. I like cats and all, but that's one at a time. Nine? Ain't no way, girlfriend!"

"Yeah, I feel you on that one."

"Oh, Kori, hold on. My other line's ringing." Persha looked at the screen and rolled her eyes. It was her mother and she knew she needed to take the call.

"Kori, let me call you back. It's my mom."

"Okay, but hurry."

"I will," Persha said as she hung up with Kori and clicked over to her other line. "Hey Ma!"

"Lawd have mercy, girl! Where have you been? And why does it sound like you on that cell phone? You know I don't like calling on these mobile phones, I know you on it 'cause it sounds funny. I still think they cause brain tumors. I know doggone well, I called your home phone. Girl, what's going on?"

"Ma, I'm not at home. I've had to move out. My house is contaminated with mold."

"With what, chile? Jesus be the glory! Chile, you been praying for the good Lord's help with this matter? Mold? That's nothing but the devil at work! Are you living right, chile? Your father, rest his soul, would roll over in his grave if he knew the way your life was going."

"Ma, please, I'm really frustrated right now. I've moved into a hotel and I just need to figure out my next move."

"Baby, put it in the Lord's hands. You can't handle this alone. But regardless of what's happening, you should've called to tell me. I'm praying for you, but I need you to pray too. This ain't nothing but the devil testing your devotion. Hang onto the good book. You got your Bible there with you?"

"Yes, Ma," Persha said, only half lying since a hotel Bible was lying on the nightstand next to the bed.

"Then open it to—"

"Ma! I'm sorry I need to go. I have another call coming in. It's the insurance people about the house. I'll call you later, love you."

"But Persha—"

"I know, Ma, but I need to run. We'll pray later."

She hung up without waiting for her mother's response. The phone wasn't ringing, but she needed a break. Before calling Kori back she willed the phone to ring, and willed it to be Clarke calling.

After a few minutes with no luck, she dialed Kori's number and sat back to pick up the conversation where they left off.

"How's your mom doing?" Kori asked.

"Oh, she's good. You know her, always with scripture at your service. Oh, Kori, that's my other line again." Persha squealed with excitement when she saw Clarke's number appear.

"I'll call you back!" She could barely contain her enthusiasm. She blew out a breath and inhaled a deep one before mustering up her sexy voice.

"Hello?"

"Damn, shorty, you sounding better and better," Clarke said.

"I may sound better, but I still don't have a place to stay."

"Yeah, that's what I was calling you about. I have an idea, but I'm not sure if you'll be cool with it. I mean, how long you talking about being out of pocket?"

"At least four weeks, Clarke. I've put in a request to borrow some money against my 401(K) and it'll take about that long to go through the red tape, then I'll be able to get an apartment until I work out this insurance thing."

"Okay, well hear me out. You know how a brotha been telling you that even though Kelsa got papers on me, it's more in name than anything else, right?"

"Yes, and I know you're telling me the truth, Clarke, that's why I try not to bug you about when you're leaving her."

With her eyes closed, Persha could hardly believe what they were talking about. She wondered if all this mess with the mold poisoning wasn't a good thing disguised as a nightmare.

And to imagine, she was just hoping he'd spring for a few more weeks at the hotel. She thought this suggested move by Clarke was even better. She struggled not to get too ecstatic with the news she was sure he was about to share; she sat and waited.

"Yeah, Persha, I am gonna leave, but right now you're my first priority. Shorty, I can't even sleep knowing what's going on with you."

She knew it was coming, what she'd finally been patiently waiting for all these months. Her mind had already started thinking about where they could get a place; maybe in Stafford or even Sugar Land.

She was sure once he proposed to her that her mother would be just as happy. She'd of course leave out the part about them living together, and the part about him having been married before. Those were minor details she needn't worry her with.

"So, Persha, you still there?" Clarke chimed in.

"Oh, I'm sorry. Yes, I am. What were you saying?"

"I asked if you were willing to hear a brotha out? Support me and stick with me so we can work this out, together?"

"Of course, Clarke. You know I have faith in you and what you tell me. I know you've been trying to figure something out to help me. That's why I love you and I know you love me."

"Okay, so here's my plan. I don't know if I told you, but Kelsa works the night shift and has a class in the mornings. She usually gets here at about eleven o'clock in the morning. You have to be at work by what, eight o'clock, right?"

She wondered just where he was going with the timetable. "Yeah, eight. That's right."

"So I think you should stay here, in the extra bed-room."

Persha dropped the phone right along with her mouth as Clarke's voice was faintly heard calling out her name.

Clarke

On the day of the move, Clarke was nervous. With so much at stake and all the possibilities of what might go wrong, he could barely think straight. And imagine he had to actually *talk* Persha into moving in, like her ass had any place else to go. He knew that at first his idea probably seemed crazy, but the plan really was best for everyone involved.

He'd thought about it for three days before presenting it to Persha. While Kelsa was at work, he and Persha would sleep in the guest room. They'd get up, shower, get dressed, and head out for work together. By the time they left, Kelsa wouldn't even be out of class for a few hours. Then by the time she was heading home, he and Persha would've already been halfway through their workday.

The way he had it figured out, he could get pussy day or night, or both if that's what he wanted. If he could, he'd pat himself on the back for the plan any man would be proud of. Now all he had to do was figure out a way to continue to get head the way he liked it. As he sat thinking about his master plan, it was easy to begin reminiscing about the place he liked to call his euphoria.

Clarke eased back and closed his eyes. He was immediately transported to the midst of his favorite activity. His eyes beamed as the moist lips became shiny with spit and parted to welcome him in. To Clarke, there was nothing better than a deep throat lodged around his member. He knew he was rendered completely useless during these sessions.

He understood the power of an excellent blow job, it could create and ease a throbbing hard-on if it was done properly. There was no doubt; Clarke was always reduced to a whiny boy when he was deep down the throat. And an experienced sucker knows just how deep, how rough, how wet, and how long it will take to trigger the elusive eruption. When Clarke was being sucked off, he didn't mind releasing his power. He knew firsthand that the tongue was a tool of teasing and torture, and his family jewels were at the mercy of a wet and wanting mouth. And when done right, the sucker was getting off on it just as much as he was, or maybe even more. Clarke didn't just love head, he was a *head* connoisseur. The stronger the jaw, the wetter the mouth, the more he enjoyed it.

As if right on time, his cell phone rang, and it was Persha. Clarke shook off the images that left him trembling at the memory of the spectacular sensation.

"Where are you?" he said, clearing his throat.

"I'm leaving the mall. I had to buy some clothes and stuff."

"You're not bringing a bunch of luggage, are you?"

"Clarke, I didn't have extra panties. Everything I have can fit in the trunk of my car."

"Okay, cool. So here's the deal. We can go grab a bite to eat, then we can get you moved in and squared away. You feeling all right?" he asked.

It was times like this Clarke wished he could confide in his buddies, but honestly, he wasn't sure if that was such a good idea just yet. He had already cleared room for Persha's outfits in the back of the guest-room closet. He was sure they'd be safe behind his winter clothes. Kelsa never even ventured into the room, much less the closet.

When Persha honked her horn, Clarke ran out to meet her in the parking lot and explained to her that they'd get her settled in after dinner. He wanted to treat her to a nice meal before they settled in.

At the Olive Garden he held the door open for Persha and two other women that were entering behind them. He then walked into the cool restaurant.

"You sure you're okay with eating here? We can go somewhere else if you want," he said to Persha.

"Nope, this is cool. I like their salad and bread sticks. Besides, a sistah could use a stiff drink."

"Well, a brotha got something stiff for you, but it ain't got nothing to do with a drink," he whispered as they followed the hostess to a small table off in the corner.

A few minutes later the waiter came to take their order.

"Need more time?" he asked.

"Just a few minutes," Clarke said.

The waiter nodded. "Okay, I'll be back with water in a few minutes." He turned and left.

Minutes later when the waiter returned, Clarke was first to place his order. "I'd like the seafood Alfredo," Clarke said, closing his menu and looking at Persha.

"Emmm, I think I'll take the chicken linguine, with an Italian margarita," Persha added.

"Okay, I'll be right back with your salad and drinks," the waiter said as he scooped up the menus and left.

As they waited for the drinks they had ordered, Persha gazed out of the window. "Can you believe it?" she asked, pausing.

Clarke didn't answer right away. The last thing he needed was her ass complaining about staying with him and Kelsa. Here he was trying to make a way for her, the only way he knew how, and she was complaining? Sometimes he didn't know what to do about women. *Just can't keep 'em happy*, he thought.

By the time Persha turned to him, she looked as if she was expecting an answer.

"Clarke, what's on your mind? I asked if you knew it wasn't even spring yet and it's so damn hot and humid outside. You didn't say anything."

"Awww, shorty, I'm sorry. A brotha just thinking about that food and when it's gonna get here. I'm starving!" He rubbed his stomach for good measure.

"You sure that's all you're thinking about?"

"Yeah, girl. I haven't eaten since I had a Krispy Kreme doughnut this morning. And I only had one, so you know how a brotha is feeling right about now."

"'Nuff said." Persha looked around the buzzing restaurant until she spotted what she was looking for. "Good, here comes our waiter, and he's got bread sticks and our salad."

"That'll work!" Clarke said.

After dinner, the two sat at the table long after it had been cleared.

"You feel better now?" Persha asked.

Clarke leaned back and rubbed his stomach. "That hit the spot, seriously." He eased forward. "So what's up, shorty. You ready to go or what? A brotha could work off all this food if you know what I'm saying." He winked before displaying a devilish smile.

Her lips pursed and her eyebrows inched up.

"Well, I guess I gotta pay for your hospitality sooner or later, right?" She grinned.

"Now you talking. So I guess you ready to step then, right?"

"Yeah, just let me run to the little girl's room real quick." She got up from the chair.

"Cool, I'll meet you at the door. Let me take care of the bill, then it's straight to the house."

Persha made her way to the bathroom and Clarke took care of the bill. After that, they headed back to Clarke's house.

Clarke instructed Persha to park her car down the street. He told her to walk ahead of him to the house. A few minutes later, he walked up and let her in.

"We don't know any of our neighbors or anything like that," Clarke said, as they entered the house, "but a brotha still didn't want to take any chances. You know how that is."

She shook her head and stepped into the house. It was hard to tell just how large the house was from the outside. But once inside, it was one large flat open room, spanning more than twenty-five hundred square feet. The kitchen was off to the left and a den was off to the right. The cascading staircase was near the back towards the den.

The furniture was contemporary, leather and cherry-wood. And lots of plants gave the house an outdoorsy kind of feel.

"You like?" Clarke asked as they stood near the door.

"Wow! This is really nice. Your wife must have a helluva green thumb! Are all these plants real?" Persha asked with excitement.

"Yup! Sure are," he boasted proudly.

"Damn. I can't get anything to live in my house—well, unless you count the damn mold!" She walked over toward the den, where several large plants were mounted near the entrance to the elegant dining room.

The house was immaculately done in navy with lots of greenery cascading all over, especially near the big-screen TV. Clarke stood and watched as she moved from one area of the house to the next.

"This is so nice," she said, gasping.

Clarke led her upstairs. A crystal vase with fresh flowers sat on a small table near the staircase. That's where Persha stopped and turned to face Clarke.

"I can't believe all the plants and flowers. This house has such a calming atmosphere. Your wife did an awesome job," she said with more excitement pouring through.

"What makes you think my wife did all this?"

Persha went still. She looked around the room again then turned back to Clarke. By the time they made it back downstairs, Persha was completely awestruck.

"What do you mean?" she asked skeptically.

"Why is it that everyone always assumes a nicely decorated house is done by a woman? Can't a brotha get any props?" he asked with his arms bent at the elbows and hands stretched out.

Her eyes widened, and she looked around the house again, taking in all the plants, flowers, and other things she had dismissed as feminine touches. By the time she swung her head back to Clarke, he was standing with arms crossed at his chest.

"You?" she muttered, bewildered.

He nodded in the affirmative. "You don't believe me, do you?"

Persha shrugged easily. She looked around the room in disbelief again.

"Okay, come here," he insisted. He walked her into the kitchen. "See those flowers on the breakfast island?"

"Dang, they're breathtaking!" She moved forward toward the vase.

"These are called four season orchids. They're an upright plant with daisylike flowers, but more fleshy. They can be massive." Clarke touched the flower. "I like them because they bloom any time of the year."

Persha moved in to sniff the flowers.

"No fragrance," he said casually. "They're just for show."

"Nice," she mumbled, still looking a bit skeptical.

He moved toward the living room. "Now, in here I decided on the African ivy. This is of Mediterranean origin and the leaves will grow to be about six inches."

Before she could say anything else, he led her back upstairs. He motioned to the first door to the left.

"This is the guest room where you'll stay. But before you go in, I want you to see something."

Persha followed him down the long hallway, admiring the plants as they walked.

"These are ferns. They're actually Hawaii bird's-nest sleenworts, to be precise. I moved them out here, but they're usually in the bathrooms. In there I've placed the annuals because this is the time of year they bloom; only from February to about April."

Clarke turned to see a stunned look on Persha's face.

"What's the matter?" he asked innocently.

"I'm just—um—I can't. Ah—I, well—I had no idea," she stammered.

"It's okay. Most people never know this side of me, but yes, I do most, if not all, of the decorating. I chose leather furniture because that's masculine, yet nice when paired with the right plants, fabrics, and wall colors."

Leaning against the banister, he waited for her to speak.

"So you did all of this yourself?" she asked.

"Sure did."

Persha looked around at all the thriving plants and artful decorating.

He figured she was probably going through what many others had once they found out he had a creative touch. He gave it a few minutes to sink in then took a deep breath.

"Now, if you don't have any more questions, a brotha would like a down payment in advance for his hospitality." He displayed a devilish smile.

Persha

It wasn't easy holding Clarke off till she had a chance to shower. But Persha wanted to wash off the grime and prepare herself for what she knew they both needed. This wouldn't be the normal bathroom she'd use, but he had insisted that she shower in the master bath. This bathroom was huge, done in a butterscotch paint with earth-toned–colored accessories throughout.

It was right off the left of the master bedroom that had a large bone-colored four-poster bed as its center-piece. There was a nice chaise near a corner with a tall antique reading lap near it. The room had matching drapes and bedspread with a throw that sat on the chaise. It was inviting, except for the fact that it was another woman's bedroom. She felt warm in the sur-roundings.

She strolled back into the bathroom. The shower was glass-enclosed and separated from the Jacuzzi gar-den tub. That was surrounded with yellow and brown candles. Persha didn't miss the pewter-colored wine bucket that looked right at home near the tub's edge.

She couldn't believe Clarke lived in such luxury on a daily basis.

The moment she stepped dripping wet out of the shower that had an upper and lower head, Clarke was standing there waiting with a fluffy bath sheet.

"Your body is so tight. I don't think I could ever get enough of it," he said with a smile, taking her into his arms.

"I won't get a chance to dry off, will I?" She smiled.

He shook his head. "Come here, shorty."

"But I'm all wet."

Clarke's eyebrows elevated, and before she could reach for the towel, he had pressed his lips against hers. He used his hands to palm her behind and pull her close. Just as the kiss started getting heated, he pulled back and looked at her through frenzied eyes. They were both breathing hard and heavy. Before she could make another move, he pushed her shoulders down and she dropped to her knees.

Persha glanced up as she opened her mouth to receive him. When she took him into her mouth, she could feel him begin to swell instantly. After sucking and slurping the way she knew he liked, she felt his body quiver.

"Oh yes! Shorty, just like that," he cried.

Instead of pulling away, he shoved himself deeper into her mouth. To avoid gagging completely, she opened wider. Persha pulled back just as he released. He took her into his arms and sighed.

"Damn, you're good, baby girl. You're damn good," he said.

Soon her feet were off the floor and he was moving her. Up against the vanity, her mind was no longer thinking about being wet. Now she was hot, her heart was racing, and she was fighting to keep up with his tongue's vigor.

He barely pulled away, before he used one far-reaching motion to shove some things aside on the sink top. Persha clawed at his back trying to hang on as he swept her up onto the countertop.

She was panting like crazy with one leg against a wall. The other was stretched farther apart. She got a glimpse of their bodies in one of the large side mirrors and was instantly turned on.

"Oh, shorty," he breathed.

"Yes, Clarke?"

His tongue moved from her mouth to her neck, to her nipples, then to her belly button. Her skin tingled as his tongue left a wet trail across her skin. Persha threw her head back and squeezed her eyes shut as immense pleasure washed over her.

Her body moved and rocked with his. When possible, she held on, gripping him forcefully. He moved her hand from its tight grip around his neck and slid it down between her own legs.

"It's so hot and wet, you feel that? Shorty, you feel it?"

"Mmm-hmm," she responded incoherently.

Clarke eased up a bit, took her hand and brought it up to his face. He sniffed. "Mmm, I smell you." Then he moved her fingers to his lips. He suckled two of her fingers, savoring her body's juices.

"You're so tasty. You're in heat, shorty," he moaned. Once her hand left his lips, he jammed the other fingers into her mouth. "Good, huh?"

She shook her head agreeing. Persha had never tasted herself, and was kind of shocked by his gesture. But she didn't want to ruin his rhythm.

Spreading her legs even farther apart, he gazed into her eyes then thrust himself deeper inside her. Persha could hardly stop squirming atop the marbletop vanity.

He was sucking and slurping. At moments she

struggled to push his head away, because the pleasure was too much to bear. But the more she pushed, the faster his tongue flickered back and forth.

Finally giving in, she felt her heart rate increase quickly as his momentum picked up.

"Oh God, Clarke! Oh, God!" she screamed.

As if encouraged by her moans, he licked and sucked faster and faster. Unable to hang on any longer, Persha released a growling cry.

"God, I love you!"

Clarke continued the assault on her clitoris, spreading her legs wider and wider with his hands.

"Oh, Clarke please!" she squealed.

The doorbell rang, but he didn't stop. He kept sucking with more vigor and strength. A few minutes later, there was knocking at the door.

He pulled back and looked down at her and then at his stiff erection. "Fuck! Who the hell is that?" he growled, angry at the distraction.

Persha pushed herself into an upward position. Still breathing heavily, she was relieved by the sudden break.

Out of breath, she managed to say, "You expecting company?"

Clarke shook his head then eased two fingers into her while stroking his manhood.

"Damn, talk about bad timing. Girl, you are so wet and hot! A brotha wants you so bad." He reached down and sucked her opening before finally pulling himself away for good.

"Let me get rid of whoever this is. Stay put!" he warned with a pointed finger as he stormed out of the bathroom.

Barely able to move, Persha shook her head and tried to recapture her wind.

"Hurry!" she called after him, easing back on her elbows.

Clarke grabbed a robe from a hook on the door and cursed as he looked over his shoulder and stumbled out of the bathroom. She heard his feet as he quickly padded down the stairs and to the door.

"Damn, dawg! Whassup?" Clarke's voice echoed through the house.

Persha couldn't hear what the visitor was saying, but only seconds later, she heard Clarke say, "Man, this is a bad time. Let a brotha holla at you in a minute. I'm in the shower."

When she heard the door close she looked down between her legs and waited for him. When he returned, Clarke stood at the door and gazed at her.

"Your ass looks so good up there like that," he said.

Persha laughed. "You can't even see my ass," she said.

"I know what I *can* see," he teased.

"Well, you gonna stand there and watch or you gonna come over here and give *her* what she needs?" Persha grinned wickedly.

"Touch it for me," Clarke said as he started stroking his fading erection. "Yeah, that's what I like. Damn, shorty!"

Using one hand to lift her breast to her mouth, Persha used her tongue to lick the tip of her nipple.

"Oh girl, damn, girl!" He dropped the robe at his feet and walked over to the vanity counter.

Before she could inch back farther on the countertop, Clarke had already thrust himself into her.

"Aahh, this is what I needed," he cried.

Persha pushed him back. "Clarke, baby, you can't go bare. I just got off antibiotics. My pills, that messes them up."

"Oh, shit! But wait. Just hold on a sec," he said, still moving his hips.

"Damn, this feels soooo good, baby. But you gotta stop," she cried. "You gotta stop."

He pushed himself deeper, spreading her legs farther apart. "Ah—I—a brotha just gotta—"

"Clarke, baby, you gotta get strapped."

"But oohhweeeeee your pussy; it's so sweet and wet, baby. This one time won't hurt. You feel it? I'ma pull out. I'ma pull out! You feel it?" he whispered as if he were in another world.

"Oh yes, baby, I do."

"It feels good?" he whispered.

"Mm-hmm. Soooooo good," she cried.

As he pushed in, she moved up, spreading her legs wider and wider. Her body started getting hot all over again as she started clawing at his chest, his neck, and his back.

"Oh, Clarke, this is so . . . I needed you, baby. I needed this."

"I know, shorty, I know. Damn, your pussy is so tight. It's good, baby." Clarke grabbed her breasts and started humping her harder.

"You gotta pull out, Clarke. You gotta pull out."

"Not now, baby. I can't. This is too good. Oooooh, it's so good. Not now!"

Bending his knees a bit, he slowed his pace, but kept his balance as his hips rocked from side to side. Suddenly, Clarke's eyes widened. He froze, grabbed her waist and then shoved himself farther into her.

"Oh, shorty," he whispered, and looked directly into her eyes.

She never felt closer to him than at that very moment. Without saying a word, he had told her so much. Then without warning and with his eyes still glued to hers, he wiggled one last time before crying out in sheer ecstasy.

"Oh, shorty. It feels so . . . a brotha can't hold it. Shhhhiiiiiit!"

When he exploded, Persha literally felt it. She held on, tightly matching his movements. Then she felt herself about to erupt for the second time. She buried her face into his shoulder as he fell onto her body. For a long time, they lay there, panting in each other's sweat.

A few minutes later he backed up. "Damn, girl! You got some good shit! No doubt about it!"

Persha didn't know if she should move or keep her position.

"Whew! You wore a brotha out, shorty!" He walked over to the shower and turned on the water.

Hopping off the countertop, Persha looked at herself in the mirror. Trying to pull her hair together she became mesmerized at her reflection.

"You coming in?" Clarke yelled over the water.

"I'll wait till you're through," she said, still staring at her reflection.

She couldn't believe what she was doing. Not only was she sleeping with a married man, but she had just moved into his house, the very house he shared with his wife! And to make matters worse, the very best sex they'd ever had happened right in the bathroom of that same house.

Persha knew she was tripping. Not only had she fucked this other woman's man in their private bathroom in their house, but she had fucked him on top of a cold hard sink in front of a mirror with absolutely no protection.

Hours later when Persha woke in the pastel-colored guest room, she immediately smelled the fresh flowers sitting next to the bed. Looking around, she wondered where Clarke had escaped to and what time it was. While she didn't know where he had run off to, the digital clock read 9:45 P.M.

She hated napping in the evening because it was so hard to go to sleep at night. By the time she found her clothes and got them on, there was a light knock at the bedroom door.

"Yes?" she stated.

"You up yet?" Clarke asked, opening the door just enough to stick his head and upper body in.

"I was wondering where you were."

"I was downstairs watching TV. I didn't want to wake you, but I'm about to call it a night so I figured I'd check up on you."

She smiled weakly.

"You okay, shorty? Whassup?" he asked, opening the door wider.

"I'm kind of hungry," she said.

"I ordered a pizza. There's still some left in the kitchen. You're more than welcome to it."

"Okay." Persha was looking at the curl of his lips. "What?" She shrugged.

"Well, I was just wondering what you're willing to do for that pizza." Clarke rubbed his crotch and smiled at her.

Good lord! She couldn't believe he wanted more sex after the evening they had had. Afraid of turning down his advance, she stopped and looked down at his crotch.

"You mean to tell me you didn't have enough?" she asked as she stood up and walked over to him.

"It's just so good, baby. But I was wondering if you could, well, help a brotha out in another area." He shrugged.

She cocked an eyebrow up at him.

"You know, after you eat, maybe you can come kiss

a brotha good night. What do you say?" He smiled, still rubbing his crotch.

"You're a hot mess!" She pushed him slightly on her way out of the room.

Chasing behind her as she made her way to the kitchen, Clarke yelled, "Is that a yes or no?"

When she turned around in the kitchen, Persha was a bit surprised to see him still holding himself. She ignored him and proceeded to get a couple of slices of pizza. She was glad he sat there while she ate. She didn't like being alone in the house, regardless of what time it was.

As she started to get up from the table, he reached for her hand.

"Oh, let me get this. You left some crumbs on the counter." He took her plate and started brushing at something Persha couldn't quite see. When he finished, he walked over to the sink and washed both the plate and glass she used.

"I could've done that, Clarke."

"Oh, I don't mind. I don't like dishes piling up in the sink, so I try to keep things tidy around here."

She watched as he busied himself with the dishes. Again, this was a side to him she never knew existed. Years ago when they dated, not only was he not interested in plants and flowers, but he could leave a glass on her table till a ring formed and still not move a muscle to lift it.

Back upstairs they were about to pass up her room when she stopped.

"I know this is probably not comfortable for you," Clarke stated, "but I wouldn't have you here if it wasn't cool, so don't trip. Why don't you stay with me tonight?" he asked.

There was something about the thought of sleeping in his wife's bed that stroked her the wrong way. What if Kelsa came home early and found them in *her* bed. Persha knew this was the making for a serious crime of passion, and no jury would convict.

"What do you mean?" she asked.

"I just thought you might like to sleep next to a warm body instead of sleeping alone."

"That would be nice," she confessed. "But why don't we go into my room, if that's okay."

"Well, to be honest, I don't like the bed in there. But if you want to sleep in there, why don't you come and kiss me off to sleep? Then you can come back here. Cool?"

"Yeah, that sounds cool," Persha agreed, joining him in his and Kelsa's bed, thinking what choice did she really have anyway?

As she laid in the bed, trying to take all of him into her mouth, Persha swore he'd grown since the last time they'd been together. She was wondering just what happened to that myth about men needing time to recuperate.

She had to jump back to dodge his fluids the first time, but all he did was use a rag to wipe himself dry and find his home back in her mouth again. Persha's jaw was sore and it was taking him longer to come this time.

Occasionally she'd open her eyes to look up at him and his face had a look of sheer pleasure on it. His eyes were closed and his expression would switch between a smile and a mincing frown.

When he grabbed her head and pushed himself even further into her mouth, she tried to back up, but his grip was too tight. A few minutes later she tasted his warm juices and started to gag.

"Damn, shorty," he moaned.

He used the same rag he had used the first time he came to wipe off. Persha got up and ran to the bathroom. By the time she walked back into the room, he was snoring, his massive chest moving up and down at a rested pace.

Her first day in the Hudson household went smoothly. She and Clarke slept together Friday night but had to wake at the crack of dawn on Saturday. He had already explained that Persha needed to make other arrangements for Saturday and Sunday. Clarke had told Persha that Kelsa tended to stay around the house on weekends because she was gone so much during the week. She was more than welcome back Monday after work.

Driving around the city of Houston before many people were even turning over in bed, Persha decided to find a twenty-four-hour restaurant and wait for sunrise.

The moment she deemed it a decent hour, she called Kori.

"Hey, girly, what's up?" Persha asked. "You feel like meeting for breakfast?"

"Mmm-hmm. Where you talking about meeting?" Kori asked.

"I'm at I-Hop near the Beltway."

"So I see you still in that southwest part of town, right?"

"Well, I thought it would be best if I stayed close to the house. I'm supposed to meet with the insurance people a few times, so that just makes it easier. You didn't tell Cricket did you?"

When Kori didn't respond right away, Persha felt her heart beating a mile a minute.

"Kori! I know you heard me," Persha said, fuming. Persha didn't need Cricket's negative comments. That was precisely why she never told either of them about her new living arrangement with Clarke.

"I asked you not to say anything to her about this."

"Well, it's not like I had a choice. What was I sup-

posed to say when she asked about you? Anyways, she
wasn't trippin'. It's not like you're staying *with* Clarke.
I just told her he was going to help you out."

Persha sighed. She could see the brilliant rays of
sunlight creeping over buildings in the horizon.

"Look, I'ma 'bout to go so I can get there. I'm
starved. You call Cricket yet?" Kori asked before hanging up.

"Oops, I forgot, I'll call her now and we'll see you
there."

Nearly an hour later as Persha and Kori were about
to be seated, Cricket ran up, out of breath.

"Hey, thanks for calling me for the girlfriend meeting at the last damn minute!"

Seated at a booth the three started studying their
menus. A few minutes later, Cricket placed hers down
and looked at Persha.

"My auntie and I have already talked. We want you
to come and stay at the house. I don't think it's right for
your married boyfriend to pay your rent. It's like you're
a kept woman."

" 'Scuse me?" Persha said, her brows twisted upward.

"Kori told me the entire story, and while I feel sad
for what's happened to you and your house and all that,
I think this is a good time to break things off with him
and move in a different direction," Cricket said as she
sat poised. "Girl, sistahs ain't got time to be harming
each other. We need to be more supportive and encour-
age one another to live right, take care of ourselves,
physically and emotionally. You could get any man you
want with your fine self. Girl, you don't need to be
sharing no two-bit punk with some other sistah." She
crossed her hands on the table with a look on her face
that said she was ready to read anyone who wanted to
step up.

"Respect yourself, girlfriend. That's all I'm talking about. You know I love you, and I know you love yourself, right? So let that dog go back home to his wife."

Persha glared at Kori, who inched lower and lower behind the menu. She cleared her throat, adjusted herself in her chair and prepared to go toe-to-toe with Cricket.

"You just don't understand, Cricket," Persha started.

Cricket's voice dropped an octave. She leaned forward and squinted one eye nearly shut. "I don't understand what? What is it I don't understand? What, that you're wasting your time with a married man, one who cares nothing about anybody but himself? Or maybe I don't understand because I haven't been on a date in more than a year. Which is it, Persha?"

Persha started backing down. She knew it was a war she wouldn't win, because she knew Cricket was right.

"I'm just going through a lot right now," Persha sighed. "I don't need y'all beating me up."

"Hey, girlfriend, that ain't even what I'm all about, you know that. You may have your head screwed on backwards, but you know I love you and I always will. That's why I'm trying to state my position right off the bat. You know I don't like his chicken ass for what he did when we were back in school, but that was damn near ten years ago. So now, all I'm saying is he's headed for disaster, and I don't want to see you go along for the ride, that's all," she said easily, shrugging her shoulders.

When the waitress arrived to take orders, each snapped out of the conversation as if on cue. And the minute she walked away, Cricket started up again.

"I say you come stay with me at my aunt's, even with the cats as opposed to being at some married man's beck and call," Cricket said, rolling her eyes. "That's all I'm saying."

Cricket leaned back in her seat, waiting for Persha's answer.

"That's kind of you," Persha said, "but I think it would be best if I stayed where I am. And no offense, but you know I have allergies, and all those cats; girl, I'd lose my mind."

"But what about your morals, about your dignity, self-respect, self-love? What's having a mind if you've lost everything else?" Cricket shrugged matter-of-factly.

"Okay, that's enough, Cricket," Kori said, jumping to Persha's defense. "If Persha wants to stay in a place her man pays for, leave her alone. You shouldn't lose sight of the fact that sometimes we just have to accept each other for who we are and leave it at that. Now, I don't want this girlfriend's day to be ruined with you two arguing and bickering."

They sat back as their food arrived.

"Now, let's eat and then hit Garden Ridge first, then the malls. We need positive energy, not chaos," Kori said. "As long as she's happy, we should be happy. I mean, you're looking a lot better, girlfriend." Kori grinned at Persha before digging into her food.

"I feel good too, now that the antibiotics took care of that mold poisoning. I'm good as new." Persha smiled.

Despite her smile, Persha wondered secretly just how long she could keep up the charade.

Clarke

Clarke was thrilled to see the weekend finally winding down. Between magnificent blow jobs with his lover, and sex with his wife, he was ready for Kelsa to go back to work and looking forward to some downtime for himself.

As he suspected, she never once opened the door to the spare bedroom. He knew his wife had a pet peeve about doors being open upstairs, so they kept all doors closed at all times. That's how he knew it wouldn't be a problem to have Persha staying there.

Although he knew for a fact Persha wasn't sleeping with anyone else, he said a silent prayer in hopes that she wouldn't need a little fine-tuning when she came back.

Sitting up in bed Sunday evening, Clarke looked over at Kelsa's mocha-colored skin. She wasn't a *beautiful* sistah, but she was all right. Her hazel-colored eyes were probably her biggest asset because, in his eyes, her body was average. It was nothing that jumped out in the tits and ass department. But she was reliable.

"What's the matter?" Kelsa asked with eyes glowing at Clarke.

"Aw, can't a brotha admire his lovely wife?" Clarke said. He had been trying to score points all weekend. When Kelsa's car pulled into the driveway just after eight o'clock Saturday morning, he already had breakfast waiting for her. It was only toast, eggs, and coffee, but it did the trick.

Not for one minute did she suspect another woman had been in her house, and to make sure she never did, Clarke shadowed her everywhere she went. Kelsa must've passed up the guest room hundreds of times and never as much as looked toward the door for more than two seconds.

Since he did most of the housecleaning, she really had no reason to even wonder if the room was straightened up.

"I'm so very tired," said Kelsa.

Clarke snapped out of it and reached over to rub her shoulders. "Here, you need some help getting to sleep tonight?" he asked.

Kelsa gave him a knowing look. She inched forward and adjusted her body to reap the benefits of the impromptu massage.

Clarke was proud of how well things seemed to be going. He knew once he got her off to class and then work, it would be smooth sailing for Persha to come back to the house.

By Wednesday, hump day, the arrangement had been working just fine. That evening he decided he'd make a nice dinner for Persha. Truth be told, he really didn't like her messing around in the kitchen anyway.

As they sat for dinner the sexual tension was floating thickly in the air. Just before she took a drink from the wine goblet, he noticed how her lips pursed as if preparing to welcome his.

The thin silk slip she was wearing showed off all her curves, from her deep settled bosom, to the small waist and her thick hips. He couldn't wait to get his hands on her.

Candlelight and soft music added to the ambiance of the evening. After wrapping up dinner, he looked across the table and winked at her. She smiled, matching his flirting.

"Why don't you go make yourself comfortable in the living room. Push play on the DVD player and wait for me. I'm about to clean this up and I'll meet you in there."

Persha was glad to take him up on his offer. Clarke watched as she got up from the table and headed toward the living room. Clarke could see her hips swaying in the thin silk fabric.

That's when it dawned on him that he hadn't fucked anyone in almost three days. Oh, he was more than ready to get his freak on.

Instead of hand washing the dishes, he started loading the dishwasher. As he stood near the machine, he could feel the bulge growing in his pants.

Now, thinking about it, he could hardly wait to get inside of Persha. She was always warm, wet, and welcoming. No doubt about it, that girl loved sex, and he loved that about her.

He saw the light glaring from the big-screen TV, but still heard the soft music blaring through the speakers. He hoped the porno he picked would get her all worked up so that he could handle his business.

After wiping down the table and counters, he started the dishwasher and was by her side within seconds. He was happy when he noticed her thongs underneath the coffee table.

"You picked this, huh?" Persha asked, referring to the porno.

Clarke smiled and replied, "Yeah, I thought you might find it interesting."

In the porno, one woman was servicing several men in a park setting. One at a time, they took turns having their way with her as the camera continued to capture her smiles.

Before Clarke could figure out whether Persha was feeling the vibe, he reached for her slip and yanked it off.

"Shorty, you make me crazy thinking about you," he said.

His mouth cupped hers and they rolled onto the floor. She was just as eager, tugging and pulling at the buttons on his shirt. When she didn't undo them fast enough, Clarke pulled it open, buttons popping off. Persha feverishly attacked his chest, slopping and kissing all over his nipples.

"Oh, shorty!" he moaned.

Clarke's heart was beating faster by the minute. He couldn't keep his hands off her, exploring and roaming her body in search of any trigger spots.

She was already wet. He leaned back to strip off his pants and release his erection when she put one hand up.

"Hold up a sec," she said, breathing heavily.

His eyes were glued to her stiffened nipples. They made his mouth water and his heart beat faster.

"Whassup, shorty?" He grabbed his crotch. "I know you want a brotha. Don't tell me you've become a tease all of a sudden."

"Nah, nothing like that, Clarke. But, baby, go get a condom. You got to be strapped."

"Aw, girl! Is that what you're worried about? We done already did it once. Another time ain't gonna hurt. C'mon!"

She shook her head. "No, Clarke. You need a condom. I already told you about my pills last time. I'm just getting back on them real good, so we need to use protection."

He fell back onto bended knees. "Damn, shorty. A brotha ain't got no damn condoms! You can't just leave me here like this. I'm harder than a rock!" He looked down at the bulge in his pants with a pitiful look on his face.

Still shaking her head, she looked up at him. "You've got to have one condom somewhere around here."

"I don't! Can't we just do it this one last time? I promise I'll go buy some tomorrow, first thing! Damn, I swear," he said with a frown.

"Nah, that's not good enough." She eased up from her wanting position on the floor and he moved toward her.

"Shorty, just let me put the head in. I just want to feel you. I won't even go in all the way, I promise. Just let a brotha feel you, and I'll pull right out! I swear, girl!" He rubbed his crotch as if to ease the desire burning in his loins.

"C'mon, Clarke. You're not thinking straight. If you don't have a condom, we should just go take a cold shower. Ain't no need to go any further. If you're not strapped, you need to step back!"

Looking at the larger-than-life sixty-two-inch screen of the woman performing various sex acts with her partners, he sucked his teeth and sat down.

"I don't believe this shit! You been with somebody else?" he questioned.

"What?"

"I mean, if you ain't sleeping with nobody else, and

you know I ain't sleeping with Kelsa's ass, I don't see what the problem is. You act like a brotha gonna give you the heebie-jeebies or something."

"Clarke, that has nothing to do with it and you know it. A disease isn't the only thing we got to think about. I don't want to get pregnant right now. We just need to be careful, that's all I'm saying."

He started pouting, hoping that would change her mind.

"Well, maybe you could kiss a brotha off to sleep. I need something, shorty!" He looked down at the bulge in his pants. "Look at this. You gonna let a rock-hard thangie go to waste, baby?"

"I'm afraid so; if we ain't got no condoms."

"Okay." He started unzipping his pants. "Well, here. Let me sit on the couch so you can get busy. How's that sound?"

"Why don't I go check and see if I have any condoms in my car?" Persha said.

His eyes lit up. "No shit?"

"It might be old, but I may have one or two lying around somewhere. It's worth a try to go look."

"Cool, okay, but hurry back," he whined.

Persha got up from the floor and picked up her slip. As she was about to put it over her head, he tugged at it.

"Quite surely you don't expect me to go out there naked, do you?" she asked with a sensual grin.

"Nah, shorty. I'm just admiring your goddess of a body. Okay, go ahead, but hurry back!" He started stroking himself again.

Persha put on the slip and stepped back into her mules. As she reached the door, she turned back and looked at Clarke.

"Dammit, my keys are upstairs in my purse. I'll be

right back," she said as she headed up the steps and retrieved her keys.

When she came back downstairs, she could barely
make it out the door before he stopped her.

"Where are you going with your purse?"

"Clarke, if I can't find a condom in the car, I'm
gonna drive down to the corner store."

With a bewildered look on his face he said, "What
corner store?"

"I'll find one," she said, slamming the door behind
her.

Ten minutes later, when Persha still hadn't returned,
Clarke thought about going to look down the street but
he figured he'd just wait. If worse came to worse, he'd
just have to beat himself off then make her work to get
it back up.

Things were getting pretty steamy on the flick, and
he didn't know how much longer he could wait. He figured he'd at least get out of the pants, that way she
could really get an idea of the seriousness of the situation.

Lying back on the sofa with his eyes glued to the
big-screen TV, Clarke was getting all worked up. His
mind kept thinking of all the ways he'd fuck Persha.
Maybe on the coffee table, standing up, or even on a
chair, or they'd try them all. But, the way he was feeling, he could probably fuck her for hours nonstop and
he'd be okay with that too.

When he looked up nearly twenty minutes later and
he was still alone, he started wondering just where the
hell she was.

"Damn!" he spat, getting up from his spot in front of
some action he'd soon try to match. He walked to the
door, and just as he was about the grab the knob, it
swung open.

His eyes widened in horror and his mouth dropped.

Kelsa took one look at her husband and started frowning.

"What are you doing up in your underwear?" she asked.

He followed her gaze down to his crotch and shrugged his shoulders. *What the fuck?* he thought. Suddenly he started perspiring.

"Hey! Kelsa!" he said awkwardly.

"Well, are you gonna let me in or just stand here blocking the doorway?" she asked, sounding irritated.

"Oh, shit! Ah—I'm—oh, yeah, of course you can come in. This is your house!" He watched as she stepped past him and into the living room.

Clarke closed the door and dead bolted the lock. He even looked out the peephole before turning to see his wife standing there with her hands on her hips.

"What the hell is going on in here?" she hissed. He knew she was fuming. He could visualize the smoke that would be coming from her ears if she were a cartoon character.

"Oh, that," he motioned toward the large screen and the people performing various sexual acts and smiled.

Kelsa stood waiting for a response. Clarke walked all the way into the living room. He was relieved he had put the dishes away and cleaned up. He didn't need her finding out about their little houseguest.

Kelsa cleared her throat and stood firm in her spot.

"I asked what is going on in here, Clarke Hudson?" she asked.

"Damn, baby, why you hassling a brotha? I was just sitting back watching a flick. It's not against the law in my own damn house is it?" He frowned, staring down her gaze.

"Are you here with someone, Clarke?"

"What?" he asked as if offended by her query.

Kelsa had eased her hands away from her hips. "I said, are you here with someone? You heard me," she snapped, twisting her neck.

"Nah, girl, you crazy. Ain't nobody here but me."

She started looking around the room, but didn't say anything. When her eyes met his again, she seemed a bit calmer.

"I don't understand. Soft music, lights dimmed, and a porno playing. What are you doing with this type of shit, all by yourself?"

Clarke sat on the sofa. "What, now you don't trust your man? You don't trust me now, because you came home and found me watching a flick?" He threw his hands up and started shaking his head.

When he saw worry starting to creep across her face, he knew he'd be okay.

"If I can't watch a flick at the house, then I don't know where I can see one. You ought to be glad your man ain't out roaming the streets and sniffing every skirt he can find. Instead, I'm sitting here thinking about you, wishing you were home, but willing to put my needs on hold anyway. I try to stay faithful and this is the shit I get for it?"

Clarke stormed over to the couch and sat down.

"Oh, Clarke, I'm sorry," Kelsa said as she walked over towards the couch. With Kelsa's back toward the front door, she couldn't see the bright blue piece of cloth that caught Clarke's eye.

"Shit!" he whispered.

"Darling, I said I'm sorry. You're right. I should be happy to find you here all alone, even though you're watching a dirty movie. The point is, most men would probably be out on the prowl somewhere. I love you." She walked over to him and leaned in for a hug.

He moved up just enough to use his foot to scoot Persha's thongs under the sofa. Clarke released a huge sigh of relief when they finally separated.

Kelsa glanced at the screen, then back at Clarke's face.

"Baby, it's okay to look at flicks." Clarke attempted to convince her. "Lots of married people do it, you know."

Bashfully, Kelsa shook her head in agreement, but purposely avoided looking back at the screen. "Why don't I go upstairs, take a shower, and change? Maybe I can help you out, if you know what I mean." She winked.

Fuck the shower, Clarke thought to himself. *How about you just let me get under your skirt, move your panties to the side, take care of my business, then you can take your ass to sleep?*

Clarke didn't feel like waiting for her to take a shower, nor did he really feel like touching her. Kelsa's body had nothing on Persha's. All he could do was think about those nice big tits and that poppin' ass of hers.

"How does that sound?" Kelsa asked.

"Oh, yeah, that'll work. I'll just watch this for a few more minutes and clean up down here while you get in the shower. I'll be up real soon."

She reached over and kissed him before walking to the staircase. When he heard her open their bedroom door, he quickly dug out Persha's panties. He picked up his pants and stood in front of the TV for a few minutes.

Clarke tried to absorb as much as he could of the X-rated images. He held Persha's thongs up to his face and inhaled long and hard. Oh, how he wanted her ass.

He could all but taste her pussy standing right there. Clarke reached for the remote and turned off the movie. Just as he turned off the radio he heard a soft tap on the front door.

"Damn! Perfect timing, Persha!" Frowning, he rushed over to the door and swung it open. "What the hell took you so long? Kelsa's here! She's upstairs taking a shower!" he whispered.

"What?" Persha said, her eyes darting over Clarke's shoulder.

Clarke could see the alarm in her eyes. She was nervous, and he hoped she could tell just how mad he was.

"Man, shorty, you fucked up! Where you been anyway?"

"I had to go to a store to find some condoms!"

"See, I told your ass let's do it one last time, but no, you had to go find your fucking condoms. Now look what you've done. I probably gotta go upstairs and fuck her now!" he huffed.

Persha jumped back. "What?" she all but screamed.

"Sssssshhhhhhh! You want her to hear us? This is your fault! She caught me up in here in my drawers watching a flick. I told her I was horny as hell. What else could I tell her?"

"I thought you guys didn't have sex anymore. That's what you told me," she whispered, hot and heavy.

"Persha, don't go getting all soft on me now. You know I don't fuck her anymore. But how else was I supposed to explain the way she found me and this place. She's not stupid, you know."

"Clarke?" Persha and Clarke heard a voice call as they turned and looked toward the stairway. "Is somebody there?" Kelsa's voice asked.

"Nah, baby, that's the TV," Clarke answered. "I'm about to come on up. You showered yet?"

"No, I'm about to. Give me a few minutes. I'll be ready soon."

"Okay," Clarke answered.

He looked back at Persha and shrugged. "So what's up?" he asked.

"Let's just go get a room," she said.

He frowned. "Go get a what? A room? What a brotha wanna spend cash for something he could get right here for free?"

Persha had a puzzled look on her face. She was speechless.

"Look, you can stay here tonight. Just wait 'till I close the door and sneak up to your room. I'll turn the radio on. But you've got to be late tomorrow, because Kelsa won't leave for class until about six o'clock. Cool?" Persha didn't answer. "Shorty? What's up?" he asked, keeping an eye on the staircase.

"I don't want you to sleep with her tonight," Persha admitted.

"What?" Looking into Persha's eyes, Clarke told himself not to feel bad. After all, he was doing what he had to, he reasoned. It was her screwup to begin with.

"Clarke, I mean it. You said yourself you don't love her anymore. You're leaving her, so I don't think you should be having sex with her."

For a moment he wondered if she knew what she was saying. Kelsa was his wife. How was she expecting him not to sleep with her? Realizing his time was running out, he reached for Persha and kissed her passionately.

"Okay, you're right," he said in defeat. "I'll just tell her my head hurts. But that means you're gonna square a brotha away later, right?"

She nodded and watched as he reluctantly walked up the stairs to go and be with his wife.

Persha

Persha bolted up from bed and glanced around the darkened room. Her heart was racing and she felt horrible. She eased back onto the bed and squeezed her eyes shut. The images haunted her thoughts, so her eyes snapped open and she glanced around the room again.

"There!" she whispered. "I know I heard something that time." She strained to hear, but all was quiet. Again, she eased her body back onto the bed and pulled the covers up around herself.

Persha couldn't sleep a wink. Throughout the night she continued to toss and wonder what was going on merely a few feet from the room she was occupying. This time when she sat up, she swung her feet around and got up out of bed. She took a deep breath and grabbed the door handle. She eased the door open and glanced down the hall in both directions. She tiptoed her way out of the room and crept up to Clarke and his wife's bedroom door.

With her ear pressed against the door, she held her breath and pushed her ear up as far against the door as it would go. Despite her struggle, she didn't hear a thing. Frustrated, she crept back to her room and quietly closed the door. She calmed herself by closing her eyes and counting to ten silently. Somewhat satisfied, she climbed back into bed and eased her body down.

After tossing a couple of times, she settled and convinced herself that her mind was playing tricks on her. Moments later, she knew for sure she had heard faint sounds of music coming from Clarke and Kelsa's. Again, she bolted upward and snuck down the hall and back to their bedroom door.

Persha had a good mind to burst in there and tell ol' wifey-poo exactly what was up; plain and simple! She burned with anger and sheer jealously as she sulked back to her room. If Clarke wasn't man enough to speak up for what he really wanted, then she'd just have to do the job herself!

For the next two hours, painful images of Clarke having sex with his wife, danced through her mind.

A couple more times Persha popped up, thinking she had heard sounds of passion coming from the room. She finally convinced herself again that it was just her mind tripping.

And what about that comment Clarke had made earlier, saying he wasn't gonna pay for something he could get for free at home? Was he talking about the room, or the sex? The thought made Persha sick with anger.

She started thinking maybe this wasn't such a good idea after all. She knew he meant well, but the pain of knowing he was in that bed with another woman was just too much. If he'd tortured her for hours and watched her die a slow and painful death, that wouldn't be as bad as what she had been feeling.

Persha believed in the fairy tale. Her mother never had it, her mother's sister never had it, but she still believed in it. She wanted to be the one who had it all. She felt deep down in her bones that with Clarke, she could have that fairy tale. They could get married, raise a family and actually have a chance at happiness. That would make her Bible-toting mother proud beyond words.

But that night, Persha's mind continued to play tricks on her. When the digital clock proved it was 4:45 in the morning, she was still determined to get some sleep. Maybe she should've let him go bare again. He did have a point. They'd already done it one time, so what was a second time gonna hurt?

But then if she had, Kelsa would've walked in on them in the act. Then what would they have done? Clarke was always talking about timing is everything, saying he couldn't leave her just yet. Persha started thinking, *If they had been caught, that might have helped the divorce move a bit quicker.*

The last thing she remembered thinking about was Cricket dressed in all white standing downstairs while she and Clarke were whispering in the wee hours of the morning.

"Self-respect! Love yourself! Where's your dignity? Have you any pride or morals left? Sistahs should be held to higher standards! We need to help, not hurt each other!"

Waking up, Persha couldn't believe she was dreaming about Cricket. She was glad her friends would never learn the depth of her lows, because sometimes even she found her actions hard to believe.

Suddenly, fear struck her heart. What should she do? It was 7:45 in the morning, and she hadn't seen nor heard from Clarke since last night. How was she expected to know if Kelsa was gone?

Persha swung her feet onto the floor. She got up and quickly made the bed. She didn't dare try to make it to the bathroom, even though she had to piss like a race-horse.

After a few minutes and she still heard no sound outside her room, she was considering leaving for the bathroom. Forget the fact she didn't get to call work and tell them she'd be late. There was usually only two of them in the small insurance office, so hopefully the agent wouldn't be coming in today.

It didn't take long for her to start wriggling and squirming to hold her pee. She wondered why Clarke hadn't come to rescue her. Suddenly her mind went from escaping to relieving her bladder any way she could.

She quickly scanned the pretty room, but the only thing she saw was the vase of flowers. Persha didn't want to, but it seemed since she looked at it, she wanted to pee even more.

"Five minutes! I'm giving him five minutes to come get me, then I'm just gonna have to do whatever I can," she said to herself, trying to take her mind off the need to pee. "Nah-ah, two minutes. I've already waited all damn night. Two minutes; that's it," she swore.

But soon she made her way to the vase. She could barely lift up her slip before she was able to move the flowers over and get the vase between her thighs.

The relief she felt was immeasurable. With her eyes closed and more pee than she had ever experienced leaving her body, she was quickly overcome with re-lief.

When Clarke cleared his throat, she nearly dropped the vase as she felt the warm fluid run along her arm.

"Persha, not in my tulips!" he screamed.

She couldn't stop the flow; especially since she was nearly finished. When she was finally done, she sighed and used the edge of her slip to dry herself.

"I'm so sorry you had to see that, but Clarke, I didn't

know what else to do. I didn't know if I should try to make it to the bathroom or just wait here for you to get me. I had to go. I tried to hold it, but after fifteen minutes, there was nothing I could do."

He didn't say anything. He just looked at the small spot on the carpet and the vase sitting next to it.

"I didn't know if your wife was leaving this morning, or if y'all were sleeping in." Her voice was laced with sarcasm.

Clarke ignored her comment and leaned against the door.

"Well, I suppose it was a good thing you didn't come out. Kelsa didn't go to class this morning."

"What's going on with her? I mean, why did she just pop up like that last night?"

He shrugged his shoulders. "I don't know. She says she wasn't feeling well."

"Is she still here?" Persha asked, wondering just how the hell she was going to shower and get ready for work.

"No, she's not, but she'll be right back. I sent her to the store for some syrup and milk. So that means you've got to hustle."

"Okay, well, let me take a quick shower and hopefully I can get out of here before she gets back."

Clarke stood at the door. "No, Persha, that's not good enough. I mean you need to leave now! You don't have time for a shower. Just grab your stuff and go! I'll call you later at the office and we'll talk about it tonight."

"What? I can't even brush my teeth?"

"Look, shorty, this ain't easy for me either. You think I wanted to sleep with her last night, especially knowing you were a few doors down? That was probably one of the hardest things I've had to do. But hey, I managed, because I know better things are on the way."

"But, Clarke."

"Shorty, she'll be back soon, so you need to leave before we get caught. You know that wouldn't even be cool."

Persha didn't want to give up that easily, but she knew she didn't have a choice. She cast her gaze down at the carpet and said, "Okay, let me grab my stuff and I'll leave."

She drove into the basement parking lot of her building in the Galleria area and made a quick dash for the restroom. No one used the basement restrooms, so she had a few minutes to give herself an Indian bath in the sink and brush her teeth.

With her clothes wrinkled, her hair half done, and her makeup looking crazy, she walked into the small office and tried to act normal. The office was small and cluttered. There were old phone books from previous years in the corners, on tables and on old file cabinets. There were a few old plants stacked on top of phone books that served as tables.

Two desks, one for Persha and the other for Brenda, the office manager sat in the middle of the office. Persha's desk was also cluttered just like the rest of the office; she had stacks of policies, files, and old pictures of herself, her mom, and her girls scattered on the desk. Buried beneath all of that was a telephone and the usual office supplies.

The office had old blinds that they kept shut at all times and a door off to the left of the room that was a closet converted into an office for the agent.

Before Brenda could say a word, Persha looked up from her desk and sighed.

"I tell you, I'm having such a hard time with this mold stuff and the insurance company," Persha complained.

"Ooooh, they still trying not to pay your claim?" Brenda asked, but her features had already softened, so

Persha knew she'd get away with being almost an hour late, despite the fact she didn't even call.

"Yeah, and look at me. I'm barely making it, living out of a suitcase at a cheap motel. I don't know how much longer I'll be able to hang in there."

"Emph! Poor thing," Brenda cried.

"I'll be okay, though."

"You know, not all the time, but if you need a place to sleep, baby, come on over to my place. I sure hate you having to go through this mess, with your mama so far away too. It's just me and Jessie, and he works the overnight post on Friday through Sunday, so you keep that in mind, you hear?"

The phone rang, so Persha didn't have to do anything more than shake her head. Brenda caught the phone and that left Persha alone with her thoughts.

At around 11:45 in the afternoon Brenda suddenly started laughing. During this time, Persha was bent over and digging for paperwork at the bottom of her desk drawer.

"I'm glad you find humor in this," she said without looking up.

"Persha!" Brenda called all giddy.

"Brenda, if Mr. Tomlin comes back and I don't have those papers, I'm dead meat." She didn't look up.

"Oh, Persha, I think you can break for a minute or two," Brenda sang.

When Persha stood up and turned around she nearly cried at the sight of Clarke standing there with a vase of tulips and baby's breaths.

"I figured you had a bad night after we talked on the phone this morning, so I was hoping these might make you feel better," Clarke said. "I'd also like to take you out for lunch if you're free." He smiled, then looked at the flowers. "And, well, I had no doubt tulips would bring a smile to your face."

"Just precious! Just precious!" Brenda sat back, clapping her hands like a child.

Speechless, Persha looked at Brenda then back at Clarke with the flowers.

"Oh, shoot! You didn't have to do that," Persha said. "You've helped so much already." Tears started rolling down her cheeks.

"Girl, you'd better take these flowers before I give them to Ms. Brenda!" Clarke threatened.

"Ooooo-wee, chile. And you know I'd love to have 'em too," Brenda joked. "Tulips are my favorite!"

After they decided the best place to put the vase in the small cramped office, Clarke turned to Brenda and asked, "Would you like to join us for lunch?"

"Oh no, I couldn't. You lovebirds go right ahead. I'll hold down the fort," Brenda insisted.

"Okay, but you want me to bring something back for you?" Persha said as she grabbed her purse.

"No, baby, I'm gonna make my way up to the sixth floor and grab something from the deli in a bit."

"You sure?"

"Yes I am. Now scoot and have a good time."

Persha looked at Clarke and then said, "I need to go to the bathroom first, if you don't mind."

"Whatever you want," he said, holding the door open for her. They walked over to the bank of elevators and waited for one going down. They then hopped on the elevator and headed down to the basement level.

On the elevator, Persha turned toward Clarke and said, "Did you have sex with Kelsa last night?"

"No, girl!" Clarke exclaimed.

She took his word and left it at that.

When the elevator doors opened, they were the only two down there. "The bathroom is over here," she said as she pointed to her right. "And no one ever comes down here." She grinned as his eyebrow elevated upward.

"So you not hungry?" he asked.

"I am, but not for food right now. We can grab a quick burger later," she teased, leading him into the ladies' room.

Persha locked the door behind them and prayed no one would suddenly need to come in. Clarke's pants were already at his ankles when she turned to him. He put his hands on her shoulders and pushed her down to her knees.

That wasn't what she had in mind, but if it was what she had to do to keep her man satisfied and out of his wife's bed, then she'd do it. After a few minutes longer than she intended, she got up and hiked up her skirt.

"Damn, you didn't have on any panties?" he asked, excitedly.

"I didn't have time to grab any this morning," she tossed at him. Before she could lean up against the sink, Clarke was on his knees and his head was buried between her thighs.

While she was enjoying that, she really wanted to feel him inside of her. She let him go at it for a few more minutes before whispering, "Clarke, baby, give me what I really want."

He moved back and looked up at her. Persha hopped on to the sink and spread her legs.

"There's just something about you and sinks, huh?"

"Guess so," she said, smiling.

"I don't have a condom on me," he warned, hesitating before making another move.

"C'mon, Clarke, we don't have much time."

That's all he needed to hear.

With all his might, he thrust himself into her. She grabbed at his neck and his shoulder, finally settling

for his hips. She pulled him in, tugging at him harder.
Every time his hips moved, she tried to match his pace.
She spread her legs wider, and pulled him closer.
Clarke dipped his head down and took one of her nipples into his mouth. He held it between his teeth and
added just a bit of pressure as he continued to push
himself deeper between her thighs. A few minutes later,
they both exploded and collapsed into each other's arms.

"I swear you got the best pussy ever!" he said.

Persha looked into his eyes and said, "Don't you
ever forget that!"

A little while later, when Persha walked back into
the office, she looked even more tousled than she had
earlier.

Brenda glanced up at her. "So where'd you guys
eat?" Brenda asked.

"Huh?" Persha frowned. She had already forgotten
the excuse she and Clarke had used to slip out of the
office.

"Oh, yeah, we went to Macaroni Grill, you know,
right down the street here on Westheimer." She opened
the desk drawer and put her purse back.

"Emph, that sure was fast. Usually it takes just
about an hour to travel up Westheimer during the day,
much less up and back too."

"Yeah, well Clarke knows his way around real well,
so he's always taking shortcuts." When the phone rang,
Persha quickly grabbed for it. She didn't feel like entertaining any more of Brenda's nosy questions.

"Hey, girlfriend! What's going on?" Cricket said
through the phone.

"Aey Cricket, nothing much. What's up with you?"

"You were weighing heavy on my mind, so I knew
that meant I needed to call you. I put Auntie down after
a sponge bath and had a free moment."

Persha wished she'd get to the point. She knew that

wasn't the reason Cricket decided to call. Cricket was the type who moved and spoke at her very own pace regardless of whether it suited anyone else.

"Yeah, so I was thinking I'd be able to get away for a few hours this evening, and Kori agreed, so you were the last one left."

"Cricket?"

"Yeah?"

"What are you talking about?"

"Girl, see, that man's got your head so messed up, you can hardly pay attention. I was telling you, we're meeting at Fandingo's for dinner and margaritas this evening."

"Okay, I didn't catch that part," Persha added.

"See, it's that man. Your mind is slipping, gurlfriend. Know when something's no good for you, and know when to walk away and stay away."

"Okay, so what time are y'all meeting?"

"Mmm, about five o'clock. I know you're on Westheimer, and it's stop-and-go traffic down that entire stretch. So how's six o'clock? Is that good for you?"

"It should be. I'll meet y'all there."

Before Cricket could start preaching again, Persha hung up like that was her way of saying good-bye.

As if an afterthought, she turned her body to face her computer and dialed Clarke's number.

"The Ad Agency," the receptionist said, "handling all of your cleaning needs. How may I direct your call?"

Persha found that greeting strange for an advertising agency, but she figured, whatever's clever.

"Mr. Hudson please," Persha said.

"May I say who's calling?" the receptionist asked.

"Can you tell him that it's Persha?"

"Yes. Hold one moment please."

A few minutes later, his baritone rang through.

"Hey, shorty, what's up?" he asked.

"Nothing, I was calling to see if you have any plans for tonight." Persha relaxed a little when she heard Brenda on the phone. Sometimes it was hard sharing such a small office, nothing was ever private.

"Actually, I was thinking about meeting a few of the fellas for a drink. Why, whassup?"

"Nothing, my girls are crying about you taking up all my time." She chuckled.

"Hold up a sec, let me close this door." Persha heard him get up from his chair. She heard the door close a few minutes later.

"Okay, I'm back," he said. "Ah, Persha, you're not talking to your *girls* about *us* are you?"

She pulled the phone from her ear and looked at it closely, as if to better examine what he was saying. She didn't want to fly off the handle for no reason.

"What's that supposed to mean?" she asked, trying to control the tone of her voice.

"I'm just saying, I don't know if it's a good idea to be talking me up to your girls. I mean, you know how friends sometimes have a tendency to start dipping into folks' business. That's how shit gets all thrown off sometimes."

"Oookay, well, without going into full details, no, I don't talk you up around my girlfriends! Now, is that all you need to know?"

"Whoa! Shorty, whassup with all this 'tude? Now, a brotha can't even talk to his woman? Why you jumping all sensitive on me?" he asked innocently.

"You know what? This isn't the time nor the place for me to get into it." She rubbed her forehead with her free hand then stopped when she remembered that Brenda rarely missed a thing.

"Shorty, it ain't like I'm telling you not to run with your crew. I'm just saying be careful what you tell folks about your business. That's all I'm trying to say. I ain't trying to get you all twisted or nothing like that."

"Well, I was just trying to touch bases with you because I'm probably gonna have dinner with them and I may be late meeting you at the house. I was just trying to make sure I didn't miss our connection."

"I feel you, I feel you. Hey look, why don't you kick it with your girls for a few hours, get a little taste, then hit a brotha on the hip when you finish doing your thang and we'll go from there? Kelsa's back at work, so it's all gravy, baby."

"All right. I'll talk to you later. I love you, Clarke."

He hung up so fast that she knew he didn't hear her. Persha busied herself around the office until quitting time. A few minutes before five o'clock she grabbed her purse and rushed out before Brenda could start asking questions. She smiled as she passed the basement restrooms on her way to the garage.

Persha pulled into a spot in Fandingo's parking lot and wondered why she had agreed to go in the first place. She wasn't really in the mood to hear Cricket complaining. And she was still a bit perturbed from her phone conversation with Clarke.

Just as she decided to pull back out of the parking spot and turn back around, Kori knocked on her window and nearly scared her to death. Persha rolled the window down.

"Lawd have mercy! Gurl, whatchu doing out here in this heat?" Kori asked. "You better come in and have a cold rita! We already got a table."

"Oh, and here I thought I was actually early," Persha said.

"Nope! We're already on round number two. You better hurry."

"I'll be right in, let me clear my voice mail." She

watched as Kori's thin frame walked back into the building. When she got to the door, her bright pink linen dress almost blended into the building's wall. Her cornbread-colored skin was the only sign that she wasn't part of the fixture.

Persha had a feeling they'd been talking about her, especially if they were already on the second round. She didn't look forward to going inside, but against her better judgment, she went and joined them inside at their table anyway.

Like magic, when she sat down at the table, a drink appeared before her. The waitress reached from behind and gave her a straw.

"Do you know what you want?" the waitress asked with a thick accent.

After sipping in silence for a few minutes, Persha looked up. She sighed. "Dang, this is soooo good. Just what I needed." No one else said anything. Persha started feeling the tension, but she wasn't in the mood. She tried to ignore it. Especially since her nerves were still frayed from the conversation with Clarke.

Cricket looked at Kori and Kori looked at Persha. Neither said anything. Finally Persha's arched brows inched up.

"Okay, what's going on?" Persha asked.

"Nothing," Kori said quickly.

"Oh, we opened a tab at the bar, you know, to keep the drinks coming," Cricket threw in.

"That's cool, but what's the problem. What's up? What are you two really up to?" Persha's patience had run out. She didn't have time for this.

"You're gonna hate us," Cricket muttered.

Persha sighed, thinking *here we go again*. "Why exactly am I going to hate y'all?"

"It was all her idea," Kori quickly added. "I was forced, so I had to follow through."

"Let's cut the crap," Cricket said, returning to her no-nonsense style of handling everything.

Persha noticed that Cricket had her hair color replenished. Cricket sported a short curly Afro, the color of burned brown sugar, and it fit her face perfectly. Her features were well-defined; thin narrow nose, high cheekbones, and lips that looked naturally lined.

"Look, we know where you're staying and it ain't cool," Cricket said. "We're your girls and ain't no way in hell we gon' sit here and let you go out like that. We're not here to judge you, we just want to support you."

Persha's eyes began to swell with tears. It was a feeling she struggled to fight. When she tried to reach for her drink, Cricket stopped her hand by grabbing hold of it.

"I don't know how you're staying with this man, or where his wife is, but I've seen too many crazy things go down in my life. And if anything ever happened to you, neither of us would be able to live with ourselves for not doing something."

"Yeah, she's right. We love you, Persha," Kori chimed in.

Before she could do anything, Cricket pulled out a large envelope.

"There's fifteen-hundred dollars in here, enough for a down payment on an apartment. Lots of them are offering a month or two months' free rent. You should have some pocket change left over to buy a few personal things you might need. We wanted to get this to you sooner, but we had to pull our resources together. You know how that is."

"And don't even insult us by talking about paying it back. We also rented some cheesy furniture for you, but you can switch it out whenever you want. I figured three months would be enough time for that insurance crap to get resolved," Kori said. "I can't stand how we pay them every doggone month then when we need help they can take us through all this red tape. And if they treat you like this and you work in insurance, I could just imagine what they'd do to us common folk," Kori added.

With tears streaming down her cheeks, Persha looked at her friends. "There's no way I can take this money from y'all," she cried. Before they could even respond, she got up and dashed out of the restaurant.

Driving like a loose cannonball, Persha quickly dashed up Briar Park and headed toward Westpark. She was sure if they came after her, they would've thought she was driving back down Westheimer.

She couldn't believe what they had done. Yeah, it was nice of them to pull that money together, but why didn't they have faith in her man? He was making a way for them and she had to believe in him.

It didn't take long for Persha to slow down. She realized she couldn't get in the house until Clarke finished hanging out with his friends. She slowed down even more when she turned onto his street.

With loneliness slapping her hard, she didn't know what to do, especially on a Friday evening with hours to burn. She was actually hungry. Maybe she should've eaten before she up and left the restaurant and wasted a perfectly good margarita.

Persha pulled into the parking lot near the Food Town off Beltway 8. She decided she'd go have a pedicure in hopes of killing some time.

Before going in, she pulled out her cell phone and dialed her mother's number. After a few rings, she heard the familiar voice.

"Hello?" her mother answered.

"Ma?" Persha said.

"Hey sugarplum. How'er you doing?"

"Oh, I've been better. How about you?"

"Whew! Chile, I'm okay, just trying to keep up with your Aunt Pam. We just got that new *Buns of Steel* video and we just finished working out."

"I thought you sounded a little out of breath, but I didn't want to say anything. I didn't know what you were over there doing."

"Chile, you accusing your mama of ungodly actions?"

"No ma'am, I'm not. I was just unclear about why you were breathing all hard like that."

"Well, rest assured your mama is a virtuous woman. God be the glory. I may have sinned before, but I now know the ill of my ways and I'm proud to say I'm blessed and highly favored."

That's why Persha avoided calling her mother as much as she had called her before the old woman found the Lord again.

"Ma, I was calling because I needed to talk. I've got some things going on right now."

"Have you been praying, going to church, paying your tithes?"

"Ma?"

"You answer me, Persha Janice Townsend!"

"That's not the issue!" Persha screamed.

"Who are you raising your voice at? If you were living your life according to the good book, you wouldn't be having any problems right now. Well, you might be having problems, but nothing the good Lord couldn't see you through."

Persha started crying. "I didn't call you for this," she mumbled.

"Well, baby, somebody needs to tell you. If you ain't living right, of course you're gonna have lots of problems. I don't approve of the way you young women allow men to abuse and misuse your temple. Get right with God and you'll be just fine."

"Ma, can't you ever just listen to what I have to say without referring to scripture?"

"Persha, I'm a child of God and what I'm telling you is that this *is* my way of listening. I don't know exactly what you're going through, but my advice will still be the same. Read first Corinthians chapter ten, verse thirteen. Baby, that states that the God-given way is the only way to get out of any predicament you find yourself in."

"Okay, Ma, I guess I need to go then."

"Persha?"

"Yes, Ma?"

"Let's pray before you go. I want you to promise me you'll drop to your knees more and take all of your problems to the good Lord!"

"Actually, Ma, I need to run. I, ah, I think we're breaking up. I can hardly hear you!" she screamed.

"Persha!"

Before her mother could get the rest of her words out, Persha hit the end button on her cell phone and sat in the parking lot and cried. Persha knew she had to do something and she had to do it fast.

Clarke

At about 11:45 P.M. Clarke glanced down at his watch and knew for sure he was deep in hot water. But he had had such a good time. He certainly didn't want to be the first one to speak up and say he was ready to go. In the back of his mind he kept thinking about Persha and where she must be waiting for him.

But when the music started and the spotlight began darting around the crowded club, he took his Bud Light bottle to his lips and started rocking to the music.

When the first girl came out, his adrenaline really started pumping. He couldn't tell what the others were doing, but he couldn't wait to see some ass.

Clarke and his buddies were at Treasures, a gentlemen's club located off Little York and Hempstead Highway. It was quite a distance from his house, but again, he wasn't concerned with being close to home. He knew Persha would wait for as long as it took.

"You know you can go behind the wall and get serviced," his buddy leaned over and whispered in his ear.

"Yeah, but not with her I'll, bet!" Clarke said as he watched the scene before him.

He looked toward the stage and saw a couple of women dancing around a pole. One wore spiked heels and a sheer tank top with a matching garter strapped around one of her thick thighs. When she jumped up, then slid down into a magnificent split, Clarke was in awe. A group of men threw bills onto the stage. She swiveled onto her back and spread her legs, revealing her pink flesh. Soon, the dancer leaned back on her elbows and elevated her hips into the air. She began gyrating her hips to the music.

On the other side of the stage another dancer worked for a small crowd posted in front of her. The dancer bent over and spread her thighs.

Normally he didn't care for these types of places because it was like being teased, but this was where Antwone and his other buddies wanted to go, so he tagged along.

More than two hours since he last thought of Persha and her well-being, he and his buddies walked out of the club. Clarke and Antwone lagged behind the others.

"Where they heading off to?" Clarke asked, motioning toward the other men.

"I think out to Heartbreakers," Antwone answered.

"Shit! That's way out there in Galveston, off forty-five, ain't it?"

"I think so," Antwone said as he smiled toward the other guys as they pulled out of the parking lot.

"So whassup with you? What're you about to get into tonight?" He stood looking at Clarke.

"Aw dawg, a brotha just trying to make it back to the house, that's all. Why? You got something else in mind? Where's wifey anyhow?"

"She went to her sister's for the weekend. I'm supposed to be working on that little carriage house in the back, but hell, I figured since I got till Monday, I'll get to it when I get to it. You know how that is."

Clarke wondered what was really on Antwone's mind. At one o'clock in the morning they were standing in a parking lot talking about his to-do list. He wanted him to get to the point and quit sidestepping the real issue.

"Who wanted to come to this place anyway?" Antwone suddenly asked.

Clarke shrugged his shoulders and leaned against his car, then stood up. He didn't want to get comfortable. "You know me; I don't need this to get off. I thought it was you or one of the others."

"Nah, it wasn't me."

"So, man, what are you about to do?" Clarke asked, irritated.

"I don't know, probably head to the house. You wanna come by and get a brew?"

"Yeah, man. Let's do this!"

Clarke thought about calling Persha's cell phone as he trailed behind Antwone in his car, but then he decided against it. *Why call now?* he reasoned. He'd just have to sit and listen to her bitch about his whereabouts.

Nearly three hours later, Clarke was taking every shortcut he could think of as he raced to beat the sunrise home. Many streetlights were blinking and he didn't even want to think about where Persha might've been or where she had to spend the night while he was out having a blast.

When he did finally pull up into his driveway just at the crack of dawn, he was surprised to see her car in its normal spot down the street.

He walked up to Persha's car and when he got close he noticed she was inside sleeping!

"Oh, shit," he said. Clarke glanced around in all directions to make sure none of his neighbors were watching, then he lightly tapped on her window.

Wiping slobber from her mouth, Persha jumped up and glared at him through bloodshot red eyes. She looked around as if to see just where she was, then turned the key to lower her window.

"Aw, shorty, I'm so sorry. I'm sorry," he cried. "Come on, let's get you inside real quick so you can shower and head out. It's Saturday, so you know Kelsa might be home in a couple of hours. A brotha is so sorry, babe."

While he was apologizing, and he did feel bad when he found her sleeping in her vehicle, she had to know what a stupid move that was. What if someone had called the police? He didn't live in the ghetto. People didn't just fall asleep in their parked cars in his neighborhood. She might as well have been sleeping on a bench.

When it appeared she had gathered her bearings and was aware of where she was, he held the door open for her to climb out.

"Why would you crash here in your car?" he asked, looking around nervously.

"You act like I had a choice!" she snapped, rushing to keep up with him as they walked toward the house.

"How could you just leave me out here like that? What if something had happened to me?"

"Persha, this is not the hood. I think these streets are safe."

"Oh, so that makes it okay?" She stopped walking.

Clarke rushed to her side, grabbed her arm and shoved her forward.

"Look, don't start this bullshit out here." He nervously glanced around. "Ain't no telling who's watching. Let's get inside and we'll talk about this later."

"How are we going to talk about anything? I probably only have time to shower then I have to leave before your precious wife gets home."

At the door Clarke paused. He slowly turned and looked directly into her eyes.

"Do you want us to be together?" he huffed. Persha slowly nodded. "Well, I thought you said you had faith in me." He pointed at his chest, using his index finger to emphasize his words.

"I do," she mumbled.

"Then why are you suddenly questioning everything I say? You agreed to this, now you've decided this ain't good enough for you?" He unlocked the door and they both stepped in.

The sun hadn't completely made its appearance so it was still somewhat dark outside. When they walked in, Clarke reached for the light switch and dimmed the lights. He was still mad at Persha, but figured he didn't have to make that big of a deal out of the situation. After all, he wasn't there to meet her like he promised.

When satisfied he had turned the situation around enough to suit his needs, he looked at her and said, "If this ain't working for you, I think you need to let a brotha know. You know I want us to be together, baby girl. But if you decide you want to step," he said, shrugging, "then I have to let you go."

"That's not what I'm saying, Clarke, you know I'm patient. And I don't think you would really have me living here with you and your wife if you didn't really care about me." She looked down. "I was just kind of disappointed that you didn't spend some time with me last night. I really needed you."

Clarke nervously looked at his watch for the second time since they'd arrived inside. He glanced toward the kitchen and noticed the light above the stove was on.

"Say, why don't you go shower, and ah, we could

talk about this later. Kelsa'll be here in a couple of hours, but we can go spend the day together somewhere else if that's cool with you."

"You promise, Clarke?" Persha started smiling.

"Yeah, you're right. I should've made time for you, but my boys and I went out last night. Then a brotha had a bit too much to drink, so I had to chill on Antwone's couch till I sobered up a bit."

"Clarke, why didn't you call me? You know I would've come to pick you up. See, that's the kind of stuff that makes me upset. I haven't met any of your friends, you talk about your father every once in a while, but not hardly enough to me. I know you guys fell out years ago, but I want to feel like I'm a part of your life."

Clarke really didn't have time for this shit. He didn't want to appear edgy, but he couldn't stop thinking what would happen if Kelsa came home early. While he was anxious about getting her out of there, Persha had the nerve to try and get all sentimental. Clarke didn't want to set her off again, but he needed her to shower quickly and get the hell out.

"Okay, well, look here, why don't you go do your thang and then we can make plans to hook up later? We'll talk about all that."

"Really?"

"Yeah, just go hop in the shower. A brotha may even join you," he teased.

After she finally went upstairs, Clarke walked into the kitchen and flicked off the light. He didn't usually make mistakes like that, but he figured his mind was just slipping with all this stress he was working with.

He was anxious to get Persha out of the house. She had no idea what he was going through. He figured once he got her out, he'd shower, make breakfast and then get in the bed and wait for Kelsa to come home. That's exactly what he did.

When Clarke and Kelsa woke up later, Clarke was thinking about taking Kesla out to Galveston. He didn't really want to do that either, but lately she'd been acting funny too. After a shower, she told him she needed to run errands and would return later. He figured he'd wait until then to decide whether he needed to make any kind gestures.

Not knowing for sure why she was suddenly tripping, he figured any nice gesture might put him back in her good graces. He did know one thing. He knew that he had to have a talk with Persha. They were wrapping up her third week at his house and she hadn't said shit about her insurance payment. Either they were going to pay for her condo or her money from her 401(K) should be coming through. Their little arrangement was wearing him out.

After straightening up the already clean kitchen, he walked out to the living room. The predawn light had made him feel even sleepier. He stretched out on his leather recliner and made himself comfortable.

He jumped when, what seemed like seconds later, his eyelashes started tingling. First he swatted toward the distraction. When he felt wet lips pressed against his, he woke to find Persha standing over him buck naked.

"Damn, is a brotha dreaming or what?" he said, rubbing his eyes.

"I just wanted to show you what you missed out on last night and give you a taste of what's to come later," Persha said as she fell to her knees. Clarke proceeded to adjust the chair to an upright position. Clarke quickly dropped his pants and underwear and put his limp manhood in her mouth. In a few seconds his member sprang to life and he eased back to enjoy the pleasure.

"Damn, shorty!" He put his hands on her head to pull her in closer. "Ssss, this is what I'm talking about." He closed his eyes and released a moan.

Caught up in the rapture, neither heard the door unlock. By now, Clarke's brain was talking to his manhood and both wanted Persha to keep sucking harder and harder. Her jaws may not have been that strong, but she was getting the job done.

"What the fuck!" a voice yelling startled Clarke and Persha.

After that, everything seemed to happen so fast. Kelsa dropped everything she was holding at the door. Clarke pushed Persha back on her bare behind and jumped up with his pants at his ankles and his erection pointing stiffly forward. He had been caught with his pants down . . . literally.

Persha

"**O**MIGOD!" Persha gasped, using her hands to cover her breasts and the rest of her body.

"What the fuck is going on in here?" Kelsa yelled. "Who's this ho in my house? You sorry-ass bastard! How dare you bring some nasty hooker into my fucking house!" Kelsa was screaming and Persha was looking around for something to cover her naked body.

Clarke tried to move toward his wife, but his pants prevented him. He took a step and fell, landing flat on his face.

"I don't believe this shit! Oh lord, I knew something was going on! I knew it, I knew it, I knew it! Oh, I'm about to kill somebody." Kelsa started pacing back and forth near the front door.

"Baby, Kelsa, wait. Kelsa, I can explain!" Clarke stuttered. "I swear, I can explain, just wait." He struggled to get up, but his pants were all twisted around his ankles, almost pulling him back down each time he moved.

"Bitch, if you don't get your skank ass out of my fucking house, we're gonna have some real big problems up in here. Shit! Where's my gun? Where is my fucking pistol? I don't believe this shit right here in my own fucking house!" Kelsa said as she started opening up end-table drawers and closet doors, frantically searching for something. Each time she moved, Clarke tried to follow her but fell over, still not having pulled his pants up.

Persha knew she couldn't make it upstairs to the guest bedroom where all of her clothes were; her purse and her car keys. Everything was up there. What was she going to do? Maybe she could get close to the closet near the front door to grab a jacket or something. That's what she'd do. She really had no other choice. She had to give it a try.

She took a deep breath and moved toward the door, but suddenly, Kelsa stopped what she was doing and dashed toward her.

"Nah-ah, bitch," Kelsa said, "get your nasty ass out of my house. Don't even try to grab cover now! You wasn't thinking about that when your nasty ass was sucking my husband's dick!" Kelsa opened the front door. "Get the fuck out!" she screamed as she shoved Persha outside.

Outside with no clothes on, Persha didn't know what to do. She glanced around using her hands to cover her breasts and midsection. She was beside herself. How was she going to make it to her car? She didn't even have her keys. At the front door she struggled to cover her body with her hands. She could still hear Kelsa cursing up a storm. Soon she heard a few crashing noises. When she heard a pop, she took off running.

Kelsa must've found that gun she was looking for, Persha thought. And while she loved Clarke, his ass wasn't worth dying over.

Next door, Persha grabbed two trash-can lids and

made her way down the street. She used them to hide
her body. As the sun was bright now, and the neighborhood was starting to come to life, she started crying.
She couldn't bare the thought of people seeing her like
that.

What the hell was she going to do? She didn't have
on any clothes, no money to use a pay phone, no nothing. She was naked with two plastic lids covering
everything she had.

Looking back toward Clarke's house she wondered
if she should go hide in his car. Quite surely he'd be
leaving soon as mad as Kelsa was. Giving up on that
idea, she sat on the curb next to her car and started
thinking.

When two cars passed by and honked, she started
crying again. The second car came back by a few minutes later and the driver rolled his window down.

"Hey ma'am, are you okay?" a good-looking white
man asked.

She ignored him. "You need help? Where are your
clothes? What happened?" Still behind the wheel, he
stopped his car in the middle of the street. "Ma'am,
what's your name? Did someone hurt you? Can I call
someone for you?"

Persha tried to block him out, but he just kept asking
questions.

"Do you live on this street?" the driver continued.
"Were you visiting someone?" By then people had
started looking out their windows.

Feeling very alone and afraid, she decided if she was
going to do anything, she'd better make her move. She
eased up from her spot and used one of the lids to slam
against her car window. She'd rather show her ass than
her breasts, so she held one lid in front of her bare
body.

"Ma'am!" the man screamed. "You can't do that!

Hey, who are you? Is that your car? Why don't you have on any clothes? If that's your car, why don't you use your key?"

The glass wouldn't break. A few minutes later, Persha looked up the street to see Clarke running out of his house. He was only wearing his boxers.

At his car he fumbled with his keys, finally jumped into the car and started it up. And a few minutes later he was backing up.

"Whew!" Persha sighed. He was finally coming to take her to safety with him. But her heart began to sink when she saw him back out, turn the other direction and take off.

Soon, Kelsa ran out of the house with the gun in her hands yelling, "You dirty fucking bastard!" She then fired two shots toward the moving vehicle.

One bullet shattered the back window as Clarke's car screeched down the street. When Persha saw Kelsa looking down the street she ducked down behind her car's wheel and started begging God to spare her life.

Two seconds later, she heard the man's car take off. She wasn't sure which way he had gone, but she looked around the wheel to see Clarke's front door still open. She didn't know what to do. The white man was gone and she needed to pee. She shut her eyes tightly and started praying again.

This time when she opened her eyes, she peeked around the tire and saw Kelsa walking down the street toward her with the gun still in hand.

"You're next, you stupid bitch!" Kelsa yelled. "You like to fuck with married men, huh? Well, I'll fix your hot ass."

"Oh shit! Oh, shit," Persha mumbled to herself. She couldn't move. She didn't know what to do. There she was hunched over, hiding her naked body behind the wheel of her car and a woman with a gun was hunting her down.

Persha started crying. She knew she'd one day have to pay for what she had done, but she never imagined she'd die like this. She couldn't move.

"I know your skank ass is out here, you nasty bitch," Kelsa shouted.

Persha didn't dare peek from behind the wheel again. She didn't know what to do, but she *knew* Kelsa was coming. She heard her walking. Persha started praying.

". . . Before I lay me down to sleep, I give you Lord my soul to keep—" Persha prayed.

"Bitch, it's too late for that now!" Kelsa said.

When Persha opened her eyes, she was looking up the barrel of Kelsa's gun.

"OMIGOD!" she cried, dropping the lids and using her hands to shield her face.

"Even he can't help you now! You should've thought about that before," Kelsa said.

As Kelsa was about to pull the trigger, Persha started peeing, right there, on herself, in front of her boyfriend's wife. Persha's sudden inability to control her bladder stopped Kelsa in her tracks.

Clarke

When Clarke pulled into Antwone's driveway, he was still a bit rattled. He couldn't believe Kelsa actually fired shots at him. What if one of those bullets would've hit him? He looked around to make sure her crazy ass hadn't followed him. When he was satisfied she hadn't, he jumped out of the car and darted toward the Johnsons' front door where he began knocking.

Standing there barefoot in his boxers, he wondered why the hell no one had answered. And look at his car! Now he had to worry about replacing the back window. He knocked again and then pushed the doorbell.

A few minutes later, the door swung open and Antwone's wife, Michelle, was standing there staring at him.

"Ah, Clarke? What happened?" she asked curiously. "Why don't you have on any clothes? Is everything okay?" She looked around the driveway.

Bitch, do you think everything's okay if I'm at your fucking front door damn near naked? Clarke thought.

"Ah, is Antwone here? I really need to speak with him," Clarke said.

"No, he took Junior to the sporting goods store."
Michelle stood there looking at Clarke.

"Well, ah, you mind if a brotha comes in to wait for
him?" he asked, trying to hide the irritation in his
voice.

"Oh, I'm so sorry! Of course. Yeah, come on in."
She let him into the house, then walked out a couple of
steps to look around.

"You didn't say why you're out here with no clothes
on," she said, finally closing the door behind her.

"Yeah, I need a pair of sweats and a T-shirt. I'm sure
Antwone must have something I can fit into."

Shaking her head, as if she was snapping out of
something, Michelle rushed to the back. "Oh, yeah.
I'm sorry. What was I thinking? It's just strange, that's
all."

*Yeah, I'll bet it is. Just go get me some clothes and
shut the fuck up,* Clarke thought to himself.

As soon as she was out of sight, Clarke walked over
to the window and started looking out of the blinds. He
didn't feel like having any more drama. So far the coast
was clear. He released a sigh of relief and waited for
Michelle to come back into the living room.

"Okay, these were all I could find," she said, returning into the living room holding up a pair of old jeans
and a Morehouse College sweatshirt.

"I'm sure Antwone won't mind if you borrow this."
She reached over to hand the clothes to Clarke then
leaned against the entertainment console.

After taking the clothes and inspecting them, Clarke
looked at Michelle. "I guess I'll have to make these
work," he mumbled.

"Well, Clarke, you still haven't said what happened
to you. You get robbed or something?"

Without answering her question, he made his way to

the bathroom and slammed the door shut. He couldn't believe she was asking all those damn questions. She had to know he couldn't stand her stupid ass.

Antwone's jeans were too short and way too damn tight, but what could he do? He squeezed his large body into the sweatshirt and took a deep breath before going back into the living room.

When he walked back in, Michelle was gone. Feeling sudden relief, he looked around for the remote and tried to think about his next move.

The front door opened before Clarke could turn the TV on.

"Jesus! What the hell happened to you?" Michelle exclaimed. "Do you know your entire back window is shattered into like a million pieces? Are you okay? You need me to call the police? Where is Kelsa? Is she . . . Oh GOD! Is she hurt?" Michelle rushed over to the kitchen and came back with the cordless phone in her hand.

Clarke rolled his eyes and prayed Antwone would be back soon. Before she could dial, he put his hand up to get her attention.

"Look, Michelle, you need to chill. It ain't nothing like that. Kelsa's cool, and actually, I don't feel like talking about this right now." He dismissed her by turning on the TV and easing back on the sofa.

Michelle walked closer to him. "Clarke, you come to my house nearly naked with no shoes and your car window shattered, and now you're saying you don't want to talk about it?"

He wasn't in the mood for any neck-twisting, hand-waving lectures. He just wanted to sit back, wait on his boy and think about what his next move would be.

Leaning back on the sofa and closing his eyes, Clarke wanted her to disappear. Wasn't any way in the world he was about to put her all up in his business.

Sometimes he wished women would just do what they were supposed to do and shut the hell up. He felt they only needed to be seen in the kitchen or in the bedroom, certainly not heard. Ever!

A few minutes after her last comment Clarke opened his eyes to find her still standing there. This time, with hands on her hips, waiting, like he owed her some kind of explanation.

"Okay, let me have it. Or am I gonna have to pick up the phone and call Kelsa?"

Shit! He didn't know why she was tripping on him. The very last thing he needed was Kelsa knowing where to find him. What if she came over there with the gun?

He slowly eased up. He sighed, rubbed his bald head twice from the back to the front and then focused his gaze on Michelle.

"Look, now's just not a cool time. I need to relax. When's Antwone coming back? What's his new cell number again?" Clarke asked.

Casting a skeptical look at him, Michelle didn't budge.

"I'm the one asking questions here, buddy. Now, are you talking or what?" she demanded.

Finally figuring he would get nowhere with her, he eased back onto the sofa again.

"What did you do?" she pressed, acting truly concerned.

After a few moments and still no response, he heard Michelle walk away. He opened his eyes when a feeling of relief washed over him. Soon he started staring off at the ceiling. He was hoping she'd stay gone until Antwone came home. And as soon as Antwone came home, he'd talk to him about controlling his woman.

How the hell did I get myself into such a mess? Clarke thought as he closed his eyes again. He figured he'd be in a better position to think things through after resting a bit. But seconds after his eyes closed, he suddenly jumped up from the couch.

"Why isn't Kelsa answering the phone if you didn't do anything to her?" Michelle said as she stood in front of him with the phone in her hand. "If you killed her, you can not hide over here!" Clarke rolled his eyes. "Did you know one out of every four women is killed by her lover, boyfriend or husband? And if *Dateline NBC* calls about this story, I'm gonna have nothing but good things to say about Kelsa. You need to know that now so you won't be shocked when you see me on TV talking about all this." Michelle shook her head. "Then I'm gonna testify against you at your trial. You need to know that too," she snapped.

"Dammit, Michelle! I didn't kill anybody!" Clarke shouted.

She sat down across from him as if they were about to have a a deep conversation. "Oh, well, that's good because we're not harboring any fugitives over here. And I mean that!"

"Don't you need to cook or something?"

She cocked a skillfully arched brow up and her face twisted. "What?" she asked.

"I was wondering if you didn't have something you needed to be working on, besides me, I mean. 'Cause I really am not in the mood to talk."

"Well, why don't you get in your car and go to where ever you came from because I need to know what is going on. I don't want you bringing any drama over here to my house. We don't need any distress in this family, and nothing good can come from whatever you've got going on. I just don't want it in my house."

Her house! Wonder how many bills she pays around this mug, Clarke thought as she looked around.

"Why can't you tell me what happened?" she pleaded, using a softer tone.

"Michelle, Kelsa and I got into it! There! You happy? We had a fight and I thought it was best if I left because I don't feel like going to jail."

"What! You guys had a fight? What happened? Why didn't you have on any clothes? And what the hell happened to your window?"

"Okay, see a brotha gives you a nibble and you want to take a huge bite. Just let it go. I don't feel like talking about it."

"Well, how do I know you didn't kill her and cut her body up in small pieces and bury her somewhere? How do I know the police didn't shoot out that window as they were chasing you away?"

"You don't!" Clarke snapped. "You also don't know if it's a good idea to get me all worked up again because you don't know if I may be capable of doing whatever I did all over again, now do you?"

"You don't have to go getting all dramatic. I was just trying to find out what's going on." She got up from the couch as the front door opened.

Antwone walked in behind his son. "Damn, dawg, who was playing target practice with your car?" Antwone asked.

"Yeah, that's the million-dollar question," Michelle said, looking at Clarke.

"Man, am I glad to see you!" Clarke said as he got up from the sofa and helped his friend with the bag he was carrying.

"What happened? And shit, are those my clothes you wearing, damn dawg. You in bad shape," Antwone said, frowning.

"Yeah, but he all of a sudden forgot what happened." They both looked at Michelle. Before Clarke could say anything, Antwone pushed his son toward his mother and said to Michelle, "Why don't you help him with this stuff in his room?"

She looked at Clarke, then at Antwone, rolled her eyes and took her son by the hand.

Clarke and Antwone walked outside to inspect the damage to his car. During that time, Clarke walked Antwone through the incident. He told him everything except about Persha living in his wife's house. When the story ended, Antwone was still shaking his head.

"Dawg, you're more than welcome to the carriage house for as long as you'll need. What are you going to do anyway?"

"I don't know yet, man. But thanks for the place."

"It's the least I could do. After all, it doesn't have to be a bad thing that you were thrown out, or actually not even thrown out, but chased away."

"Yeah, man, thanks for not getting all bent out of shape because of Persha."

"Hey, dude, you're allowed to have a little dip on the side. Besides, you know how *we* do it. We ain't all emotional and wrapped tight like women," Antwone said, flashing his brilliant smile.

"Ain't that the truth," Clarke said.

They walked around the car one last time, then stood staring at the damage.

"Whassup with Michelle? She sure had a million questions before you came in. You think she'll figure it out with me being so close?"

"Man, if her ass ain't got a clue yet, what makes you think she'll suddenly wake up?"

"Good point," Clarke said, extending his fist out for a pound. "Damn good point, dawg."

Persha

"**D**rop the gun!"

Persha couldn't remember a time when she had been more relieved to see the law. But minutes had passed and Kelsa was still pointing the pistol right at her face. Hadn't she heard the cop? And why didn't the cop shoot her since she didn't follow his instructions? Persha looked at the officer, praying he'd feel threatened and shoot Kelsa in the back, leg, arm or hell, even in the head.

"Ma'am, I need you to drop your weapon. Now!" the cop ordered Kelsa.

Okay, that's better, Persha thought. *But maybe she's just one of those people who need to learn by example. Shoot her ass! Please!*

When another patrol car pulled up, Kelsa looked around. She then looked back at Persha.

Persha had never seen so much hatred in anyone's eyes, and certainly not directed at herself. Persha wanted her to drop the gun more than she wanted anything else.

Soon, the officer gave his warning again.

"Ma'am, ease down slowly and drop the gun. Put your hands on top of your head."

Finally, Kelsa did what she was told. She then just stood there staring at the officer. When it appeared that she was out of harm's way, Persha used her lids to cover her body as she got up from the ground.

"Okay, I don't know what's going on here, but we'll need to go downtown to get statements," the officer said, removing his hand from his holster.

Still holding the lids as shields, Persha was confused.

"Go downtown? Why?" Persha cried. "I wasn't the one with a gun pointed at another person. Shouldn't you arrest her, not me! That's attempted murder!" she insisted.

Officer number two walked up to the commotion after he had urged onlookers to go back into their homes. When he walked over to where Kelsa stood, he looked at the first officer and said, "Why doesn't she have on any clothes?"

His fellow officer just shrugged his shoulders. "I don't know. When I pulled up, this one was holding a gun on that one over there." The officer pointed. "That's how I found her. I think my slicker is in the trunk if you want to give it to her."

"But I didn't do anything," Persha cried.

"Calm down, ma'am. We'll get to the bottom of this," the first officer on the scene assured her.

When the second officer got the slicker for Persha, she grabbed it out of his hands before he could even extend it to her.

"Thank you so much!" she cried. After putting the raincoat on and buttoning it up, she was ready to tell her side of the story. But before she could begin, the stranger in the car stepped forward.

"Officers, I'm the one who called," the white man who had tried to help Persha said.

The officer pulled a small notepad from his pocket and started asking questions while the man spoke.

"Well," the man started, "I saw this naked woman trying to break into this car. Then this one . . ." He pointed at Kelsa. "She shot at a man down the street and then came looking for her." He looked at Persha. "I was trying to help her because I figured something was seriously wrong, but she wouldn't talk to me. When I heard the shot fired, I knew I'd better call for help."

"Yes, sir, and thank you. We actually received several calls," the officer taking notes said.

Persha listened to the stranger's version of the story, then raised her hand. "Can I speak now? I don't want to go downtown. I didn't do anything. So I shouldn't have to go to jail."

The first officer looked at her and said, "Ma'am, we're *all* going downtown. So you can speak now or you can speak later. But either way, we're going downtown to get to the bottom of this."

"But I didn't do anything!" she screamed. "This has been humiliating enough."

The second officer walked over to Kelsa and started reading her her rights.

"Shut the fuck up!" Kelsa snapped at the officer.

The other officer began reading Persha hers.

"Why am I being arrested? I didn't do anything," Persha went on.

"Yes you did, you skank bitch. Tell them how I caught you in my house fucking my husband! You didn't do anything, huh?" Kelsa screamed as she was being escorted to a patrol car.

"Ma'am, we need you to be quiet," the arresting officer told her. "We'll take care of this downtown. Are you the registered owner of that pistol?"

Kelsa shook her head and replied. "It's my husband's gun," she said just before they pushed her head down to let her into the back of the patrol car.

Hours later, Persha was still waiting in the holding cell with the borrowed raincoat on. When the jail guard came to the cell, she looked in and called out, "Persha Townsend!"

Persha jumped up. "Yes! That's me!"

"You made bail. C'mon."

Persha followed closely behind the jail guard. As she walked, she tried to avoid making eye contact with Kelsa when they approached the cell she was being held in.

"I can't believe that bitch is leaving before me," Kelsa said.

"I am, thanks to your husband!" Persha teased.

The guard looked back. "Don't start nothing, it won't be nothing. We can turn around, you know. You're not out of here until the papers are signed," she threatened.

When Persha arrived in the waiting room, she was so happy to see Cricket and Kori that she nearly ran and jumped into their arms.

"Gurl! Where are your clothes?" was the first thing Kori asked. "They really make you strip when you get locked up, huh? I thought they only did that shit on TV."

Cricket didn't say anything.

"No, silly, the police let me borrow this," Persha answered.

"Well, where are your clothes?" Kori asked again.

"It's such a long story; I don't know where to start. There's really no point in even going over it again," Persha said as they proceeded to sign the required papers needed for her to be released. They then headed out of the jail.

Outside in the parking lot, Persha wanted to take in all the fresh air her lungs could hold. After spending several hours in jail, she was glad to be free again.

"So what did they charge you with?" Cricket asked, finally breaking her silence.

"Indecency," Persha replied. "I have to go to court and everything. I just want to put this mess behind me."

Persha climbed into the backseat of Cricket's car, but she had no idea where to tell them to take her. She still had no place to go, and since they'd used the apartment money for bail, she was sure she'd be out on the streets.

"Where's your car?" Cricket asked.

"At Clarke's house," Persha answered. "So are my keys, my purse, my clothes, and everything else I own."

She didn't have time to beat around the bush. She had no idea where Clarke had gone and she was determined to get back on her feet before catching up with him again.

The girls went to Kori's where she loaned Persha some clothes to put on. They then headed out to put a decent meal in Persha's belly. During this time, Persha told her friends how Kelsa had caught her and Clarke in a compromising position. She told them that if the officer hadn't shown up when he did, she was sure she would've been dead. Persha relived the horrible incident over and over again all the way to the restaurant as both Kori and Cricket had their share of questions.

Persha was sitting in Cheddars restaurant located off Beltway 8 with Kori and Cricket wearing a borrowed dress that she never even liked when Kori wore it. Not to her surprise, Kori and Cricket were still full of questions.

"Is she still in jail?" Cricket asked.

"She was when y'all came to get me. I don't know about now," Persha answered.

"Well, I think we should go get your things from over there. Ain't no telling what she'll do with your stuff," Cricket suggested.

"That story is just off the hook! I can't believe he went out like that!" Kori said. "And what kind of man just runs out and leaves a sistah hanging like that?"

"Well, I can't believe she came after me with a gun!" Persha stated as the reality of the situation seemed to just sink in. "I could've died!" she mumbled quietly under her breath.

"Yes, we tried to tell you that was a very dangerous situation you put yourself in," Cricket said, saying *I told you so* without really saying it. "Well, I'm just glad that even though it nearly cost you your life, you've decided to leave that sewer rat alone."

When Persha didn't respond, Kori said, "Don't judge her, Cricket." For the rest of the meal, conversation was limited to whatever was necessary to get through the evening.

After eating, the three rode out to Clarke and Kelsa's house in hopes of retrieving Persha's belongings.

"You think anyone's home?" Cricket asked as they sat parked outside of the house.

"Looks kind of dark," Persha said, "but I really need my stuff. My purse, keys, and clothes are in there. I need to get them now because there is no way I'm going to deal with her again."

Kori looked at the house. "Sure is a nice house. What does she do anyway?"

"She's an RN. She works the overnight shift and then takes a class in the mornings."

Cricket looked at Persha through the rearview mirror. "So what are we going to do? I really don't feel like catching a case over some loser. And if she's packing, I really don't want to be bothered. Bullets don't have any names on them, and they don't care who they hit."

"She has to get her stuff, Cricket!" Kori snapped.

"Yeah, well, she should've thought about that before she started disrespecting that woman's house like that."

"What about him? He brought her there. How come all your comments are always geared at Persha? It takes two, you know!"

"Yeah, but I don't give a rat's ass about him. I know a loser when I see one. I care about Persha. Where is his punk ass now? And the way he left her, he could've driven down the street to pick her up. He knew her ass was out there naked, but he only cared about himself. Damn coward."

"Can we stop this please?" Persha screamed.

A few seconds later, Kori spoke up. "I'll go up to the door first and try to talk to her. When it's cool, I'll come back and get you if necessary, or I'll just see if she'll give your things to me."

Persha and Cricket watched as Kori strolled up the walkway like she'd been invited. At the door she stopped and tried to look in a window. She pushed the doorbell, then turned and waved Persha up.

"Gurl, you better not go up to that door," Cricket warned her. "If that woman comes running out here with her pistol, I'm leaving both of you."

Kori came back to the car. "No one's home and the door isn't locked because I can see where it's not completely pulled closed. I think we should go in and get your stuff before one of them comes back."

Persha looked at Cricket for guidance. She hesitated at first.

"You're on your own," Cricket said, looking around the neighborhood.

Persha opened the car door and took a deep breath before following Kori up to the door. They rang the doorbell again, and when no one answered, Persha pushed the door open.

"Kelsa? Clarke?" she said as she stepped inside. "Is anyone here?"

Still, no one answered. Reaching for the switch near the door, Persha turned on the dimmer and immediately her eyes focused on the smoldering fireplace. Her heart started racing.

"No!" Persha screamed.

Rushing from her lookout spot at the door, Kori walked into the house. "Shit! What's wrong? You scared me!"

"Look!" She pointed to the fireplace that was still smoking.

"At what?" Kori moved in closer.

"That bitch burned all my clothes! My new underwear, the outfits I bought. I don't believe this shit." Persha stood there as she identified some of her half–burned-up articles.

"Oh snap! Yup, gurl! Ooo-wee was that silk!" Kori bent forward for a closer look into the fireplace. "It's crispy now. Damn, she wasn't playing, huh?"

"Shit! Kori, I'm about to run up to the room to see if, by chance, there's anything left of mine that she didn't roast. Stay here. I'll be right back," Persha said as she headed up to the room.

Once Persha got up to the room, she noticed that the bed had been stripped of the sheets. The vase she used as a bathroom was knocked off the table and clothes were strewn all over the room. Kelsa had found her things, no doubt about it, because all she saw was clothes that belonged to Clarke. And most of those were cut into pieces. Looking around the room, she could tell that Kelsa had gone mad.

Persha walked back down the stairs to meet Kori.

"All my stuff is gone! What the hell am I going to do?"

"What about your purse or your keys?" Kori asked.

"Gone! Everything was gone from the bed."

"Did you check the trash cans?"

Shaking her head, Persha walked toward the kitchen. She couldn't believe she was once again without any clothes.

"Damn, this bitch hooked this house up. It's nice with all these plants," Persha heard Kori say.

"Oooh! Here's the stuff from my purse!" She reached into the trash can. Persha retrieved her purse, wallet, and even her car keys. When she walked back into the living room, Kori was looking at several plants.

"Damn, she got good taste."

"Hmmmm." Persha looked around the house. "Let's get the hell out of here. At least that fool didn't burn my purse up."

As they made it to the car, another car pulled into the driveway.

"Wait!" Kelsa jumped out of the car screaming.

Before Persha could even get her door closed completely, Cricket had already taken off down the street.

"Shit, I'm not about to get shot over that loser. You need to come back for your car later," Cricket said, as she careened around the corner.

Persha's heart started racing as she turned and looked out the back window. It nearly stopped when she saw Kelsa in the middle of the street. She was about to duck when she saw Kelsa waving her hands, until she realized they were empty.

"Gurl, if this ain't a wake-up call, then I don't know what to say about you," Cricket said, shaking he head. "And if you still love that fool, then all I have to say is I hope God never gives me that kind of love, because I don't need this type of shit in my life."

"Amen to that!" Kori said.

Persha didn't say a word. She just rode in silence thinking about Clarke, as they dropped Kori off at her house and then headed to Cricket's, where Persha would stay until she could get back on her feet.

Persha had grown sick and tired of being in Cricket's aunt's house. All of those damn cats were driving her crazy. Even Persha's room reeked with a strong feline odor. It didn't take long for her to start counting down the days to her insurance settlement.

The house was always dark and gloomy. Regardless of how loud Persha played the radio, she still heard the various machines the old woman was hooked up to, and there was never any food. Well, there was always pounds and pounds of various types of cat food, but no human food.

She was grateful for the place to stay, but honestly, it was depressing. Most of the times Cricket would whisper everything she said, and the volume on the phone was always kept just above a whisper.

There were so many medicine bottles on the kitchen counter that Persha hated going in there. And everywhere she went, she could count on at least five or six cats following behind her. They'd rub up against her ankles. She'd even caught a couple in her bed. And when they were in heat, there was no peace in the house. Everything, what little she owned, was always covered with cat hair.

There was a large garden in the backyard and it may have once been lovely, but now, it was just swarming with cats and kittens. Persha never complained because she knew the emotional task Cricket was facing. For the most part, she tried to spend as little time in the house as possible.

For the next few weeks, Persha's calls to Clarke went unanswered. Every time she called his office, he was either out, or too busy to take her call. Her heart ached for him. She knew they'd be able to work things out. She wondered where he was staying and what he was doing with himself.

In a couple of her weakest moments, she'd even driven by the house when she knew Kelsa would be at work to make sure she didn't see his car. Then when it was obvious it could've still been in the shop, she started calling. She'd use star 67 to block her number and hoped that he'd pick up the phone.

When none of that worked, she started feeling sick. She knew for sure this was way beyond her control. The heart wanted what the heart wanted.

Persha still loved him, and she wanted him back. She didn't dare say anything to Cricket about it, but she had already made up her mind, she'd get him back at any cost. They were meant to be.

She had to find Clarke and get out of that house. There was just no way she could survive much longer. Most mornings when she got up out of bed, she'd feel light-headed and her stomach was always weak.

At one point she'd even considered taking nosy Brenda up on her offer to spend a few days in a normal setting. But she knew better than that. Friday afternoon, she sat at her desk and realized all she had to do was pull out the card Clarke had given her and go up to his job. But when she found it, there was no address printed on the damn thing. Feeling defeated, she took her paycheck and walked a few blocks to the bank to make a deposit and to keep a few dollars for her Friday-night evening with her girls.

The three of them, her, Cricket, and Kori, were meeting for happy hour. They agreed to meet at Chuy's on Richmond, and since she arrived first, she opted for a table on the patio and waited for the girls to arrive. Kori arrived first and she and Persha sat out on the patio and waited for Cricket.

"So, what's it like living among the cats?" Kori joked.

"I'm about to lose it!" Persha replied. "I can't take it much longer. I really can't. I'm starting to get sick all over again."

"Really?"

"Yes."

"Is that why you're not drinking?"

"I don't feel right. Just the smell of alcohol makes me puke."

Kori's eyebrows squeezed into a tight line as if they were being forced together. She looked at Persha before she sipped her drink.

"I really wish I could help you," Kori said, "but, gurl, I'm about to kill that family I live with. I told you how they started counting food, right? Well, in addition to the notes, they've come up with a schedule for when I am allowed to turn on the air conditioner, and even take baths!" Kori crunched a tortilla chip and said, "Can you believe that? You know we need indoor air here in Houston!"

"How much longer do you have on that lease?"

"I'm counting the months. I've got three more to go, and I can't wait to get out of there. Maybe you and I can get a place together."

Persha started shaking her head. "Ain't no way in the world I'm staying in that house for another three months. I'm saving up now. In the next two weeks, I plan to make some kind of move," Persha said right in time as Cricket was heading to the table to join her and

Kori. She was glad they'd gotten that little talk out of the way before Cricket showed up.

The last thing Persha wanted to do was commit to moving in with Kori. She was getting a place with Clarke as soon as she caught up with him. He probably thought she blamed him for everything that went down and was scared to face her. But that was the furthest thing from the truth. She wanted nothing more than to be with him in spite of the situation. All of that was in the past. She wanted to work on their future.

Over the weekend, Persha didn't start to feel any better. Come Monday morning, she had to call in sick. She wasn't sure if it was the stench of the cat-filled house, or something she'd eaten at the restaurant on Friday, but every five minutes she was rushing to the toilet to throw up. Even as she looked up over the toilet bowel, several cats were looking up at her as if they were wondering just what the hell she was doing.

When she called in to work, Brenda told her if she didn't feel good the next day, she should stay home again. Later that evening, when she was finally able to pull herself out of the bed, she walked around the house looking for Cricket. She wanted to see if she possibly had anything in that homemade pharmacy of theirs that could maybe settle her stomach. She couldn't find her anywhere, though.

It's probably all the better anyway, Persha thought. *Something tells me that nothing she has in this house can come even close to curing what I have.*

Persha struggled to slip on some clothes and decided to hop in her car and go to the nearest convenience store. Sitting behind the wheel she started crying as she pulled up into the parking lot. She parked and just sat there wondering why things couldn't go right in her life. Before this mess with Kelsa and Clarke, she hadn't done anything to anyone. And she only did the move-in thing with Clarke because she really didn't have another option. She knew deep down inside he'd eventually call her and they'd patch things up, but she wanted that right away. She kept checking her cell phone every second, just to make sure the ringer was on. She didn't want to jump the gun and get a place without his input, but she really needed to hear from him.

After she had cried her eyes raw, she finally got out of the car. She went into the store and bought what she needed. Later that night, the test confirmed what she already knew was true.

She was pregnant by a married man who left her outside naked after his wife started waving a gun, trying to shoot them both. And she hadn't seen him, nor heard from him, since he sped away to safety without her. . . . Yep, pregnant as the day was long.

Clarke

Clarke didn't know what else to do. While he was ignoring Persha's calls and messages, he had been calling Kelsa for nearly two weeks straight with no luck. He had no idea how, but he knew for sure he had to get back in her good graces and get his life back to normal.

Him and Antwone had already agreed, in spite of the occasional problems, their lives were better with wives. And Clarke felt like a fish out of water without his. A few days ago, he had gone by the house when he thought for sure she'd be at home, but he tried his key and it didn't work. Finding it hard to believe Kelsa had changed the locks, he stood in amazement and then left feeling crushed. He didn't want to believe all hope was gone concerning their marriage.

While he sat at his desk, he wondered why things had such a strange way of working themselves out. For instance, he'd been seeing someone for the entire five years he and Kelsa had been married with no problems. But he and Persha start kicking it and in less than six months his entire world was turned upside down.

A knock on the door interrupted Clarke's thoughts. But before he could answer it, Antwone had already stuck his head in.

"I came to take you out to lunch. Whassup?" Antwone said.

"Ah, nothing, dawg, just sitting here thinking about this mess my life's turned into," Clarke replied.

"Well, forget about your problems for a little while and let's go grab a bite to eat."

At Dave and Buster's on the Richmond strip, Antwone and Clarke were seated quickly. They had lunch then headed to the bar.

"You know you can stay in the carriage house for as long as you need, right?" Antwone said.

"Yeah, that's cool and all, but a brotha just feels out of the loop. You know how it is."

On Mother's Day weekend Clarke watched as Antwone unloaded several large packages from the trunk of his car. Clarke started feeling jealous, but he figured he'd keep himself busy around the house to take his mind off his problems.

Suddenly he decided that maybe if he went by the house with a gift for Kelsa, even though she wasn't a mother, she'd at least let him in so they could talk. When Antwone went inside for the last time, Clarke walked out and got in his car.

He drove to First Colony Mall and quickly bought the cheapest tennis bracelet he could find. With the Zales bag in hand, he strolled up the walkway to his old front door and rang the doorbell.

After a few minutes there was no answer so he backed up and looked up to the second floor. A window was open and he considered climbing up to get inside.

"Kelsa," he yelled, first with his voice kind of low because he didn't want to disturb any of the neighbors.

He didn't know if she was home, but he had to try something.

"Kelsa, baby let's talk this out. I'm sorry," he cried a little louder. "Just open the door and let me come in and talk to you."

He looked up and down the street to make sure no one was looking out of any windows or anything like that. He didn't want somebody to call the cops. Gazing up at the open window again he called out his wife's name. "Kel! I know you're in there, I can hear the TV. I came by to wish you a happy Mother's Day and give you a gift, baby. C'mon, just let me in. I just want to talk. I promise. I don't want anything more. Just talk to me."

"Sir?"

Clarke jumped when he heard the deep voice. He turned to see a police officer standing behind him.

"Ah, yeah?" Clarke asked, looking confused.

"I'm going to have to ask you to leave. The lady doesn't want to be bothered," the officer said.

"What do you mean?" Clarke asked, still looking up at the open window.

"Mrs. Hudson called and asked us to ask you to leave her property and not to return."

"But I just want to talk."

"Well, it's obvious that the lady doesn't want to talk to you."

Clarke was growing more upset by the minute. He tried to gather his composure. He didn't want to go to jail, but he didn't appreciate the way Kelsa was playing him either. It was completely unnecessary for her to call the law on him.

"Look," Clarke said to the officer, "I live here. My wife and I had a disagreement and she changed the locks. But I should at least be able to get some of my personal belongings even if she doesn't want to talk to me."

For a second the officer didn't say anything, but then he nodded. "You're right. Let's try this. Why don't you get back into your car? Sit there until I tell you to come out. Let me try and talk to her first."

A few feet away from the officer, Clarke climbed back into his car. He rolled his window down as the officer used his shoulder radio to call in. A few minutes later, the officer walked up to the door and knocked.

"Mrs. Hudson, this is Officer Daniels. May I have a word with you please?" he said.

Clarke watched as Kelsa opened the door and whispered something to the officer. For a second it looked like the two were arguing, but Kelsa eventually stepped aside and let the officer in.

"Shit, I thought he was going to get me in," Clarke said to himself. He was tempted to get out of the car and go up to the door himself, but then thought better of it. So, he waited.

After nearly twenty minutes in the car, the front door opened. He saw Kelsa first, then the officer, who was carrying a large black trash bag.

Clarke's heart sank. He didn't really want his belongings. He was just trying to use that to get in the house. He knew if he could have a few minutes alone with Kelsa, he could get her to change her mind about him and their breakup.

The officer stopped at the door, said a few quiet words to Kelsa and then the door closed behind him as he walked up to Clarke's car.

"Mr. Hudson, here are some of your things," the officer replied. "I regret to inform you that your wife has taken out a restraining order against you. She says she does not want to talk to you nor does she want to see you. So I have to warn you, if you return, we will be required to arrest you."

"What?" Clarke screamed. "What does that mean? A restraining order? What am I supposed to do? I live here!"

"Sir, I need you to calm down. She produced a signed court judgment. It expires in thirty days, but for now you are not to come on the premises. And you're to stay away from her in public."

Clarke couldn't believe what he was being told. He rubbed his head and leaned forward onto the steering wheel. He didn't want a stranger to see him cry, but he couldn't believe Kelsa had done this to him.

He knew deep inside if she just gave him five minutes, five minutes to tell her how sorry he was and how much he missed her, they could go back to the way they were before all of this mess.

"Sir?" the officer called. Clarke lifted his head ever so slightly and turned toward the officer. "You need to get your things. She was nice enough to give them to me. But you can't stay here. I need you to take these things and leave."

"What?"

"Mr. Hudson, there is a restraining order against you. That means if you violate the judge's order, you can and will be arrested!"

"Arrested?" Clarke shook his head. "But this is my house too."

"Well, not according to the papers Mrs. Hudson has. She says the house is in her parents' name, and yours is nowhere on the deed. Regardless of that, a judge signed the order and you're no longer allowed here. It's like trespassing."

Clarke was confused. He shook his head, hoping to wake from the nightmare he was submerged in. Clarke refused to believe what the officer was telling him.

This had to be some kind of huge mistake. There was absolutely no way Kelsa would think to do something like this, not on her own anyway. That he was sure of.

"If I could just talk to her for five minutes," he mumbled.

The officer started saying no. "There's no way! I can get in trouble by letting you stay this long. You really need to leave. Take your things and go. I don't want to have to haul you in, but I will if you refuse to obey the judge's order."

"Man! This is wild! I can't believe this. I just want to talk to my wife!"

"Yes, sir, I know. I understand what you're going through. I've been there myself. But I'm trying to tell you the best thing for you to do is leave. I suggest you get yourself an attorney and let him take care of this for you. There's no need for you to go to jail because of this. She doesn't want to talk right now, so you have to respect that."

"Okay, okay, you're probably right. An attorney, huh?"

"Yes, sir. That's just so you can protect your interest. I really don't know what else to tell you. But you have to understand you can't come back here. Like I said before, if she calls the police again, you will go to jail. Absolutely no questions asked. So why don't you take this bag, and go look for an attorney."

Clarke got out of the car to put his things in the backseat. That's when his eyes fixed on someone he didn't want to see. Persha's car slowed as she drove past his house.

"Oh shit!" he mumbled under his breath. "You're right, I better get out of here," he said to the officer. "I do need to get an attorney. Let me put this stuff in the trunk and I'm out."

The officer stood back and watched him. He also

saw Persha make a U-turn and pull up in front of Clarke's car.

"See, this is what I don't need. Officer, can you tell this woman that I can't stay here and talk to her! Please help me out here," Clarke pleaded.

"Okay," the officer said as he looked at Persha. When she got out of the car, he walked over to her. "Ma'am, you need to let this man go. He can't stay here. You're blocking his vehicle and this driveway."

"Oh," Persha replied as she quickly got back in her car and pulled up. As soon as she turned off the ignition, Clarke pulled off.

Persha

She couldn't believe he didn't even wait to talk to her. Persha saw him whisper something to the officer, but why he pulled off without talking to her was beyond confusing. It was actually painfully embarrassing.

She saw the direction he turned and quickly pulled off to the left. If she had to follow him, she would. Persha wanted to have her say and she wanted to be heard. But mainly she wanted to tell Clarke she wasn't mad at him. At least not anymore. She was ready to move on and she wanted to move on with him.

After tailing him for nearly thirty minutes, he finally pulled into a gas station. She turned in right behind him. She parked out of the way and was smiling when she got out of the car. Persha quickly ran up to his window.

"Hey! What's going on?" she asked. "You haven't returned any of my calls. I can't reach you at work and your cell's turned off. What gives?" Suddenly, Persha's hand went up to her chest, her eyes widened in surprise, and a smile quickly spread across her face. She saw the Zales bag on the seat next to Clarke and her eyes began to water.

Following her gaze to the bag in the seat next to him, Clarke quickly pushed it onto the floor.

"Oh, don't even trip. That's for my moms," he said.

Persha tried to mask her pain. She quickly looked away. Her heart rate returned to normal and she tried to remember what she was thinking before she saw the small bag, which no doubt contained jewelry.

She fought back tears and tried again to speak. "Ah, I was just wondering why you never call back anymore," she said, thinking about why Clarke had lied. He told her long ago that his mother died of cancer. Didn't he remember that? She didn't even want to entertain the idea of who that gift might have really been for.

Clarke sighed, shook his head, and shrugged his shoulders. "You don't get it, do you?" he said in an exhausted tone.

Persha shrugged. "Get what, Clarke? What? Now you don't want to talk to me? You don't want to have anything to do with me or something? What is it I'm supposed to be getting?"

"Look, I need to work some things through, that's all."

"Yeah, but what happened to us? You don't live with Kelsa anymore, so what's up?"

"Nothing, I'm just trying to figure out a few things. That's all."

"Yeah, but while you're figuring things out, what about me? What about us?" She let out a breath but he didn't say anything.

"I'm just going through a hard time right now; this mess with Kelsa. And I'm just having problems, that's all."

"Yeah, but you said we'd be together soon and now that you're not with her, what's the problem?"

Clarke rubbed his bald head and sighed again. He looked forward instead of up at her.

"It's not that easy, Persha. That's all."

"What's not that easy? I don't understand. What are you talking about?"

"Shit! You ruined my marriage. Now I'm probably gonna be sued for everything I own; my house, my car, money! Everything!" He slammed his palms against the steering wheel.

Persha stepped back. "What are you saying, Clarke?"

"Damn, isn't it clear to you? I don't have time for this right now. I need to get myself and my shit together or Kelsa's gonna take me to the cleaners. Is that what you want?" He finally looked up at her.

"Well, no. But I thought—"

"Yeah, I know what you thought. But what I'm telling you is, not right now. We need to cool it. She probably got somebody watching my ass this very minute."

Persha looked around the gas-station parking lot. It didn't seem like anyone was paying attention to them.

"So what do you want me to do?" she asked in defeat. "I never hear from you anymore. You never call or page. You won't even take my calls. And your cell, the number is no longer in service. What am I supposed to do?"

Clarke sighed and eased back in his seat.

"Look, Kelsa's really tripping hard. I had to call the cops just to get some of my clothes and stuff. You saw that officer. I have a restraining order against her," Clarke lied. "Ain't no telling what she might try next. She's pretty desperate. That's why that cop was there. I couldn't talk to you in front of him."

"Oh, well, I didn't know what was going on."

"See, that's what I'm trying to tell you. There's a lot of shit you don't even know about. You need to let me handle this and trust me."

"But Clarke, there's something I really need to talk to you about."

"I'm sure there is, but what I'm saying is I can't do this right now. I have some other stops I need to take. I need to hook up with my attorney and try to get this shit cleared up."

Persha suddenly got excited. She couldn't believe her ears. "Attorney? You have an attorney?"

"Yeah, shorty. A brotha gotta protect his interest. This is about to be an all-out war and I can't just go in unprotected. Kelsa's really tripping, that's what I'm tryin' to tell you."

"Damn, I had no idea."

"I'm sure you didn't. You probably thought I was sitting up chilling somewhere. But a brotha is actually gearing up for a fight. And it's gonna get ugly too. See, I was trying to avoid all of this in the beginning. She knew her days were numbered, but now I see I gotta act the fool because that's apparently all some women understand."

"Well, how can I help? What do you need me to do? I want to help you get through this."

"I just really need you to be understanding. This is not going to be easy on a brotha and I don't need another person tearing me down right now."

"Oh, I would never do anything like that, Clarke, you know that. I care about you too much. I just want this to be an easy transition for us. I'm willing to wait until this mess is cleared up because I know that we will eventually be together."

"Well, actually, right now I'm not sure what I want to do. I know I don't ever want to go through this sorta mess again."

"Oh, I can just imagine. Well, I know you don't want to sit here too long, but I wanted to tell you that I finally got a place. It's nothing big and fancy. It's only month to month and it's right off the beltway."

He didn't seem impressed with anything she was saying. Clarke actually appeared a bit restless, looking out his rearview and side mirrors.

Persha wanted his undivided attention. She'd thought about telling him right then and there that she was pregnant, but wanted the moment to be special. She didn't think a gas-station parking lot was a good place to break the news, especially after what they'd been discussing.

"Well, a brotha gotta hit the road. I'm already late for my meeting with my attorney. I can't keep him waiting."

Persha smiled at the thought of finally getting her man all to herself. She reached for him, but he moved beyond her reach.

"What's wrong, Clarke? I just need to touch you again. It's been so long."

"Persha, didn't I just tell you Kelsa probably got folks watching me? You think it's a good idea for us to be out here acting all affectionate and shit? That's not smart."

She pulled her hand back like a scolded child and looked around the gas station again.

"You're probably right. But when can we see each other? I want you to check out the new place. I really need to see you. You know, in private, behind closed doors." She smirked.

Stone-faced and serious, he looked up at her and said, "It's almost like you haven't heard a word I said to you. That, or you just don't care. If Kelsa ruins me, like I think she's trying to, there's nothing for you to have. It's all but over between us, Persha."

Persha couldn't help herself. She stood and struggled to fight the tears that were again threatening to escape her eyes. Her hand went up to her stomach. She couldn't help herself.

"Over?" She gulped, shaking her head in denial. "It can't be."

Clarke's eyes darted between her stomach and her head. His face flinched in shock. Before she could do anything he reached for the handle and said, "watch out." She inched back with tears rolling down her cheeks.

He jumped out of the car and grabbed her by the shoulders. He looked around one last time then leaned into her, so close, she could feel his warm breath on her forehead.

"I know your ass ain't trying to act like you pregnant or nothing like that, right?" he whispered through clenched teeth.

With trembling lips, Persha's eyes fixed on his cold stare. Unsure of what to say, she started shaking.

"Don't give me that scared little-girl shit. Answer my question, Persha! You're not pregnant, are you?" They were nearly leaning against her car.

"Uh, you're hurting me, Clarke."

"Ma'am, is everything okay over there?" a man asked.

The strange voice came as much-needed relief.

Persha looked to the right without moving her head. It was a mechanic who had asked the question.

"Ma'am, are you okay?" he repeated. "You need us to call the police?"

Clarke let go of her shoulders, stepped back, and turned to the mechanic.

"Aw, come on, man!" Clarke said. "It ain't nothing like that. No need to call the man. Can't a brotha have a little disagreement with his woman anymore?"

"Ma'am, are you okay?" the mechanic asked, completely ignoring Clarke's explanation.

Free from Clarke's grip, Persha turned to the mechanic and forced herself to smile. "Yeah, I'm fine." She shook her head up and down. "I'm okay. Thanks for asking."

After looking at her for a few minutes, the mechanic finally turned around and walked back into the garage.

Persha sighed. Clarke started smoothing out his clothes. Leaning against his car, he looked at her for a long time without speaking.

"I wasn't trying to upset you," Persha explained. "I just want you to know how much I need you. After all I've gone through with the insurance company, you were there for me. I'm about to get the money from my 401(K) so I can put something down on another condo. I just want to do for you what you did for me."

He tilted his head and folded his arms across his chest. "So you got a place, huh?"

"Yeah," she said, sniffling.

"Well, maybe I could come by and check it out." His eyes were closely inspecting her body. And suddenly, under his close scrutiny, she began to feel very uncomfortable.

Persha started thinking it might be best if she told him now. She didn't need him coming around, staying at her new place and then seeing her belly swell up with no warning.

"Ah, Clarke, there's something I do have to tell you." She swallowed hard and looked in the direction of the mechanic, but he was no longer in her view. Clarke slowly shook his head up and down, concentrating his gaze on her every move.

Persha shifted her weight from one leg to the other, took a deep breath and slowly said, "Ah, well, um—actually I'm um . . . I'm pregnant, Clarke."

It was sudden. One minute she was standing, the next she was on the ground and her face was stinging. When she looked up, the mechanic and another man were running toward her as the tires on Clarke's car screeched out of the gas station's parking lot.

"Ma'am, are you okay?" one man screamed, hoisting her up by one elbow while the other man took her other arm.

"You want us to call the police?" the other asked.

"Oh, no, I'm fine, I really am. He's just . . . I don't know. I need to sit down. I don't want to hurt my baby."

"Plus you pregnant? I can't believe a brotha would go out like that! Why he flash on you like that?" the other man asked, with his gold-capped tooth shining.

Persha shook her head. She had no idea why she was talking to these men. She couldn't believe Clarke had done that to her. Only weeks ago he was protesting his love for her. Or was that love for her wet tight pussy? She couldn't remember now.

Pregnant and more alone than she'd ever felt in her life, Persha walked into her small apartment and checked her answering machine. Deep down inside she was hoping to hear from Clarke. She wanted to hear a tearful apology, his pitiful voice, begging for forgiveness.

Two weeks after Persha's very painful encounter with Clarke, she had faced the fact that she was going to be a single mother. How the hell was she going to tell her mother? The lectures, the scriptures, the times her mother had her pray to keep her legs closed until she was married. Now this?

Persha's belly was taking shape and when she walked into the office one morning, Brenda's eyes were on her stomach. As Persha sat behind her desk she wondered where things had gone wrong. She and Clarke should've been embarking on the new chapter of their lives together. Instead, she was alone; pregnant and alone. She was pregnant by a married man who slapped her in a gas-station parking lot when she admitted what would soon be hard to hide or deny.

"You put on some weight?" Brenda said. Her way of getting information came as no surprise to Persha.

Persha sighed, dropped the folder she was working on, and looked toward Brenda. Before she could answer, her attention focused outside the office door.

"Oh, what are they doing here?" Persha said as she jumped up from her seat and walked to the door to let Cricket and Kori in.

They exchanged hugs and kisses.

"Heeey! What a surprise!" Persha said. "What are you two doing here? Who's with your aunt?" she asked Cricket.

"Oh, I've hired another nurse to come in and help out," Cricket replied. "We're getting closer to the end and it's becoming too much."

"You guys remember Brenda, right?"

Kori and Cricket smiled and greeted Brenda.

Standing in the small office Kori looked at Persha. "We've missed you. You don't call anybody anymore, and goodness knows we haven't seen you. What's the matter, are our girlfriend get-togethers not good enough for you anymore or what?"

"Nah, that's not it," Persha said, looking down at the floor.

"Well, Kori figured if you didn't want to come to us, we'd come to you," Cricket said. "You want to go grab an early bite?"

"Not really. My appetite has all but disappeared ever since—," Persha said before stopping herself.

"What's going on, Persha?" Cricket asked, noticing the intense look in her eyes as if she had been caught with her hand in the cookie jar.

As if someone released the floodgates, Persha started crying. And once the tears started rolling, it was nearly impossible to stop them.

Persha fell into Cricket's arms, and Brenda quickly produced a wad of tissue, as if breaking down and crying was a normal act around the office.

"It's gonna be okay, baby," Cricket said. "It's gonna be just fine." She patted Persha's back a few times.

Kori fell to a nearby chair anticipating some kind of bad news because she knew these were not tears of joy.

"I'm pregnant, and Clarke wants nothing to do with me or the baby. I haven't seen him in nearly a month, ever since I told him about the baby," Persha confessed.

"That bastard!" Cricket spat. "He's a no-good snake."

"Oh, baby, I knew it!" Brenda cheered. "Chile, women done raised kids alone for hundreds of years. Don't waste your tears on him. If he don't want no parts of you or your child let him be!"

"She's right," Kori said from her chair, leaping up to go to Persha's side.

Cricket leaned forward. "Don't even tell me that's why you've been avoiding us. Girl, we're family. Your mama ain't here. We're all you have. Don't ever do anything like that again," she chastised.

"I just don't know what to do," Persha said, wiping away a few tears. "How am I supposed to tell my mother? You know how crazy she can get? After all she had to give up to raise me alone, and I fall into the exact same trap she did. Well, I mean my father died when I was a baby and there was nothing she could do about that. But she was a single mom and it was hard for her. What am I going to do?"

"You're gonna pray that God blesses you with a healthy child and you'll do what you have to do in order to take care of it. Plain and simple," Brenda interjected.

Kori threw her hands up. "Yeah, girl. It's a no-brainer to me. We thought you had some real bad news! A baby, that's not all that bad. Okay, so he skipped on you, but like Ms. Brenda said, he ain't the first and won't be the last. Straight up."

With newfound courage, Persha thought she was ready to face her mother, or at least to call her and deliver the news. Her mind was definitely made up. She'd have the baby without Clarke. And unlike her mother, she'd be very up-front about their relationship. When the child was old enough, she'd explain why she and Clarke were no longer together. Her own mother didn't like talking about her father. All Persha knew was that he was killed in a military training exercise.

Even though she'd made up her mind to tackle this alone, still, deep down inside, a little part of her wanted to give Clarke another chance. She had to admit to herself that he was going through more than any one man should have to bear alone. And when he slapped her, well, that was just sheer reaction. She knew he didn't mean anything by that. He loved her, and when the baby came, he'd love it too.

With the phone ringing in her ear, Persha couldn't wait to share her news with her mother. Persha had already told herself that she would not allow anything to make her feel bad about her decision.

"Hey Mama!" Persha said through the phone receiver.

"Chile, where've you been! Lawd have mercy! I prayed and prayed the Lord would steer you to me. I haven't been sleeping well. I've told you time and time again that I don't like when we don't talk."

"I know, Ma, but I've been going through a lot lately. I needed to get my head on straight, get my thoughts together so that we could really talk."

"Well, let's pray. Chile, I need the Holy Ghost to

take over and become a moving force in your life! I hope you see the light before it's too late. God said—"

"Ma, I'm pregnant!" Persha said, cutting her off. There was no point in prolonging the inevitable. She saw where the conversation was going and she wanted to get it off her chest so she could take whichever scripture her mother was about to unleash.

"Ma? Are you there?" Persha asked. Still, nothing on the other end. She could barely hear her mother breathing.

"Persha? You've been fornicating?" Her mother actually sounded surprised by the revelation. Persha shook her head as she listened to Paula. "I told you what would happen. Didn't I warn you, chile? You need to humble yourself before the Lord! Oh sweet Jesus! What have you done? Chile, what in God's good name have you gone and done?"

Persha rolled her eyes. She didn't feel up to the emotional trashing from her mother.

"Well, I just wanted to let you know," Persha said. "I'm having a baby for a man who may be involved with someone else and does not want to have anything to do with me or the baby. He's married. I just thought you should know. That's all!"

Persha knew what she was doing wasn't right, but better her mother hear the news before it got too late. Initially, she had no intention of mentioning the fact that Clarke was married, but then decided she might as well get it over with. She was causing her mother enough distress. She might as well do it in one big heap.

"Laaaaawd, have mercy! Whew, chile. In the good book, Matthew chapter five verse thrity-five, says anyone who causes one to commit adultery is himself an adulterer. And in Mark chapter ten verse eleven, any man who divorces his wife to marry another woman commits adultery against her. Persha, what have you done, chile? What have you done?" Paula shrieked.

"Ma, I never said anything about him leaving his wife for me. What's done is done. They will divorce, but it's not because of me. The damage was done long before me."

"In Luke chapter twenty-four verse forty-seven Jesus says repentance and remission of sins should—"

"Ma! That's enough. Either you're with me or you're not! I don't need scripture. I need support right now."

"Persha, that's what I've been trying to tell you all this time. Everything you need is right in the good book, baby. Everything!"

As a tear ran down her cheek, Persha sighed and rolled her eyes again.

Clarke

Clarke had been in a steep drunken stupor for days after his last encounter with Persha. What the fuck did he need with a kid right now? He was hoping Kelsa wouldn't find out about it, and maybe somehow she'd take him back.

He knew for sure that if she found out about the baby, there was no way in hell they'd get back together. Lying on the sofa in Antwone's carriage house, the game was watching him more than he was watching it.

His mind had been to so many places and back, and still nothing. No matter how much he struggled, his mind could not come up with a simple solution.

He wondered if he could somehow make Persha abort the baby. That way, they could make a clean break and go their separate ways again . . . and for good this time! *Nah, that wouldn't be cool*, Clarke reconsidered.

Clarke hadn't even told Antwone about the latest development in the fucked-up scenario. He didn't need any more stress in his life, well, not any more than he already had. Besides, sometimes Antwone whined more than any bitch he'd ever been involved with did.

Like yesterday, Antwone said it was cool for them to kick it up at the house, watch the game and have a few cold ones because Michelle's stupid ass was going somewhere. Then when Clarke started talking about the restraining order and how he needed to go by the house for more stuff, Antwone suddenly sat up with his face twisted. Clarke was under the impression that Antwone felt the same way about that crazy restraining order as he did until Antwone asked, "Why would you do that if you know you could go to jail?"

With his face unable to mask his own confusion, Clarke shrugged and asked, "Man, whose side you on?"

Antwone shook his head. "It's not a matter of being on sides, it's common sense. If you would've handled your business the right way, you wouldn't be all caught up right now. That's all I'm saying. And while it's been cool for you to kick it here, Michelle is starting to ask about how long you're gonna stay." He sipped his brew. "She really talking about letting you stay is like picking sides."

"No shit?"

"I told you I was getting this place ready for her mother. That bitch is supposed to come here for a couple of weeks and ain't no way in hell she staying in my crib. So this is where she stays." Antwone looked around as if he was inspecting the place.

"Aw, dawg. Well, that's why I need to get back over to the house and talk to Kelsa. She's got to see how crazy all this shit is; changing locks, restraining orders, and not letting a brotha in the house and shit. All my plants are probably dead by now."

"Clarke, what I'm trying to say is you may need to get your own place. Man, she had way too much control over your life to begin with. You don't need her. And you know I'll take care of you whether you're here or not."

"Aeey, look man, kicking a brotha a few duckets is different from what I have with Kelsa. Some of that shit is mine too. Why should I just walk away and let her win?"

"Because you had another woman living up in her house, bro. You oughta be glad you still alive!" Antwone snickered. "Yeah, Kelsa told Michelle the whole story, dawg."

They both leaned back. Clarke watched as Antwone sipped his brew, but he was seeing something different in his friend.

"So you're saying I should just throw in the towel then?" Clarke asked.

"Nah, that's not what I'm saying. But, man, you don't want to be a liability to nobody. I mean, think about it, Clarke. What do you have to offer anybody? And you know I'm down with you and all, but selling that magic wand of yours all the time ain't even cool."

"Why you gotta go there?"

"I'm just saying. Just because I don't pay for it anymore, it don't mean you ain't still selling in a sense."

Clarke started fuming. So now Antwone all of a sudden thinks he's better than somebody because his shit's all intact. Well, Clarke knew how to set him straight, but first he had to make sure he'd have a place to stay until Kelsa took him back.

"Well, when you're married you become one. So it's not like Kelsa didn't know what she was getting into. And besides, it ain't like you kicking a brotha down like you used to either."

"Shit, man, priorities change. That's all I'm saying. By your age, you should have a few things in your own damn name so that regardless of what any of these hags do, you still got your own when they're gone. Look at you now, man. If I didn't let you chill in the back, where would you be? And if I didn't give you the down payment for your ride, shit, you'd probably still be driving around in that old bucket you used to have."

"Well, everybody ain't got a education with a masters degree and such like you. That don't mean a brotha ain't trying to hook things up. Besides, you said the money for the car was a gift, now you trying to throw it back up in my face and shit?"

"Nah, it ain't even like that, bro. I'm just saying, you dropped out of college, never went back and stop talking to your pops because he was trying to set you straight. You married Kelsa because I got married, and all the while you're sitting up in this dead-end job passing out those misleading-ass business cards and not doing anything to make your life better."

Antwone looked at Clarke. "All I'm saying is, what if something happened with us?" he said in a sincere tone. "This shit with Kelsa should be a wake-up call for you. If she files for divorce, you just out there, man, all exposed and shit. That's all I'm saying. And trying to go over there when she can get you locked up ain't gonna make things any better. Leave her ass alone and get *your* shit together. That's what I'm really saying."

"Hmm. I peep." Clarke tipped his head back slightly.

Oh, he heard just what Antwone was saying loud and clear. He knew for sure he needed to get back with Kelsa, and real quick like. And once that was settled, he might even bring Antwone back down to earth. It was clear that brotha must've forgotten just who the hell he was really dealing with.

Thinking about how he wanted to sock Antwone in the jaw after all that, he was glad he didn't. With time running out, he knew he'd have to find a way to get back in Kelsa's good graces.

When Antwone walked out of the carriage house, Clarke laid back. He suddenly had an idea and Antwone was nowhere close by to talk him out of it.

Clarke picked up the phone and dialed Kelsa. After the first ring, a recording came on announcing the number had been changed, at the customer's request, it was unlisted.

"What the fuck?" Clarke said as he looked at the receiver, then down at the numbers on the phone's screen, thinking he had to have dialed the wrong number.

When he called right back and got the same recording, Clarke slammed the receiver back into its cradle and cursed again.

Clarke searched for a phone book. When he didn't find one, he picked up the phone and dialed the information directory.

"Yes, I need the number to the Yellow Taxicab Company," Clarke said after the operator picked up. He knew the effects of the beer were already sinking in, and since he planned to have a few more to give him liquid courage, he didn't think it wise to drive.

After waiting about ten minutes, he was in the back of a cab being whisked off to his old house. At the corner he gave the driver a fifty-dollar bill from his *emergency* stash and told him to park one house up and wait.

"If I'm not back in twenty minutes, just leave and keep the change," he said, slamming the door behind him.

Clarke walked up to the front door and stopped. He frowned at the sound of music blasting loudly from the house.

"What the hell? Is Kelsa having a party or something?" he said to himself. He inched closer to the door, listening to voices and laughter ringing out. The sounds of fingers snapping and people cheering nearly sent him into a fury.

Damn, he thought. *How in the hell is she having a party and I don't know nothing about it? It's not even her birthday.*

He started figuring that it must really be over, because Kelsa wasn't even the type to have lots of people all up in the house. She was just private like that.

At the door he considered turning back and leaving. He really didn't need to see any other brothas trying to push up on his wife. She was still *his* wife. But then he thought maybe this could be a good thing. If someone was trying to get close to Kelsa, he'd straight knock that fool out, and quite surely that would show her he meant business.

After ringing the doorbell a few times and there was no answer, he started pounding on the door. To his amazement, it swung open and the music was still blasting while a few women he didn't recognize were standing next to each other in a line looking like they were about to bust a serious dance move.

Others were in the kitchen hovering over a table of various snacks. And nearby a chair was decorated with ribbons, streamers, and other things. He didn't see Kelsa right away.

"Ohhhh, lookie here lookie here! Look who decides to show up for the party," Kelsa's friend, Menesha, said.

Suddenly the music stopped. She all but pulled Clarke inside. It wasn't until he was damn near surrounded by all of the guests when he realized that there were nothing but women up in there.

"So, you came back to the scene of the crime, huh?" someone taunted.

"Yeah, wanted to see if there was anything else you

could squeeze outta our girl, right?" someone else interjected.

Clarke looked around. He wasn't really afraid, thinking what's the worse that could happen? It was a bunch of women after all. If he was forced, he'd go straight for the tits, start swinging and make a break. But for the moment, he was cool.

"Yeah, that's a dog for you. When he finds a good spot to piss, he keeps coming back to piss some more." Menesha giggled.

Clarke looked around hoping to see Kelsa. He didn't need this shit.

"Whaaat's going on here?" he asked. He didn't mean for his voice to sound so shaky.

"Well, if you must know," the group parted enough for Kelsa to emerge. She had a roll of duct tape in her hands. "Everyone's having a pity party for little ole' me," she said with a grin. "Imagine the cause of my pain and embarrassment showing up, right on cue!" She winked with a wicked smile on her face.

"Let's string his ass up!" someone yelled.

With his hands up in a defensive mode, Clarke stepped back. "Whoa! Hold up! Wait a minute here. Ain't no need for anybody to get hurt. Let's just chill out for a moment."

Before he could swing at a single breast, he was on the floor and hands were coming at him from all directions. Soon Clarke felt himself struggling to breathe. He wanted to tell someone that he couldn't breathe and that they really needed to get off of him. But someone was sitting on his chest and when he opened his mouth to speak, the words wouldn't come out.

Clarke couldn't believe this shit. Maybe the cab-driver would sense something was wrong and come to see about him. If only he could send a signal out to

Kelsa that he was just here to talk and to try and work things out. But soon the music was back up again.

He told himself not to panic. He wasn't scared. These were just women; *all* women were loving and docile creatures. Most had a soft spot and wouldn't hurt anybody. He should know, he left many hurt and heartbroken, and most of *them* still wanted him back.

He figured the best thing to do was to just let them have some fun, get out their frustration and then he and Kelsa would send everybody off and they could talk. And if she behaved right, he'd even consider tapping that ass. He knew she was long overdue, probably horny as hell.

But his chest, it almost felt like it was caving in. He wasn't about to panic though, they'd get up soon. Besides, he couldn't let them see him sweat.

A few minutes later, Clarke felt as though he was living a nightmare. His eyes fixed on the clock. He wondered if he'd been in the house for twenty minutes already. He wished for a way to call the cabdriver in, to send a message of distress, but he knew that brotha was long gone and fifty dollars richer.

Later, sitting in a chair with his hands tied behind his back and each foot strapped to the legs of a chair, Clarke was in disbelief. And to make matters worse, his mouth had been taped shut. This, he finally decided, had gone way too far. He had had enough and he wanted somebody to release him. It wasn't funny anymore.

At the moment, Kelsa was pacing back and forth in front of him.

"Made fun of me all those times, talking about doing a thangie smell check and so forth," she said snickering. "When all along you had some skank ho right up under my nose, living in my own fucking house!" She slapped her chest. He'd never seen her so expressive.

"Umph, umph, umph, umph," someone chimed in.

Clarke didn't have time for this mess. He couldn't believe how these bitches had him strapped up like he was some kind of animal.

"Now whatchu gonna do, Clarke?" Menesha said. "Kelsa, didn't you say you walked in on some chicken head sucking his dick?"

"Yeah, chica," Kelsa answered. "He's got a thing for blow jobs. As a matter of fact, I want to say that exactly where he is sitting may have been the exact spot he was getting his dick sucked! Yup! Right here in my fucking house, the house I pay for 'cause his sorry-ass paycheck goes toward plants and flowers and shit like that."

"Wwwwhat?" another woman screamed. "Gurrrl, you better than me! I would've cut his dick off! Sliced it up then served it to him and his nasty-ass ho!"

"Sho' nuf!" somebody screamed. Then they all started laughing and giving each other high fives.

Shit! Clarke thought. He couldn't believe they were talking about cutting his dick off. He started wriggling to free himself, but it did no good. He was strapped tightly to the chair. All he knew was that if these crazy bitches thought he was gonna sit here and be sliced to pieces, they had another thing coming. But no matter how much he wiggled, he couldn't break free.

"Aw, look!" Menesha screamed, drawing everyone's attention. "I think he's nervous. Are those little sweat beads forming on his forehead?" Her laugh was mincing. She pranced over to the chair.

And to imagine, he had once thought about getting with her back in the day when Kelsa first brought her to their home and introduced them. It was after they'd both worked a double shift. He actually thought she was fine, even with that long ass-weave she wore.

But now, after spending some time around her ignorant ass, he knew for sure that she was way too loud for him. All up in his face now. *Oooooooooh, if only I could get my hands free. I'd slap the shit out of her ass.*

"Kelsa, you notice how men start sweating when you start talking about cutting thangs off? Kind of remind you of that Lorean Bobbitt!" Menesha taunted.

"Forget about Lorean. What about that Mexican woman? Remember, it was right here in Houston? She cut off her man's thang then fed it to a damn dog!" someone chirped in.

"Oh yeah! She was the girl!" Menesha replied. "But I'll bet he wasn't sweating like this when that skank ho was on her knees sucking his dick. What y'all think?"

The cheering section went wild. Everybody was laughing, slapping high-fives, doing a few girlfriend snaps, and so forth. Clarke didn't like the situation. He didn't like how they were going on and on about him being a dog and talking about damaging his family jewels.

He needed them to keep things in perspective. He was very uncomfortable with this kind of talk.

But, trying to relax, he sighed a bit, because so far that's all it was, talk, and he wanted it to stay that way. He had to remember not to roll his eyes and watch his facial expressions. He didn't need to piss them off any more than they already were.

Just when he was about to relax and ride this thing through, his heart sank to his toes when he heard Kelsa say, "Let's take off his pants and see if we can't cut that thangie off. You know, since he ain't shy about sharing it and all."

With dread, Clarke closed his eyes as the cheers grew. Obviously everyone agreed with that idea. *Now* he was scared.

Persha

Persha felt like some silly little teenager; knocked up, abandoned, and fat. But she wasn't a teenager, though. At the age of thirty-three, she was far from it. She couldn't believe she'd allowed herself to get into this situation.

And for whom? It had been way past a month since she saw that worthless bastard, Clarke. Well, in her opinion, maybe *worthless bastard* was a bit too steep.

She was trying to understand what he must've been going through. After all, he was about to have to fight for everything he had worked so hard to obtain. She thought about him possibly losing that beautiful house, his luxury car, and maybe even his prestigious position at the ad agency. Men don't take things like that lightly.

If only she could get through to him. She wanted to let him know they could work this thing out. She'd wait until the divorce was final, but she still thought it would be a good idea for them to move in together.

Maybe instead of buying another condo they could put their money together and get a house. She had to find a way to appeal to his sensible side. Persha was watching *Girlfriends* on UPN, Urban People's Network, as she and her friends referred to the network that showed more black sitcoms than any other. Just as she was getting into the show, the phone rang.

Her caller ID showed her mother's number and she was tempted not to answer. But then she figured that she might as well get used to the nagging calls. She had no intentions of severing ties with her mother. They were still all each other had.

"Hi Ma," Persha answered the phone.

"Persha, baby, are you okay?" her mother asked.

"Yes, I'm fine. Why do you ask?"

"You didn't sound like yourself, that's all."

"No, Ma, I'm doing just fine." She smiled at one of the character's antics.

"How's the baby?"

"Huh? What'd you say?" Persha pushed mute on her remote and sat up.

"I asked how's my grandchild doing? Despite what you think, I do care about you and *my* grandchild." Paula cleared her throat. "I know we don't see eye to eye on lots of things, but I was kind of hoping we could get a fresh start and I think that's what this baby represents for us both."

Persha listened as her mother went on about their fresh start. She looked at the clock and realized that she had been on the phone for nearly ten minutes with her mother and there had been no scripture quoting. *This had to be a record,* she thought.

"Lord knows." Paula paused. And Persha figured she'd spoken too soon. She braced herself for a religious reading. "Lord knows I haven't been perfect. Maybe if I'd been honest about some of the things I went through you'd be on a different path today. You know I only wanted you to have more opportunities than me. When your father died, I knew the task ahead, and I was prepared to take on the challenge of being a single mother. Honey, fate dealt me that hand and I did the best I could. I may have wanted better for you, but just because you didn't take the route I wanted you to, it doesn't make me any less happy with the outcome."

By the time Paula paused a second time, Persha was in tears. That was the first time in years her mother had been so forthcoming. She wasn't critical, and most importantly, she didn't beat her up about her spirituality, or lack thereof.

"Persha, baby, you still there?" her mother said into the phone.

"Yeah, Ma, I am. I'm just—I can't believe what you're saying."

"Why? You know I'm still your mother no matter what. I will love you whether you're a wife or a mistress. I may not agree with your choices, but that will never change my love for you. And don't you ever doubt that. Now, with that done, I need to check for airline tickets."

"Airline tickets?" Persha asked, still sniffling.

"Chile, I've got to come see my grandbaby, and your worrisome auntie is already talking about pictures 'cause she can't picture you with child!"

They laughed. "Well, Ma, the baby won't be here for another five months. I think it's a bit premature for visits, don't you?"

"Chile, hush your mouth. If I want to come see my babies, I can come whenever the good Lord carries me. I'll be there next weekend."

"Really, Ma?" Persha started smiling and wiping her eyes.

"Just as soon as Southwest Airlines or the Greyhound in the sky, gives me the stamp of approval. I'm staying for a week. After that I'll be back once a month until you have the baby."

"Oh, Ma, I love you! I can't wait to see you. I'm gonna take a couple of days off so I can show you around Houston. You'll like it here."

"I'll like seeing you, but I sure hope you have an air conditioner there in that apartment of yours. I've been looking at the Weather Channel and, chile, every day they're talking about hot temperatures and humidity there."

Persha started laughing. "Yeah, Ma, most places out here come equipped with central air."

"Good. Well, let me go make my reservations. I'll call you later with my flight information okay, baby?"

"Okay, Ma."

"Oh, and Persha?"

"Yes, ma'am?"

"I'm still keeping you and the baby in my prayers 'cause we all need as many blessings as we can possibly get."

"I know, Ma, and thanks. See you soon!"

Hours after the phone call, Persha still got chills when she thought about it. It had to be the very best conversation she and her mother had ever had. There wasn't much that could change her good mood, she thought, as she leaned back in search of something to watch on TV.

The next day, Persha nearly floated into the office. Brenda noticed her new attitude right away.

"Oooohh chile, you sure look perky today. Must've got some good rest last night," Brenda guessed.

Persha turned to her and smiled. "Actually, I did. I had a great evening."

"Is that man of yours finally acting right? I sure hope so. These men these days . . . boy, I tell you."

"My good mood has nothing to do with a man and everything to do with my mother. As a matter of fact, I need Thursday and Friday of next week off and I'd like to invite you to a dinner party I'm throwing."

Brenda's bushy eyebrows eased up a bit. She smiled and shook her head. "A party? I'm thrilled to death you'd think to ask me. Of course I'll come, chile. What we celebrating?"

"We're celebrating my mother. She's flying in Saturday night and she'll be here until the following Sunday."

Making a clapping motion like a thrilled child, Brenda smiled. "Yippee! I get to meet your mom too! That sounds wonderful. You want me to bring something? I make mac and cheese from scratch and folks just rant and rave about it. Or I could bring a cheesecake. I make that from scratch too."

"Hmmm, let's see. I want mac and cheese, but," she touched her portly stomach and said, "this one might enjoy the cheesecake." She and Brenda both laughed.

"Well, cheesecake *and* mac and cheese it is!" she said. Brenda looked up. "And by the way, you can have those days you want off. And if you need any help getting the party together, just call me."

"Thanks, Brenda," Persha said with a smile.

When Persha pulled up to the airport, she wasn't sure how to react at first; she'd been thinking about it all day.

But that uncertainty didn't last long, when she saw her mother walking out of baggage claim, Paula dropped her bag and pulled Persha into a tight embrace.

"Oh, how I've missed you," she said, pulling back to look at her daughter.

"I've missed you too, Mom." Persha grabbed her mother's bag, and walked toward the car holding her hand. She felt good having her mother at her side. As she drove her mother kept touching her, rubbing her shoulders, touching her stomach and running her fingers through her hair. Persha felt at ease about her pregnancy and her mother was not her normal judgmental self, so that made things even better.

By the time Friday rolled around, Persha and her mother had fallen into a comfortable groove. Each morning Paula woke and fixed breakfast, then she'd drive up to the office and take Persha out for lunch and have dinner fixed before she even came home.

The small apartment was decorated and various aromas were floating from the kitchen. Paula had even dug through some of Persha's CD's and was playing one of Michael Jackson's songs. She always did love that boy, even with all his strangeness.

Persha came into the kitchen after a trip to the store.

"Dang, Ma, you got it smelling so good up in here," she complimented. "I'm gonna miss you when you're gone." She was looking over her mother's shoulder as she focused on the pot on the stove.

"You won't have to miss me for long, baby." Paula turned and wiped her hands on an apron. "I'll be back next month and the month after that."

"And we can't wait." Persha smiled, trying to dip into one of the pots on the stove.

By seven Brenda and her husband Jessie, along with Kori and her date Will and Cricket had gathered for dinner. Paula had the apartment lit with tall pillar candles and soft music was playing in the background. The menu for the dinner party started off with a leafy salad drenched in Paula's secret caesar-dressing recipe.

"Ooooh-wee this dressing's so good, it's tasty," Brenda's husband exclaimed between stuffing his mouth with bites of the salad.

When the orange roasted Cornish hens stuffed with

fresh baby vegetables, and Brenda's three-cheese mac and cheese came out, Kori's date didn't try to hide his lip licking.

Paula presented the homemade sweet butter rolls like they were royalty, shining and glossy on a silver platter and everyone dug in.

"Save room for Ms. Brenda's strawberry swirl cheesecake," Paula teased.

By the flicker of candlelight, the seven ate and ate until a few had to ease back and loosen belts and buttons.

Persha looked over at her mother. "This is so nice. I'm so glad you're here, Ma. Thank you so much for everything."

Paula looked around the table. "You know, I worry so much about my baby being out here all by her lonesome, but now that I've had a chance to spend time around all of you, I can rest a bit easy. I know God is watching out for her. Thank you all," Paula said.

"Awww," Kori managed as her date helped himself to his third plate.

Everyone else smiled and soon it was time for the cheesecake.

Persha was actually dreading Sunday. She didn't want her mother to leave, but she knew it was inevitable. When she woke to use the bathroom at 5:30 A.M., she jumped at the light being on.

She tiptoed to the hall and watched quietly as her mother kneeled in front of the coffee table in a praying position. Never before had she noticed the cunning likeness they shared. Her mother's features mirrored her own in an astonishing way. They had the same nose, same cheekbones, and thin lips.

While her mother's skin looked the color of maple syrup, Persha's was several shades lighter, but there was certainly no denying their kinship. And while her mother's long dark lashes bunched up indicating just how tightly her eyes were shut, Persha could hear her voice. It was at a pleasant octave just above a whisper.

Persha's eyes began to water when she realized her mother was praying for her. After a few minutes, she crept to the bathroom and then went back to bed. Unable to sleep, she got up after about an hour and found her mother busily making breakfast.

"Ma, you don't have to do all of this on your last day here. You should be resting for your flight back home."

Turning her ample hips and leaning against the counter, Paula looked at her daughter. "I don't mind, I'm glad to do for you again. I'm so glad we were able to patch things up and you know there are some things you and I should probably talk about before this baby comes."

Persha sat at the table and reached for one of the homemade biscuits and syrup.

"What's going on, Ma?"

"This isn't the right time for us to get into it, but just know that I love you and after we talk I really hope you'll still love me too."

Persha got up, walked over and hugged her mother. "There's not a thing you could ever say that would prevent me from loving you!"

Paula pulled back slightly. "I really hope so, child. I really do. I've been praying about it, and when the good Lord moves me, I'll be ready." She smiled. "Until then, why don't we enjoy our breakfast, then we can go for a walk before we head out to the airport."

"Sounds great," Persha said.

Throughout breakfast and during the walk, she and her mother shared small talk, but her mind was on what it was her mother had to talk about and why her mother would think that whatever it was would be enough to put into question Persha's love for her. She wanted desperately to ask, inquire about it, but something told her to wait until her mother was ready.

Persha was genuinely pleased when she looked back at their time together. Not once did they share a cross word. They had actually gotten along better than they ever had. And a couple of nights, Paula had rubbed Persha's stomach until she fell asleep.

Paula told her she felt a deeper connection to the baby and that made Persha feel special. All and all, the entire visit had been a complete treat, and both ladies looked forward to next month's trip.

After a tearful good-bye at Hobby Airport, Persha drove back home feeling loved and energized. Her excitement about the baby grew with each passing day. If only she would've been able to get Clarke on board, things would've been that much better. But she wasn't quite ready to give up just yet. No, she could and would still fight for what was rightfully hers, and soon, they'd be a real family.

Clarke

When the two pairs of scissors came close, Clarke thought he was going to piss on himself right in front of those broads. And mind you, some of them were fine. Menesha used her pair to cut the right leg of his new slacks and Kelsa cut the left. Each cut from the ankle all the way up to his waist.

"Ooooweeee, look at his silk boxers. He must've thought he was about to get lucky," a voice he didn't recognize screamed.

At his waist, both women cut his belt. Menesha stepped back. "Okay, on three let's pull the pants off," she said like it was some kind of project they were revealing.

On three, they pulled one time and his pants came off, revealing his silk boxers that he'd bought especially for the make-up sex he and Kelsa were gonna have.

Next, they cut his boxers to reveal his prized possession. Clarke could hardly believe he was sitting in a chair, surrounded by fifteen or twenty women, naked.

Oh, he was all hanging out, and it wasn't a good feeling.

"What's up with this shit, Kelsa? Where's the beef?" someone said laughing. A few minutes later, the cheering section started back up again.

Clarke closed his eyes. He wasn't a spiritual man, not by any means, but something inside told him if there was ever a time to pray, this was it. Closing his eyes tightly, he could feel a tear threatening to burst through when he heard Menesha say, "We need a butcher knife. Scissors ain't gonna cut this little thang!"

"I'll get it!" someone screamed, far too cheerfully for Clarke's liking.

He didn't know what to do. He didn't know what to think or what to feel. He could bleed to death. Didn't they realize this? Didn't they know that you don't just cut off a vital piece of a man and expect him to survive?

The moment he dreaded had finally arrived when a voice said, "This should do the trick!" Clarke's eyes snapped open and he focused on the enormous butcher knife in a woman's slender hand. The blade sparkled like light enjoyed bouncing off of it. He swallowed and fought back tears. They had already seen him sweat, he couldn't let them see him cry.

Clarke wanted to tell them they could go to jail for this; that they could be arrested. He wasn't sure, but this had to be a felony. When you consider kidnapping, the assault, and what if something went wrong. What if someone decided to really cut his dick off?

Menesha, the obvious ringleader, looked toward the blade. She smiled and her eyes lit up. Clarke imagined her head magically twisting to a 360-degree spin. But when she looked at Clarke, her voice deepened, and she said, "You'll pay, you bastard. Not just for what you did to Kelsa, but for what Ronnie did to me, for what David did to Sandra, or what Keith did to Melonie and for what Curtis did to Sylvia. Oh, you'll pay!"

At the end of that speech, the cheering section went absolutely crazy. Clarke swore some were screaming in support of the upcoming amputation. His heart started beating faster and faster. *They can't be serious,* he prayed.

Soon, Kelsa appeared at Menesha's side. Clarke didn't see her walk up next to her, she just appeared. His eyes and attention had been on the blade. With the duct-tape roll in her hands, Kelsa leaned in close to him.

"This ain't gonna be pretty," Kelsa said as she ripped off a long piece of the tape and fell to her knees. "You really don't need to see this." She reached for his head, but Clarke quickly moved it in the opposite direction.

He wanted to appeal to her with his eyes. He wanted her to know this wasn't right. What happened to the love? Didn't she know this wasn't the thing to do? Didn't she still love him? Clarke was struggling to talk with his eyes. He squinted, tilted his head, and shook his head before staring into her eyes.

She had to be in there somewhere! This was his very last chance to connect with her and prevent a tragedy. But someone must've taken his moving head for resistance, because soon, a set of hands appeared and held him in place.

All the wiggling and head shaking did little good. Once the hands were able to hold his head straight long enough, the duct tape went right over his eyes. He didn't even get a chance to close them properly.

"Trust me," Kelsa said. He could smell her perfume. "You'll thank me for this later. You don't want to see all the blood and mess this is gonna cause."

Another voice spoke up and said, "Kelsa! Hold up. Maybe you should let the low-down dirty bastard see what's going to happen. That way the dog will think twice before he screws another sistah over again."

"You know, that's not a bad idea," another stranger's voice chimed in.

"Besides, by the time we're done with him, he won't be screwing a damn thing!" another woman yelled.

The room fell silent. Clarke grew incredibly nervous and restless, but he knew it was best if he remained still.

He heard Kelsa sigh. He even felt the breath she released. He knew she was still near. He struggled not to move. He wanted to break free. This could be a last-ditch attempt to win her trust before the blades grew closer to his Johnson. He didn't like this shit at all. But what could he do and why was she taking so long?

At that very moment he started reminiscing about just how much he missed Kelsa and how badly he wanted her to give him another chance. He felt somewhere under all of the bravado, she still had feelings for him. The silence told him she was considering what she was about to do. He started smiling on the inside. Despite what the mob of bitches thought, he knew Kelsa was a good woman. He also knew about the faith he had in her.

For a moment, he wondered if they were alone. The cheering section was so quiet he considered it, but he knew better.

The calm had jump-started his imagination. What would life be like without his Johnson? Just the thought of losing his manhood made him want to die. Is a man still a man without it? How could he be? Clarke wondered if they understood the severity of their threat. It was just a few months ago when he saw that news story about that crazy bitch who cut off her man's dick right here in Houston.

He remembered wondering what the hell that man would do. Back then he had laughed, saying they might as well kill him if he had to live without his dick. He didn't feel that way now, not sitting in that chair sweating. The stillness alone was enough to make him quiver. The hairs on the back of his neck remained at attention.

He wanted desperately to hear what Kelsa would say. He knew she'd think twice and tell the hags to vacate the premises. Or at least that's what he thought until she spoke.

"I guess you've got a good point," he finally heard Kelsa say. And without warning, his face started burning, right at his eyes. He wasn't certain his skin was still in place. Kelsa had ripped the tape right off his eyes. His skin sizzled like someone had set it ablaze.

If only one of these bitter hags could have a little sympathy and spare him some agony. He knew a warm towel would help. He could barely keep his eyes open, and all of this while fighting back tears. He was emotionally exhausted and physically worn out.

But nothing could prepare his eyes for what he saw when his vision was finally fully restored. Void of the tears and temporary blurriness from the duct tape, he could see the angry mob was ready for blood. He had to be a man because Kelsa wasn't even looking into his eyes.

The assault weapon had already been passed to Menesha's hands, so he knew he was doomed. There was definitely no turning back at that point.

"Kelsa, are you sure you can handle this? 'Cause a sistah, wouldn't mind helping you out!" Menesha snickered.

Clarke watched as Kelsa's eyes settled on the blade. She didn't flinch, just nodded and reached for the knife. His heart sunk at her move. He thought she loved him.

"Not only can I do this, but I *want* to do this," Kelsa declared. "And trust me, I won't be as kind as Lorena! I'm gonna cut that mug up into a thousand pieces." She shrugged her shoulders. "Since a sistah's gonna do some time for this, I might as well go out like a champ, right?"

As if on cue, and to Clarke's dismay, the cheering section came to life again. He couldn't believe this was how he was set to die. There was no way he'd survive such an injury, and looking around the room at all the liquor and snacks, it was clear the women could go on celebrating for hours and hours while he lay bleeding to death.

With the blade in Kelsa's hands, he noticed the knife was far larger than it looked at first. Slowly and quietly at first, the crowd cheered her on. Confused, but more frightened than anything else, Clarke tried to keep his eyes on Kelsa, and that knife. He tried to block out everyone else.

Before he could figure this all out, Kelsa made one quick practice movement. It was almost graceful. She reached from behind her ear and swooped down toward his crotch. Incredibly, his dick was standing stiff, pointing straight ahead at full attention as if it knew it was the target. He couldn't control it. He wanted it to go limp. Maybe that would change the crowd's mood.

His eyes followed the blade as it quickly came close to his skin. It was all he could do to hold his bladder.

When Kelsa's eyes connected with his, he didn't know what that meant.

"The next time, it won't be a practice swing," she

said. His eyes grew wide as he watched her reach from behind and looked as if she would bring the blade down with even greater force.

Clarke held a pregnant breath.

Persha

She wasn't sure whether it was going to work, but it was her last hope. Persha wanted to give Clarke one final chance to be a part of her and their child's life. It was no accident that she picked Maggioni's restaurant. She was positive he wouldn't act up in the elegant Italian restaurant.

She looked at her watch again. She had already given the waiter her order for raspberry iced tea and waited for Clarke to show. If he didn't, then she'd be forced to face the truth. An entire thirty minutes had passed since he was supposed to be there, but she was willing to give it another few minutes. After all, their future was at stake.

Another fifteen minutes had passed before she finally decided to leave. She felt defeated and discouraged before she decided it was hopeless to keep trying. He obviously was not interested in her or the baby, so she'd pay for her two glasses of iced tea and leave.

Just as she was about to step into the revolving door, she saw him on the other side and her heart simply melted. A part of her knew he'd show up, and she was happy. That meant he wanted to work things out. *Finally!* she thought. Persha stepped back and waited for him to step through the revolving doors.

Immediately after coming through the door, Clarke reached down and kissed Persha on the cheek. *Good sign*, she thought as she slightly turned her head to accept his greeting. He looked good too. Persha was suddenly proud to be in his presence. She was so glad he came.

Back at the table she had abandoned only minutes before, Persha couldn't wait for the waiter to return. She was hoping he hadn't noticed that she was gone.

Sitting across from Clarke, she was still mesmerized by him. As they sat across from each other, she wanted so much for their relationship to work. But when the words fell from his mouth, she wanted to back up and start all over.

"Damn you big," he said easily, picking up the menu as if he'd just dropped a compliment.

Persha frowned, then struggled to find her bearing. He simply could not have said what she heard. *Wasn't he there to talk about their future? Didn't he want to work this out? What about the baby?* she wondered.

The waiter appeared, interrupting Persha from asking Clarke what was on his mind. Persha sat like she was studying the menu, but she was still reeling from his comment.

After the waiter left, Persha folded her hands on the table and sighed. "Well, I wanted to see if you had changed your mind about us." She looked down at nothing on the table. "And . . . ah, all I'm saying is, I think we should try to work this out."

Her gaze reached up to his. Unable to read his eyes, she glanced away.

"I just wanted you to tell me face to face that it's over for good. And if it is, we need to talk about the baby," she said softly.

Clarke reached for her hands across the table. Persha felt somewhat at ease by his touch. It was nice. But she didn't want to get too excited too soon. She'd hear him out first. That's what she'd do, listen to what he had to say and then take it from there.

"I, ah, Clarke . . . " Persha started.

When Clarke's finger left her lips after silencing her, she locked her stare into his. It was a moment of great intensity for her. She knew this was the defining moment of what would be their relationship, and she didn't want to miss a moment.

She wanted to remember how she was feeling; what he looked like, his expressions, every movement, every sound, and every gesture he made, but nothing could prepare her for what he was about to say. Fearing the venom from his words, she choked back tears and tried to calm her breathing. She knew what was coming, so why was her heart tripping? Maybe because deep down inside, a part of her wanted something other than what she was expecting.

"I've been thinking about this quite a bit," Clarke started. "Actually, a brotha's been trying to make plans about the future. Since my attorney says he's got it all under control with Kelsa, I've decided I need to move on. Now I know you said your place isn't all that big, but you're still expecting that insurance money, right?" He reached for her glass and took a sip of her iced tea. "So I figure I'll move into your place now, then when the money comes in we can go in together and buy a house."

Persha stared blankly at his face. She saw his lips moving. She even noticed when his expressions changed, but out of everything he said, only one word stuck out in her mind. Clarke said we. And with that one word, he had changed her life in a matter of mere seconds.

Immediately her posture changed. Her vision seemed suddenly better and her heart rate was back to normal. *Did he say "we" as in "we" together? As in a couple?* Persha thought. *Did he mean he'd thought about the future as in her and him, together?*

She blinked a few times, then cleared her throat. Before speaking, Persha wanted to make sure she understood him correctly.

"Lemme get this straight," she said, shaking her head. "I thought I had ruined your marriage. I thought you weren't sure what you wanted right now. What's changed since the last time I saw you? You do remember slapping me so hard that I felt like I had fallen into next week, right?"

Clarke held up his hands in surrender. He leaned back a bit. "Whoa! Hold up a sec. I thought this was what you wanted."

"I do, but this . . . It just wasn't what I was expecting. You slapped me, Clarke," she whispered.

"A brotha's sorry for that. It's just at the time so much was going on with Kelsa. I didn't know if I was coming or going. But like I said, I've had time to think this thing through, and with the baby and all, I just think it's the right move."

"But how do I know this is really what you want? I don't need a man because I'm about to have a baby. You said some pretty hurtful things back then."

"Yeah, I know, and I'm sorry for that, but understand a brotha was under an incredible amount of stress. But now that I've had time to talk with my attorney and he's told me that everything's straight, I'ma sit back and let him handle his biz. That is what I'm paying his ass for."

Persha decided to back off for a moment. She was unable to truly grasp all that Clarke had said. She had done it. She had single-handedly reclaimed the love of her life. And he made it clear that the divorce proceedings were going full blast. He even insisted that he'd asked for it finally, just like he said he would all along. She'd be satisfied when he made it official, but for now, she could work with the progress. She felt really good, she'd finally gotten information on the mix-up that had caused the delay in her insurance payment and things were finally falling into place.

Nearly two hours later, Persha and Clarke were in the restaurant's parking lot.

"Where'd you park?" he asked her.

"Oh, I'm near the back," she answered. "It was crowded when I got here." She turned away from him.

"Well, shorty, I'll walk you to your car, then I'll drive around and meet you here."

Persha stopped. "Okay. Are you coming over to see the place or something?"

Clarke cast a suspicious glance her way. "Haven't you heard a word I've been saying all this time?"

Persha didn't want to get him upset. Lord knows she was thrilled things had turned out the way they had, but she also didn't understand what he was talking about. She shrugged one shoulder and looked at him for clarification.

"Shorty, I said I'm moving in with you. Dang, girl. Now where do you live?"

"Ah, oh, yeah. I live off Westheimer. I knew you were moving in, but quite surely you didn't mean right this second. Don't you need to go get your clothes and stuff?"

"Ah, girl, I told you, a brotha's been thinking. I got that all under control. My stuff is in the trunk. I just need to pull around so I can follow you to your spot."

Persha held her tongue. She had tons of questions, even wanted to know why the hell he was driving around with all of his belongings in the trunk of his car, but then thought better of it. She didn't want to make any waves. She'd simply go with the flow. The important thing was that he was going home with her . . . . For good!

"So is this cool or what?" he asked.

"Yeah, like lemonade in the shade on a Texas summer day." She smiled.

Persha couldn't wait to get in her car. She wanted to be alone so she could pinch herself and make sure this was not some crazy dream. It had all happened far too fast, and way too easy. She swore to herself she'd keep him happy at all cost. And there was no way she'd go out like Kelsa. None at all. She'd know where her man was at all times and what he was up to, and more importantly, she'd take care of all his needs.

"Persha?" Clarke called to her. She looked up to see Clarke staring at her. "Shorty? Whassup? You day-dreaming on a brotha or something? I was talking to you."

"Oh, I'm sorry, I didn't hear you."

"I said, we need to stop at Wal-Mart before we get to the house."

"Wal-Mart? What for?" she asked, trying to ease herself behind the wheel gracefully.

"Well, a brotha needs a key to the crib, right?"

With her mouth hung open, she looked up at him. "Ah, a key? Yeah, right, right. You will need a key."

"I'll follow you to Wal-Mart first, then," he said over his shoulder as he strolled away.

Could things finally be falling into place? Had their time finally come? She wondered as she watched him walk away.

Clarke

With his feet propped up on an old coffee table, Clarke looked around at what had become his home. He started thinking about how Persha had helped re-kindle his relationship with his pops.

At first, he was mad when he found out what she'd been up to, but then as they started talking, he realized just how much he missed his old man. Persha had even told Hudson Senior about the baby, and the three had made plans to meet Saturday night for dinner. Pops was planning to drive down from San Antonio.

In the few weeks he'd been at Persha's place, she'd done everything she could think of to keep him happy and that's the way it should be. A woman was supposed to take care of her man. But no matter how hard she worked, wobbling most times to pick up after him, or to have dinner ready, she still wasn't Kelsa. Lately, Clarke had been missing so much about Kelsa that he thought he'd die.

Clarke never realized just how much freedom he had with Kelsa. Most of his evenings were spent doing whatever the hell he wanted, if anything at all, because she was at work. And her salary allowed them to live in a certain way that was appealing and pleasing to him. Looking around the room now, there were no plants, no fresh flowers, and the place actually looked a little gloomy.

"I wonder what Kelsa's doing anyway?" Clarke said to himself. He sucked his teeth and leaned back on the sofa. There was no way in hell he should've been thinking about Kelsa while he was all up in Persha's place. He knew that, but damn, how he missed Kelsa's ass.

The more he thought about finding an excuse to go over there, the more he talked himself out of it. All it took was him remembering what happened the last time he was there. He had busted up one of those passion parties. Male dancers even showed up. What the hell had Kelsa been thinking?

It pissed him off just to think about what could've happened. It looked like an orgy was about to go down up in there. The women who had been up in there bad-mouthing him and other men suddenly changed when the brothas burst into the house. The women suddenly turned sweeter than sugar. In the middle of all that was going on, one of the strippers untied him. They must've thought he was part of the entertainment.

Once the angry mob saw all the G-strings and bare asses, they behaved worse than men. That gave Clarke the chance he needed to sneak upstairs amid all the groping and dancing and carry out some of his personal belongings.

Rubbing his crotch, he closed his eyes to be closer to Kelsa. The irony didn't miss him one bit. When he was with Kelsa, all he could do was think about Persha and that tight pussy of hers. It always greeted him wet and hungry.

But now that he had Persha right there, every damn day and night, her pussy was still sweet, but now Persha had picked up a few pounds with the baby and all. Her ankles and legs were all swollen, so was her nose and her neck. The shit wasn't cute, so when he fucked her, he couldn't help but think of Kelsa.

If he was pressed, he'd admit he missed the way she'd sway with his hips when he was giving it to her, and how she'd dig into his back at just the right time.

In the midst of his thoughts, he realized that he hadn't talked to Antwone in weeks. But that didn't keep him from thinking of how to bring his ass back down to earth. So there he sat with limited ass and no head. Clarke tried not to waste too much time or energy on things he could no longer change, but he had plans for Antwone and those plans included a reality check with wifey, Michelle.

When the phone rang, Clarke bolted up off the sofa. Looking around the room, it took him a minute to realize just where he was.

"Shit! A brotha was cold knocked out," he said, wiping his mouth and trying to find the source of all the damn ringing. By the time he got to the cordless phone in the kitchen, it had stopped ringing.

Clarke reached for a glass to get something to drink and then decided that he was going to see what his other boys were up to. *Ain't no way in the world a brotha should be all closed up in the house on a Saturday,* he thought. Persha was out with those nosy broads, and he was happy for the break. She and that belly of hers, with all the swelling, had become too much for him. He thought she might need to go to the doctor, but then figured, he really didn't care, so he kept that suggestion to himself.

After swallowing the last of the water he had poured himself, he walked toward the phone. It rang just as he reached for it.

"Damn," he cursed, grabbing the receiver. "Hello?" he growled.

"Ah, Clarke? Is this Clarke?" the voice on the other end of the line asked.

Who the fuck else is it gonna be answering Persha's phone, he thought. "Yeah, it's me. Whassup? Who's this?"

Clarke hoped it wasn't any of Kelsa's friends. How could they've found out where he was staying? His heart started beating faster, but he didn't want to over-react. He hadn't told Kelsa about the baby yet. *Shit! How did these bitches catch up with him?*

"Claaarke, it's me, Kori," she sobbed.

Now he was confused. *How the hell was Kori calling him?* Clarke thought. *Persha's ass supposed to be out with her and that other one?* He knew for sure Persha's ass bet' not be creeping on him. After all he done gave up to be with her. *Boy, women.*

"What's the matter with you? Persha ain't here," he said. "Hmmm, she said she was gonna be kicking it with y'all."

"Clarke, I know where Persha is, that's why I'm call-ing."

"What the fuck are you crying for?" is what he really wanted to ask. *Forget about why you calling.*

"Okay, so whassup? Why you all crying and shit?"

"It's Persha," Kori said, still boo-hooing. Clarke rolled his eyes. He wanted her to just spill it. "Clarke, Persha was hurt. We're at the hospital. That's what I'm trying to tell you."

Clarke jumped up. "What happened?" he sighed.

"It's the baby! You need to get down here right away." She cried some more.

Clarke moved the phone from his ear and quickly looked up at the ceiling. This couldn't be happening, he thought.

"Ain't no way Persha's in the hospital because something's wrong with the baby?" he said, faking concern. When he looked back down, he could hardly contain the grin that had spread across his face. "Um, damn, I'll be right there," Clarke assured Kori after she told him about the hospital where Persha had been admitted.

"Finally! My prayers are being answered!" he said after hanging up the phone. He then grabbed his cell phone and headed to the hospital.

Persha

Lying flat on her back with a thick pad lodged between her legs, Persha stared up at the ceiling tiles. Tears streaked both sides of her face, every now and then and she'd sniffle and sob quietly. Her ankles were so swollen that her legs looked the same size from the bottom to the top.

"God please, don't take my baby," she cried. "Please don't take my baby, whatever you do."

Her lips trembled as the words spilled from them. She blinked back the tears and tried to focus on the ceiling. Every so often, she'd squeeze the sheet her swollen fingers clutched tightly.

Persha heard people shuffling outside her room. The door stood ajar. She also heard the footsteps leading up to her bed, but she didn't move.

"Please God, don't take my baby," she continued. She knew something was wrong because no one bleeds so heavily at six months pregnant. She couldn't lose this baby.

Soon, she smelled Kori's perfume. Again, Persha

didn't move her head. She just laid there blinking back her tears, and struggling to think positive thoughts.

"Did you talk to him?" Cricket asked Kori.

"Yup! He's on his way. What did she say?" Kori asked, looking toward the bed.

"God, pllllleease. Don't take my baby!" Persha moaned.

"She's been mumbling that all day. It's all she says," Cricket reported.

"What did the doctor say?" Kori asked. By now they were both holding onto Persha.

Cricket motioned Kori toward the window. As they moved, Persha's stare followed them. Before Cricket could answer, Persha said, "Please don't leave me alone. I'm scared."

"We're not leaving you for a second," Cricket assured her. They moved back toward the bed. Persha looked at her friends.

"Cricket, my mother told me to live right. You tried to warn me. You were right all along about Clarke. I was wrong to do what I did to him and Kelsa. Do you think this is my punishment? Do you think God is punishing me for breaking up their marriage?"

"Nah, girl," Kori comforted her. "You shouldn't be thinking about that kind of foolishness right now."

"She's right, Persha," Cricket agreed. "God doesn't work like that. I can't tell you what to do about this thing with Clarke. I know you probably feel like you're ahead of the game because he's living with you, but all I'm gonna say about that is if a four-legged dog needs a license to be living in your house, then a two-legged one should too. But we'll get into that later. We shouldn't be talking about this right now anyway. He could walk in here any moment."

Persha started crying harder. "I know you're right

and I tried to leave him alone, Cricket, I really did. But once he put that taste in my mouth, I longed for him like a fiend on crack. I felt like I wouldn't survive unless I had him all to myself. And now that he's mine, I don't want to push him away by talking about getting married, but I know for sure, I can't lose this baby. It's all I've got to ensure my future with him. I can't lose this baby. I just can't," she bawled.

Just then, the door swung open and a nurse walked in.

"Is everything okay in here, ladies?" the nurse asked as she walked up to Persha's bed. She started checking the machine and Persha's pulse. "It's not a good idea to get her all worked up. She really needs to rest."

"Yes, I understand. I'm a retired RN myself," Cricket offered.

"Oohh, then you know what I mean. She just needs to rest."

"Can we stay? She's very uncomfortable being in here alone," Cricket threw in.

"Yes. No need for you guys to leave, but try to keep her happy. Nothing too heavy." The nurse stuck her hand forward. "I'm Menesha Michaels. Just holla' if you guys need anything, okay?"

When she left the room, Kori and Cricket reclaimed their places next to Persha's bed.

"She was nice," Kori said.

"Yeah, but when's the doctor coming to talk to me?" Persha whined.

Cricket stroked her hand. "He'll be in here soon, hon. You just hang in there and try to relax, for yourself and the baby."

Suddenly, Persha's eyes lit up. "Did you get a hold of my mom?"

"Yes, I did. She'll be here tomorrow," Kori said.

Persha started crying again. "It must be bad if

Mama's coming in early. Shit! I hadn't gotten around to telling her about Clarke moving in. What am I gonna do? She knows about him, but she's gonna have me crucified for living in sin!"

"You will simply have to worry about that later," Cricket snapped. "Right now, all you should be concerned with is getting better for yourself and that baby."

When the door opened again, all eyes turned toward it. Cricket sucked her teeth at the sight of him, Kori was indifferent by his presence, but Persha immediately began to perk up. Her heart felt at ease, a bit.

Clarke hesitated for a second then said, "Aeeey y'all."

"We'll step out so you guys can have some alone time," Cricket said drily as she and Kori moved toward the door.

Persha took in a calming breath and slowly exhaled it. Just the sight of Clarke had a soothing effect on her heart. She knew they were meant to be together.

"Whassup, shorty?" Clarke said as he looked around the hospital room. "Sorry it took a brotha so long to get here, but I called Pops on my way here and he was all panicked. I think he's coming down."

She couldn't discern his mood as he stood there taking in the equipment in the bland room. Persha didn't like the idea of him seeing her in that state, but what else could she do? And she didn't have a single thing to talk about. She did feel happy about his father being concerned enough to fly in from San Antonio. That had to indicate they'd be together for the long haul.

"So what did the doctor say? About the baby, I mean?" Clarke asked.

He appeared so nonchalant about the situation. But in her current state, there was nothing she could do to stress the importance of her condition to him. Persha blinked back more tears. How exactly could she say she still didn't know? But she didn't have to. When the door opened this time, the doctor walked in.

"I'm Dr. Blendshe," he said, reaching for Clarke's hand. Before Clarke could introduce himself, the doctor turned to Persha. "How are we holding up, Ms. Townsend?"

"I'm fine now that he's here," she said, motioning over to Clarke.

"Ah, I'm . . ." Before Clarke could properly introduce himself, the nurse walked in. When he and the doctor turned toward the door, Menesha dropped the folder she was holding and Clarke closed his eyes.

Clarke

Clarke's head started twirling and he began feeling like the room was closing in on him. He needed air, fresh air. It had been way too long since anyone spoke, and he knew it was looking suspicious.

What the hell is she doing here? Clarke thought as he quickly looked around the room. Even if they weren't, it felt as though every eye was on him; waiting for him to speak or move; waiting for him to do anything, but he couldn't.

Menesha's abrupt halt gave him serious concern. He watched as her eyes made contact with his. He knew everyone else noticed it too. Why couldn't she just play it cool?

She stood at the door empty-handed and looking dumbfounded. But he could only imagine what he must've looked like, standing there next to Persha's bed while the doctor looked on. How could he not be there for Persha? How could he make this seem like he was just in the area and walked into this room? There was nothing he could do or say.

"Nurse Michaels? Is everything okay?" The doctor

asked, finally breaking the silence that blanketed the entire room.

She looked at Clarke, down at the papers scattered at her feet and then at Persha. "Ah, I'm fine," Menesha said. "I—ah—I have the test results and I—" she stooped down to pick up the papers.

"I just got back from the lab and her tests are in. I didn't know if this was a good time to—"

"This is a good time," the doctor said, cutting her off. "Actually, this is the father of Ms. Townsend's baby, so we can certainly go over all the details right now." He then reached for the shuffled folder.

Clarke sighed and his eyes quickly filled with grief. He didn't need this shit right now. What the hell was Menesha doing here? How could he not remember that she no longer worked with Kelsa, she'd moved to Herman Hospital almost a year ago.

As the doctor skimmed through the shuffled paperwork, Clarke tried to read Menesha's reaction to the news that he was having a baby with this woman. The same woman Kelsa caught him with, the same woman he lost everything over. He knew it was really over between him and Kelsa now. Menesha had all the ammunition she needed to destroy him and Kelsa and he was sure she'd use it.

Persha looked at Menesha, then at Clarke. "You two know each other?" she asked. Persha looked Menesha up and down then her stare transfixed onto Clarke.

"How do you know her?" Persha demanded to know.

At a loss for words, Clarke stood there, slowly shaking his head. What could he say? Oh, don't worry Persha, this is just my wife's best friend, don't you remember her from the restaurant months ago?

The doctor looked up from the notes he was reading. "We have a situation here," he murmured.

"If you don't need me, doctor, I have another patient I need to look in on," Menesha said.

Looking back at the notes, the doctor shook his head. Every eye in the room suddenly turned to the dark man who stepped through the door carrying a large bouquet of exotic flowers.

You could tell he was related to Clarke. Their features were similar as was their build. But this man's hair was cut close to his head with gray sprinkled at his temples. He had a cleft in his chin, with broad shoulders and muscular legs.

"This is Persha Townsend's room, right?" the man asked.

"You're in the right place," the doctor said, closing the folder. "Nurse Michaels, why don't you place that arrangement near the window?"

"I'm Clarke Hudson Senior," his baritone rang out. Clarke Sr. walked up to Persha's bed. "And you must be Persha," he said with a smile.

"I am," she replied. "I wish you didn't have to see me like this." She ran her hands down her hair as if she was trying to flatten it out.

"Pop? What are you doing here so soon? I wasn't expecting you till tomorrow!" Clarke exclaimed.

"I was on my way to the airport when you called on my cell. I was heading to New Orleans and switched my destination to Houston. Southwest has flights leaving nearly every thirty minutes, son," he said as he approached Clarke. "You didn't think I'd leave you and Persha to go through this thing alone, did you? This is my first grandson we're talking about here."

By the time Clarke was released from his father's embrace, Menesha was gone. Everything in him went still. He couldn't believe things continued to get worse for him by the minute. He wasn't even looking forward to leaving the room. He knew for sure that Menesha had bolted out of there to call Kelsa and he dreaded what would be waiting for him on the other side of that door.

Persha

Persha could barely control her heart rate. The nurse and doctor kept telling her it was imperative that she remain calm and not get too worked up. But what else was she supposed to do when her man looked like he was the cat who swallowed the canary at the sight of the beautiful nurse. Then as if that wasn't enough, the doctor said, "we have a situation," and then left the room saying that he needed to check something and hadn't been back. She pressed the nurse's button.

"Yes, Ms. Townsend, you need something?"

"Ah, where's my doctor?" she asked.

"Ma'am, he'll be with you shortly," the voice from the box barked back.

Persha rolled her eyes and swallowed back tears. She needed to know what was going on, even if it wasn't going to be good news. Some news was better than no news at all, she had determined.

Now lying there with Clarke and his father whispering in the corner, Persha had never felt more alone. Why wasn't anyone talking to her? Didn't they know what she was going through? The anguish was killing her. As if reading her mind, Cricket stuck her head in the room.

"You okay over there?" Cricket asked. When Persha didn't respond, Cricket walked over to the bed. "You've got to remember what the doctor said. You can't sit here stressing and worrying."

"I know, but I just wish he'd tell me something. It's killing me not knowing," Persha said.

"Just be patient. I think they got your results mixed up or something, so your doctor had the lab rush over the right ones. Just stay calm," Cricket said sweetly.

Persha closed her eyes and begged sleep to take over. She wanted this mess wrapped up so that she could go back home and relax. She just wanted to have her baby that they already knew was a boy, then her, Clarke, and the baby could enjoy their future together as a real family.

The next afternoon, Dr. Blendshe walked into the room with another doctor. Persha looked up at the two and immediately started crying.

"Ms. Townsend, this is Dr. Kingston," Dr. Blendshe stated. "She's a high-risk pregnancy specialist."

"Cricket!" Persha started screaming. "Cricket!" She grabbed at the sheet and tried to lift her body into an upright position. "Cricket! Oh God, Cricket," she hollered.

The doctors started looking around. "Ms. Townsend, we need you to calm down. This isn't good for you or the baby."

A few minutes later, the door swung open.

"What's the matter," Cricket said, rushing up to the bed.

"I know I'm about to get bad news. I just feel it. Have you heard from my mother yet?"

"Yes, Kori went to meet her at Hobby. She's on her way. Try to calm down," Cricket urged.

"What do they want? Why are they both here? What's a high-risk pregnancy specialist? Why do I need one of those?" Persha questioned.

Cricket started stroking her hand. "You need to calm down and hear them out. You're so panicked right now. This isn't good for the baby, Persha."

"Dr. Kingston, this is Ms. Townsend's good friend," Dr. Blendshe, said. "She's a nurse."

Dr. Kingston shook her head, taking in the information.

"Please, just tell Cricket," Persha begged. "I don't want to hear it. I don't want to know. Is the baby okay? Oh, God! My baby's gonna die!" Persha started crying. "Oh, God! Wwwhhhy!" she shrieked.

"Ssssssh," Cricket said, reaching down to take Persha into her arms. "It's going to be fine; you and the baby. But you've got to calm down. Let's hear the doctors out. If you didn't need a specialist, she wouldn't be here. That doesn't mean it's going to be bad news."

Persha looked up at Cricket. "You've always been straight with me," she said. "Don't start sugarcoating things now. I may be stupid when it comes to that man of mine, but if things were okay, I wouldn't need a specialist," she snapped.

Dr. Blendshe stepped forward and said, "Ms. Townsend, there is a problem, but I think your friend is just trying to help you calm down a bit."

Persha pushed a button and eased her bed to an upright position for comfort and to be at attention to hear the doctor's every word. She knew it was bad news all the way around. Cricket held her hand tightly, but that wasn't providing the soothing effect she needed. What she needed was comfort from her man. He should be there with her, he should be holding her in his arms.

"Just tell me. Cut the crap and tell me," Persha said

as she blew out a breath then looked at Cricket. "Tell him I can handle it. I can. I just need to know."

"You have Preeclampsia," Doctor Blendshe started. "At this point what we'd like to do is a test called amniocentesis."

"Amnio what? And what is Preeclampsia?" Persha asked. "How'd I get it? What are you saying?" She turned to Cricket. "Cricket, what's he saying?"

"He's trying to tell you, sweetie," Cricket said, rubbing Persha's hand, "You really need to calm down right now, that's the best thing you can do."

"Okay. Okay. But what does this all mean?" Persha snapped. She could feel herself sweating. She wondered where Clarke was. She didn't want him walking in on any of this. If he knew there was a chance that his son wouldn't survive, she didn't know what that would mean to their relationship. But she did know it wouldn't be good.

"In simple terms," Dr. Blendshe continued, "preeclampsia is pregnancy-induced hypertension."

The specialist stepped forward and added, "This is a common disease and it only occurs during pregnancy." Persha's eyebrows were squeezing together. She still didn't get it.

"The swelling, the high blood pressure; you must deliver now," the specialist said.

Persha looked back and forth between the specialist, the doctor, and Cricket. She didn't know what to do or say. Where was her mother? Why couldn't anyone understand just how much she needed this baby? There was no way he'd survive.

"I'm not ready to deliver. This baby, he won't make it," Persha wailed, placing her free hand on her stomach.

"Where's the child's father?" Dr. Blendshe said.

"We need to move on this right away. We need you to take the test then we need to deliver the baby."

"I want my mama!" Persha shouted. "Cricket, please, tell them. I can't have this baby right now. He's not ready to come. I can't lose this baby!"

"Persha, if they say it's time," Cricket said, "it's time. It's that simple. Now you said you could handle this! Handle it!"

"But how did I get this?" Persha sobbed. "Where did it come from and what's this amnic-whatever test? Why do I need it?"

"Hon, they're going to insert a needle into the uterus and remove some fluid from around the baby," Cricket explained. "After that, they'll decide if he's ready to be delivered."

Cricket's head turned when the specialist touched her shoulder.

"Normally that would be the procedure," Dr. Kingston said to Cricket, "But at this point, we need to deliver Ms. Townsend's baby right away."

"Is it that severe?" Cricket asked.

"Well, based on our tests," Doctor Kingston continued, "her placenta is damaged. We'll need to take the baby by C-section. Actually . . ." She looked at Persha. "Is there any way we could talk about this over there?"

Persha's eyes lit up. "What?" she hollered. "No! You talk right here. What's wrong? Tell me! Is my baby going to make it? Is he going to be okay?"

"That's why you need to take the test, and let them do what they need to do, Persha," Cricket said firmly.

Still clutching on to Cricket's hand, Persha sighed. She knew they were right. She needed to do whatever was necessary to save the baby.

"Okay, I'll do it," Persha gave in. "Please, just save my baby."

As they prepared to wheel Persha into another room for the test, her mother Paula appeared at the door. Kori was standing next to her.

"Oh, Persha!" Paula squealed. "Baby, you just hang in there and be strong. You're gonna be just fine. I've been praying since I got word. I'm only sorry I didn't get here faster, but God's got this under control."

"Keep praying, Ma. I can't lose this baby. I just can't," she yelled as she passed her mother, Cricket, and Kori.

"Where's this Clarke person?" Persha heard her mother ask. Suddenly she was glad she was being taken to another part of the hospital. She knew the moment her mother realized Clarke was nowhere to be found, heads would roll, and scripture would begin to flow nonstop.

Clarke

"**S**o you see, Pop, that's why I'm sitting here all confused," Clarke explained to his father. "I don't love Persha, not like I love Kelsa, but I know that once she finds out about this baby, it'll be over for good."

Clarke popped the last shrimp into his mouth. He and Clarke Sr. were enjoying a late lunch on the patio at Papasitos restaurant near the hospital.

He had stayed with his father in his hotel room the night before, and they'd had a long, overdue talk. Clarke told his father what he'd done to Kelsa, and how he wound up crawling back to Persha. He left out the part about slapping her because he knew his old man wouldn't tolerate that no matter what. But other than that, he was open and candid.

"Son," Clarke Sr. started, "I don't have to tell you where your mistakes started. I'm no saint. I had an affair once, and your mother, bless her soul, found out about it."

Clarke moved to the edge of his chair. "What happened?"

Clarke Sr. cleared his throat; he waited for the waitress to refill his drink, smiled at her, and then watched as she walked away. "Well, Son, your mother threw me out. It's just that simple. She threw my cheating ass out on the streets and tossed out everything I owned."

"No shit, Pops? I can't believe you ever cheated on Ma. It looked like y'all had it all wrapped up; a real solid relationship, even after she got sick."

"We did, and if she were alive, I'd still be trying to make it up to her. I was young and dumb. Extra pussy is not all it's cracked up to be. So after staying in a cheap motel for about a month, your mother finally took me back. But trust me, I had learned my lesson."

With a perplexed look on his face, Clarke scratched his head.

"What's the problem?" Clarke Sr. asked, coolly sipping his tea.

"Nothing. I just don't remember you ever leaving for a month."

"Son, this was shortly after you were born. It was a mistake and I spent the rest of your mother's days paying for it. Sometimes the wrong head goes to thinking and we get into trouble."

"No joke!" Clarke leaned back. "So who was this woman anyway? Whatever happened to her?"

"I met her on a business trip. Her lips were red, her skirts were short and tight, and her sweaters were even tighter. She was a real hot number. Problem was, she said she understood about me being married, but when I wanted to cut it off, she wasn't ready and didn't agree. She even moved to the same city we were living in back then."

Clarke's eyes widened. "What? Pops, you had a fatal attraction going on? How come you never told me about this before?"

"Son, there's no pride in lying and cheating. I was

wrong. I was just lucky your mother was able to forgive me. See, when you young guys try to chase as many skirts as you can, I look back and laugh. That's not what life's about." Clarke Sr. sipped his tea again. "Life's about finding someone you love, settling down, and building a life together. Marriage isn't easy, but shit, nothing good ever is. You've got to work hard for what you want. If your mother were still alive, I'd still be loving her more and more each day. I don't need a string of women to prove my manhood. One good woman who loved me was enough, and once that sunk in, I was good to go."

"Yeah, Pop, I know you're right. But when I was with Kelsa, I couldn't stop thinking about Persha. Now that I'm with her, all I want to do is make things work with Kelsa again."

"Son, sometimes what you want and what you get are two different things."

"Did you ever see that woman again?"

"Didn't need to. She had her own agenda. She wanted a husband and it didn't matter that he might belong to someone else. I wanted my life with my wife and son, so I didn't give her an option. I ended things and never saw her again."

"You make it sound so easy," Clarke said.

"But it is. It's just that simple. Now unlike you, I didn't have a child with my lover to deal with, so the decision to go back to my wife was easy once she agreed to take me back."

"So you think I still have a shot with Kelsa?"

"I can't say. You've been married for what? Five years? That's nothing to throw away. But son, if she doesn't want you back, you need to respect that and move on. And I don't mean move on to Persha. I mean move on. Support your child, but move on. You've caused enough pain for both women. If you still love your wife, you're not doing Persha any good by sticking around. Soon you'll start comparing her to your wife, then you'll start making life miserable for you both."

"I'm ready to step, Pop, but honestly, I feel so trapped with the baby and all."

Clarke Sr. shook his head. "I can see how you'd feel that way. But staying with a woman you don't love won't help that child one bit. Now, I'm gonna love my grandson no matter where you lay your head." Clarke Sr. leaned in. "And more importantly, I'm gonna love you too."

For a moment they sat there taking in the noises of the atmosphere; drivers sped along the Highway 59 feeder road. People were honking horns, other customers were chattering and laughing. Clarke Sr. was glad to be with his son. Their dispute, years ago, had eaten away at him.

Clarke Sr. knew Persha just about as well as he knew Kelsa. Since he and his son weren't talking, he never had a relationship with either one of the women.

"Pop? What would you do?" Clarke asked.

After hesitating a second, his father looked him in the eyes and a grin spread across his face. "Son, I'd do the right thing. People can't fault you when you do the right thing. They may not like it, but they can't fault you." He looked at his glass. "And speaking of the right thing, I think we need to head over to the hospital. I don't want to miss my grandson's first day on earth."

Clarke prepared to go, but he didn't want to. And more importantly, he knew for him, doing the right thing wasn't quite as easy as his father made it sound.

Persha

After the test, the decision was confirmed and Persha was afraid. Even with her mother at her side, reassuring her, she still couldn't shake the fear that struck deep in her bones. Something was wrong. There was no way in hell she should be having her baby so soon. And if something went wrong with the baby, she knew for sure she'd lose Clarke.

"So where's Clarke, honey?" Persha's mother asked.

This was exactly what Persha was hoping to avoid. One single moment alone with her mother and she wanted to know where the hell Clarke was. Well, she wished she knew her damn self. And where were Kori and Cricket? She didn't want to be alone under her mother's close scrutiny.

"Ma, I don't want him around right now. I need to rest and I don't need him stressing me out," Persha answered.

"Stressing you out? Chile, please! He's the father of your child. What happens here has as much impact on him as it does on you. I don't like this one bit. If he ain't around when you need him, then what's gonna happen when this child is born? I don't like this, Persha."

"I know, Ma. I know you don't like it, but trust me; he'll be here soon. I hope I have the baby before he gets back, actually."

When the door opened, Persha saw Kori with a pissed-off look on her face. Cricket was close behind. She was hoping for a distraction, but something mild, like someone offering to take her mother to the cafeteria for a snack.

"Look, I don't know who told you it was okay to come here, but she's about to have a baby right now!" Kori screamed after the stranger who strutted into the room without waiting for an invitation.

What now? Persha thought. She didn't need anything else weighing on her mind or her heart. The last thing she needed was more confusion, especially with her mother standing so near.

The little blond man who had intruded into Persha's room looked around the hospital room. "Ms. Persha Townsend?" he said. He looked like he wasn't quite sure who might answer.

"Yes?" Persha said as she eased herself up in the bed. Looking at the IV in her arm, she tried not to move too quickly.

"You've been served!" he screamed as he dropped an envelope on her bed and quickly dashed out of the room. At the door, Kori and Cricket stood speechless. Paula was confused.

"What the hell?" Persha said, then catching herself and looking towards Paula. "Oooops! Sorry, Ma." She reached for the envelope but it fell to the floor. By the time her mother reached down to pick it up, Cricket and Kori were both standing next to her bed.

"What's that?" Cricket and Kori asked in unison.

With an offhand shrug of one shoulder, Persha reached for the envelope her mother held. She sniffled, and ripped the top open. Pulling the legal document out of the envelope, she grew more curious with each movement.

"OMIGOD!" Her eyes widened in horror as she read the document. With her mouth hanging open, her heart skipped a beat as she continued reading. "OMIGOD!" she squealed again.

"Baby, don't say God's name in vain," Paula said as she smoothed out the wrinkled sheet.

"What is it?" Kori asked. Not waiting for Persha's answer, Kori and Cricket moved closer to the bed.

With her eyes filling quickly with tears, Persha's lips started quivering. She swallowed dry and hard and then mumbled, "Kelsa's suing me and some man named Antwone for ruining her marriage with Clarke!"

By the time her head started spinning, her doctor and the specialist had appeared.

"Ms. Townsend, it's time to go," Dr. Blendshe said.

Persha was embarrassed. She was hurt and confused. She wanted desperately to get up from the bed and go find Clarke.

Why was this other guy being sued too? Persha thought. She had so many questions and so many fears, but she had to be strong. Everyone would say it's for the baby, but how could she be strong for him when she couldn't be strong for herself.

A part of her was glad she was being taken into the delivery room. She needed to be alone and away from everyone, even if alone meant being surrounded by a group of strangers. They wouldn't know why she was crying. They'd think she was crying for the baby, the baby that she was sure wasn't ready to come. But the doctors said their tests indicated otherwise.

Just before the doctor closed the door, her mother squeezed in and said, "I'm her mother. She needs my support."

Persha kept thinking about the papers. When they talked about the epidural, she wasn't even listening. She remembered her mother asking a few questions. But her mind was on the document she had been served. It mentioned something about Kelsa and Clarke's divorce filing. And it was Kelsa, not Clarke, who requested the divorce.

How could that be? Persha thought. Clarke had told her that he had a lawyer. He said they were taking care of his interests. Clarke said it was Kelsa who was trying to hang on. But if that were true, why did she finally decide to ask for the divorce now? And what about that nurse? She saw the way Clarke looked at her. The passion was all but burning in his eyes.

The next thing Persha knew, she was groggy, but after a few minutes of blurry vision, she was seeing clear. Persha turned her head and saw her mother, Cricket, and Kori sitting in the room. *When did I get back to the room? Is it over?* She wondered. *Where's my baby?*

Persha reached down to touch her stomach. But it was flatter than before. Not completely gone, but the baby was no longer inside of her. She immediately sat up in bed. She rubbed her eyes and looked around the room.

"Ma! Where's my baby?" she asked. "Where's my baby?" Every eye in the room instantly dropped to the floor.

Clarke

Clarke Sr. dropped his son off at the hospital's entrance while he went to park. Walking out of the elevator, Clarke was hoping he'd get into Persha's room before Menesha's evil ass showed up again. As he walked, he searched the halls with his eyes, eager to make it to the room before he might be spotted. Man, he was sick and tired of these bitches!

So far, real good, he thought as he rounded the very last corner. Only a few steps from her door, when it looked like he'd make it okay, a voice called out to him.

"Mr. Hudson?" he heard someone call.

Clarke stopped in his tracks. For a second he just stood there, not acknowledging he'd heard his name.

"Mr. Hudson," the voice repeated.

Clarke finally turned to see Persha's doctor. "Yes?" he answered, feeling relieved that the doctor was alone.

"Have you talked to Ms. Townsend yet?" Dr. Blendshe asked.

Clarke shook his head and thought that if this quack didn't let him go, he'd never get a chance to talk to her.

"I'm just getting here. Why? Is everything okay?"

Clarke said as his jaw tightened. He wanted to finish the conversation inside the room and not in the hallway where Menesha could possibly notice him.

Dr. Blendshe looked down at the floor and then back at Clarke. "There is a problem, but I think we need to discuss this with you both."

Clarke really didn't care what was wrong. He was just thinking about how much this crumb snatcher was going to cost him every month for at least the next eighteen years. His mind was made up. He'd see Persha through the mess, but the minute she and the baby were released, he was outta there, even if that meant he'd have to get a roommate.

When he walked into the room, he sensed the tension immediately. Everyone grew quiet even though he knew they had been talking prior to him entering because he had heard voices as he approached the door. Clarke lifted an eyebrow when he spotted the older version of Persha. Their likeness was somewhat surprising to him. She was sitting off in the corner with Cricket. When he walked all the way in, they all got up as if they were ready to throw down. He immediately turned his attention to Persha. He wasn't looking for drama. He actually wanted to avoid it at all cost.

"Aeey! Whassup, Persha?" he said as he thought about how bad she looked. Her face was all fat, shit swollen all over, and even though her stomach wasn't as round as it was before, she was still big as hell.

"Is this him?" Paula screamed.

"Ma! Please don't!" Persha begged.

"Persha, baby, you've been here all day giving birth and where was he?" Paula shouted. "He comes strolling in here like he owns the place and didn't even ask how you're doing." Clarke looked toward Persha. She closed her eyes.

"And let's not forget the gift we received a few hours ago," Cricket threw in.

Still uninterested in what they were bickering about, Clarke was hoping his father would come in soon. He could use the help. He felt himself breaking out in a sweat, but he wanted to remain cool.

"Hey, doc, what were you talking about out there? I really don't have time for this shit in here," he said casually, lifting his shirt as he rubbed his stomach. He was full and could use a nice long couch.

"What? Boy, didn't your mama teach you any manners?" Paula said, stepping toward him, but Kori gently pulled her back.

"Ma, please don't!" Persha begged, cringing at the scene.

"I don't think I've ever met anyone so rude. He didn't even attempt to introduce himself or even apologize for not being here when you needed him most. He's just Gawd awful!" Paula spat.

"Ma! I don't need this right now. Please. You know I have a lot on my mind," Persha said nervously.

Paula started biting her bottom lip. Cricket rubbed her back, and Kori didn't say anything.

"Let's not forget why we're here," Dr. Blendshe said, looking around the room. "We're still not out of the woods just yet. The baby is grossly underweight and his lungs aren't fully developed." He flipped open the folder he'd been holding. "Normally, we would've tried to prolong the pregnancy, but at this point, it could have put both mother and child at risk, so we felt the Cesarean section was necessary.

Clarke looked up and said, "Baby? Oh snap, she had it already? Does he look like me?" he asked casually, already thinking two steps ahead of the game.

Maybe if the baby wasn't his he'd be able to walk

away from this thing without any scars. He was hoping he'd be able to reason with Persha before she left the hospital, but not with the lynch mob standing by.

Again, Clarke looked toward the door. He wanted his father to come in. He needed help and he needed it quickly. At least his pops could put this old hag in her place. He wasn't worried about Persha or her friends, they knew better.

When Clarke looked her way, Paula rolled her eyes and shook her head. Clarke could care less; he just wanted to see if the baby looked like him. If he didn't, then he'd walk out right away. And even if it did look like him, he might have to request a blood test, just on GP (general principle).

He just needed his father there to back him up.

Persha

Just when Persha thought things had finally calmed down, her mother spun around. She was waving legal documents in her hand that Persha had received before going in to deliver.

"What's this all about?" Paula turned to Clarke and snarled, leaping out of Kori's reach.

Clarke looked up at the papers then back at Paula's face. He sucked his teeth and turned back toward Persha.

"Young man!" Paula shouted. "Don't you hear me talking to you? I asked you a question. Don't you turn your back on me," Paula screamed.

Closing her eyes, Persha wanted to evaporate. *Could this get any worse,* she wondered. And why didn't Cricket or Kori drag her mother away? Didn't they know when to step in and help? Running the tip of her tongue over her lips, Persha tried to count to ten. Maybe once she opened her eyes it would only be her, Clarke, and the baby in the room.

"My daughter is being sued because of you! I want to know what you have to say about this!" Paula said.

Before the words fell from her lips, Persha knew they were coming. Paula despised being ignored, and Clarke didn't know, but he was only making matters worse. When he didn't say anything, Paula walked up on him.

"Your wandering hands need to be dipped in the blood of Jesus," Paula said, "and those hands will turn into praising hands. This—" she waved the papers. "This is nothing but the devil at work. And you need to drop to your knees and beg for forgiveness. You have no integrity; no morals."

Clarke turned to find her too close. He backed up and looked over at Cricket and Kori and said, "Y'all need to do something about her. A brotha don't know how much more he can take."

Persha started praying. She didn't know what else she could do. Once Paula started quoting scriptures, it was all over. She wanted to tell Clarke to just agree with what her mother was saying and save them the entire forthcoming sermon.

"Ma?" Persha tried to no avail.

"This is what happens when you neglect to treat your body like the temple that it is," Paula preached to her daughter. "You are a virtuous woman. You've got to maintain your Christlike character in a contrary community."

Clarke closed his eyes and then sighed. "Why don't I leave?" he offered as he headed toward the door to leave the drama behind him, not realizing that it was already shackled to his feet, and it was sure to follow him with every step he took.

Clarke

"Please! Don't leave. Think of our baby, your son!"

Persha pleaded to Clarke as he opened the door to exit the room. He turned and looked into Persha's eyes just as he was about to close the door behind him. She had never seen that look in his eyes before, but something told her she had finally reached him.

"The doctor needs to talk about our son, so let's hear him out."

Persha had had enough. She didn't need to see her mother looking at Clarke with daggers. They needed to talk to the doctor and they needed to do it alone.

Looking up, Persha took a deep breath and said, "Can you guys all leave the room, please? I think Clarke and I need to hear what the doctor has to say. We need to work this out."

Paula, Cricket, and Kori all looked at each other, and then back at Persha. "I think we need a few minutes alone. That's all I'm saying. Maybe you guys can go see the baby."

"That's not a good idea," Dr. Blendshe interjected.

Persha made eye contact with him. She didn't need

any more bad news. Silence blanketed the room until there was only the sound of the door creaking open. Persha welcomed the distraction.

Standing there was a gentleman who looked somewhat familiar to Persha, but she couldn't place where she had seen him before. He was wearing a pair of white linen pants and a matching shirt. Although the cloth was freely flowing around his body, you could see his muscular shape. His skin was the color of burnt yellow and his eyes were dark brown. The scent of his cologne followed minutes after his arrival.

"Yo, Clarke man," the stranger said. "I need to holla' at you real fast." He then looked around the room, but didn't greet anyone. He looked as though his patience was running thin.

"Antwone!" Clarke yelled. "What the hell! How'd you know where to find me?"

"Antwone!" Cricket screamed.

Kori pulled up a chair and said, "Oh, this is about to get real, real good."

The doctor looked around the room. He wore a look that implied he wasn't sure what to do.

By the time the entire scene registered in Persha's head, Antwone had already moved toward Clarke and grabbed his arm. Clarke looked down at Antwone's hand on his arm.

"We need to get out of here. We've got trouble brewing," Antwone said. "I don't know if Michelle followed me here, but when I left the house she was talking to Kelsa. *We* need to talk."

"Hold up a sec," Clarke said as he pulled away and held his hand up.

"I don't think you understand," Antwone stressed, "we need to bounce! I mean like right now. I don't know what's going on here, but you don't want Kelsa and Michelle in the same room together."

Unable to figure out just why she'd suddenly become nervous, Persha started looking at the two men standing near her bed.

"Did you have to bring this here, to my hospital room? Don't you know we just had a baby?" Persha said.

Antwone gave Clarke a look no one else could read, and then produced his papers. "A baby?" Antwone howled, with a frown on his face. "Ww—hhat's going on, man?"

"Not now, dawg. We'll have to talk later," Clarke said as he tried to dismiss Antwone with the wave of a hand, but Antwone wouldn't go away.

"So you're the Antwone Johnson named in the lawsuit?" Persha asked. "Why would Kelsa be suing us both for ending her marriage?"

"Yeah, something ain't right with this picture," Kori said, eyeing the two men suspiciously.

Confusion washed over Persha. She wished her mother was gone. Maybe she could handle what was coming next, but she was positive her mother wouldn't be able to.

"Kori, why don't you take Ma down to the cafeteria?"

Shaking her head, Kori blurted out, "Nah-ah. I ain't stepping foot out of here till we find out what's going on with these two." She looked at Antwone and Clarke. "What are y'all waiting for? Start talking!" she demanded.

As if recognizing the others in the room for the very first time, Antwone sighed. Again he looked into Clarke's eyes and tried to appeal to him.

"We really need to go some place *private* to talk about this," Antwone said. "I don't want Michelle and Kelsa to come and find us here."

Clarke looked at his friend and said, "At this point, it

really doesn't matter what they say. I don't want Kelsa back."

"I don't think you understand the seriousness of the situation here. Man, we really need to talk," Antwone insisted. "You know, in private," he hissed.

"Obviously, he ain't leaving, so why don't you just go ahead and spill it?" Kori urged.

"Michelle and Kelsa know, man. It's over," Antwone said somberly.

"What?" Clarke asked.

"That's how I knew you were here. A friend of Kelsa's from here called her up. She had us all served with these papers, then she called to tell Michelle about it. Man, it's about to go down. We need to split so we can talk."

"How the hell did she find out?" Clarke asked, thinking out loud as he took the papers from Antwone.

"What's about to go down? Find out what?" Kori asked, out of her seat and near Persha's bed.

Antwone looked down his nose at her. "Ah, this is a private matter," he said.

"Clarke, you are not going to leave with him. This is our child we're talking about here. You need to decide what's important to you," Persha said with authority.

Turning to face Persha, Clarke glanced down at the paper, then back at her. "I don't have time for this. You need to let me know what's up with the baby and I'll get back with you some other time." He looked at Antwone. "I don't have my ride, so I'm gonna have to roll with you."

After hearing that, Paula stepped forward. She held up one elegant finger and started up again. "Okay, so let me understand this. My daughter risked her life and that of her unborn child while you were off doing God-knows-what, then you show up here for a hot minute, bringing all this mess in with you, and now you're skipping out because you don't want your wife to catch you in your mistress's hospital room?" Paula stepped in front of the door and placed her hands on her hips. "As far as I'm concerned, she needs to come and find your trifling tail. Now I'm a Christian woman, so I'm not gonna say too much about what it looks like with you and Mr. Antwone and whatever secrets you two got going on, but maybe my daughter needs to talk with this wife of yours."

The look on Antwone and Clarke's faces were indescribable. They looked at each other, then back at Paula. Horror had found its home in their stares.

"You'll leave this room over my dead body!" Paula finally stated.

"Ma'am, this has nothing to do with you or your daughter. I just need to talk to Clarke and we can't do it here. So if you'll be kind enough to step to the side, we can take this elsewhere to sort things out."

"Ah, I don't mean to break this up, but does anyone want to know about the baby?" the doctor spoke up.

All eyes focused on him, but no one spoke up. Persha was afraid to hear what he had to say. Cricket, Kori, and Paula were more interested in what Clarke had to say, and he and Antwone had other things on their minds.

Before Dr. Blendshe could provide information to the new parents and others concerned, his pager went off. Looking down to the pocket of his smock he grabbed the pager and started pressing buttons.

"Oh, my," he exclaimed as he reached for the phone. Again, everyone in the room grew silent as they watched him make his call. "Yes, this is Dr. Blendshe. Ah, yes! I'll be right there." He slammed the phone back into its cradle and headed toward the door. Paula couldn't move fast enough. "Ma'am, it's imperative that I get down to the neonatal unit. It's the baby. I'll send word as soon as I know something."

Paula didn't move.

"Ma! Please, move away from the door! If something's wrong with my baby, he needs to go," Persha hissed.

As if she suddenly snapped out of something, Paula quickly stepped aside. But as soon as the doctor walked out, she resumed her post in front of the door.

Persha closed her eyes and turned her back to the group. She said a silent prayer, again begging God to spare her child's life.

Clarke

*T*his shit has got to be straight outta the *Twilight Zone,* Clarke thought. *This can't be happening; stuck in a room with a bunch of crazy bitches and a flaming fool! Think fast! Think fast! There's got to be a way out before any other parties to the drama decide to show up.* Clarke didn't know what to do.

He thought Antwone was stupid for showing up at the hospital. He should've known things weren't cool. Hadn't he gotten the message when none of his friggin' calls or messages were returned? Shaking his head, Clarke was tired of mad-mugging Persha's nosy-ass Mama.

He threw his hands up in the air and shrugged his shoulders. "Let the motherfuckin' chips fall where they may!" he said in exhausted defeat.

"What? Dawg? What are you saying? Are you saying what I think you're saying? I can't go out like this! You don't understand. I'm not some fucking maid. I got way too much to lose."

Fire started raging in Clarke's eyes. His jaw tight-

ened and his fist began to ball at his thigh. He just
knew this fool wasn't trying to flash on him like this.

"Maid?" Kori said as her arched eyebrows shot up.
She rose from her chair, taking center stage. She
looked at Persha then looked back at Antwone and
Clarke who were about to square off.

"Girl, I thought you said he worked for some ad
agency," Kori said to Persha while looking at Clarke.

Clarke didn't need this shit. He knew it would come
out, but never envisioned it happening like this. He
closed his eyes. He was fuming. He wanted to use his
bare hands to rip Antwone's head off, then he'd take
care of this loudmouth, who was slowly pissing him
off.

With her back still turned to the circus, Persha
willed herself to a better place. She didn't need the
drama.

"Persha!" Kori screamed. "He is a maid?" she
shouted.

Turning slowly, Persha looked at Clarke. He didn't
have the courage to look her in the eyes. She didn't
know. No one knew but those who were closest to him.

"Clarke? What's going on? This is all scaring me,"
Persha confessed.

"Look, stay out of this. It ain't got nothing to do
with you!" Clarke snapped, still staring Antwone right
in the eyes.

"It does have something to do with me. What are
you saying? We have a child together," she reasoned.

"Okay, hold up a sec," Kori said as she approached
the bed. "Is he some big-shot ad executive or is he a
maid? That's what I want to know."

By now, Paula had slacked off on her post. She and
Cricket stood near the window watching the drama un-
fold. No one answered Kori's question.

"I repeat," Kori screamed, louder than before, "is

this man a maid or does he work for an advertising agency?"

"Well, that depends on who you talk to!" a voice entering the room answered.

At the sound of the familiar voice, Clarke looked toward the door. His heart took a nosedive when he saw Kelsa stroll into the room with Michelle and Menesha in tow.

Persha

"Who the hell are you?" Kori asked, glancing in Kelsa's direction.

With one look, Kelsa dismissed her. After making her dramatic entrance and answering Kori's original question, she stood there poised, like the winner in the Ms. America pageant. After a brief second, Kelsa pointed at her own chest and said, "Me? I'm wifey. But then again, I'll bet your girl knew that!" she spat.

"Lawd have mercy!" Paula cried.

Menesha and Michelle high-fived each other, then Kelsa.

With pain from her stitches burning like an out-of-control wildfire, Persha still managed to inch her body into an upright position. At the sight of Kelsa, she wanted desperately to get up out of that bed and walk over to physically claim what was hers. She hoped the woman wasn't there to try and get Clarke back.

"Why are you even here? It's over between you two. You can't have him back," Persha cried, before she could think better of the comment.

Persha was struck by Kelsa's beauty. There wasn't any one thing that stood out more about her, except maybe her brilliant hazel eyes that seem to light up the room. She was dressed in a tailored navy suit, her hair freshly done, and her body was thin, but shapely. She oozed confidence.

How could she not be good enough for him? Persha wondered. Persha winced at the pain, determined to appear half as confident as Kelsa looked. She fought the urge to break down. Why wasn't Clarke speaking up? Why hadn't he thrown Kelsa out of the room? And what was she doing there in the first place?

"As I stated before, it really does depend on whom you talk to about good ole Clarke here. See, his crafty business cards that he ordered off the internet himself would lead you to believe he's the vice president of some huge ad agency here in town. But what he fails to tell most people is that, ad stands for artistically domestic," Kelsa said as Menesha reached up and gave her a high five again.

"Read 'em girlfriend," Menesha said.

"And for those of you who are slow, Artistically Domestic is a cleaning service," Kelsa continued. "You know, like Maggie Maid. So while he no longer cleans the houses of the River Oaks elite, he does clean their offices."

"Wait, hold up," Kori interjected. "You mean to tell me this boy ain't running things over at some up-and-coming advertising agency, but instead he cleans houses?"

"Houses and office spaces. He has been promoted. He is talented after all." Kelsa snickered, looking at Clarke.

"So it never really surprises me when some little silly trick sees the card, the car that I helped buy, the jewelry that I bought, and thinks she's struck it big with a real baller. I'm used to it. But I know what's really popping."

"I know you not talking about my baby, calling her a silly trick," Paula snapped.

Kelsa's stare quickly turned to Paula. "Well, let's see. If she's the same woman who moved into the spare bedroom of the house I pay the mortgage for, at the urging of my husband, while I was working hard to maintain our lifestyle; the one who snuck in and out of my bed sometimes while the sheets were still warm from my own damn body; the same one who was caught buck naked, sucking my husband's dick in the middle of my living room like the place and his dick were hers, then she is the silly trick ho' I'm talking about," Kelsa said with no shame.

"Emph Emph emph," Menesha added.

With her mouth dropped wide open and a hand over her chest, Paula stumbled back into her chair. When she looked at her daughter, her eyes were filled with tears.

"Is this true?" Paula managed to ask Persha.

Persha cut her stare away from her mother. She was struggling not to break down. How could she? How could Kelsa walk up in this room and turn her world upside down like that? Where was her mercy?

"Girl, speak up when your mama's talking to you," Kelsa urged with a smirk on her face.

Michelle snickered.

Persha rolled her eyes at Kelsa and Michelle. This wasn't supposed to happen. And right in front of her sanctified mother. If she could, she'd take Paula into her arms and say just how sorry she was for letting her down. She could only imagine the pain and shame her mother was feeling.

"Okay," Kelsa said as she shifted her weight to one

side and used her hands to express her words. "Since the cat got her tongue, let me answer that for you. Yes! It is true. All of it."

Paula turned to Persha and just shook her head.

"Girl, you didn't tell your mama how lover boy here ran to save his own skin when I turned that gun on him?" Kelsa directed at Persha. "How he left you outside naked running down the street, or how he left you sitting up in jail after all that mess?" Kelsa sucked her teeth. "Well, quite surely you told her how he pimp-slapped your ass down to the ground at the gas station about a month or so ago. Well, shoot, you were pregnant then, right?" She turned to Clarke. "Yeah, I saw your ass. Saw the entire thing. Boy, if that was me, your ass would be six feet under right now!" Turning back to Persha, she said, "Well, I guess I wouldn't want my mama to know that kind of stuff about me either." She tisked, "Shame on you, girlfriend. Shame, shame shame!" Kelsa shook her head.

Visibly shaken, Paula stretched out her arm. "Please stop it! I can't take it anymore," Paula cried. "I don't want to hear this mess. It ain't nothing but the devil. Pure devil at work." She used both hands to cover her ears and started crying.

Cricket walked to the bathroom and came back with tissue. "Are you okay?" she asked as she gave Paula the wad of toilet paper.

In between sobs, Paula nodded, but didn't say another word. She accepted the tissue.

Persha looked at Kelsa and said, "Okay, you've done enough. Can you leave now? I hope you feel good about upsetting my mother."

Extending one finger, Kelsa stepped closer to the bed and replied, "Oh, baby, I'm far from done. After I take this maid for everything he's got, which ain't much, I'm bringing you and his lover boy over there down right along with him. When you fuck another woman's husband, you should expect to pay the price!" She looked at Antwone. "And that goes for you too. While this one ain't got nothing more than the shirt on his back, I know you stand to lose a lot. I sure hope the booty was worth it." Persha's eyes bulged. Kelsa looked between Persha and Clarke. She snickered. "Oh, girl! Don't even tell me you didn't know! Yeah, I was like that at first too when I found out. Yeah, Michelle has the proof, trust. It's true, Clarke here likes boys too. Isn't that right, Michelle?"

Antwone's wife looked at her husband and shook her head. "I was such a fool for you," Michelle said to Antwone. "I had no idea. And who knows just how long this has been going on?"

Finding all of this too hard to swallow, Persha closed her eyes. "Clarke, you're gay?" she asked, her shaky voice barely above a whisper.

"Hell-nah. We ain't gay!" Clarke and Antwone snapped in unison.

Persha looked at the two handsome men standing in front of her. How could she have known? There were no signs, or maybe there were but she chose to ignore them.

Clarke stepped forward. "Persha, we're not gay. They got it all wrong," he pleaded. "Kelsa's hurt. She's trying to say whatever she can to make you leave me."

"Oh, no you didn't!" Kelsa screamed. "Don't make me pull out the pictures," she threatened.

"We're not gay!" Antwone insisted.

"Well, I've got a tape that says otherwise," Michelle threw in. With confusion on his face, Antwone shook his head and asked, "What are you talking about?"

"Well, let's just say I've always looked out for my best interests. I put a security camera up in the carriage house," Michelle said. "I'll admit when I did it at first, it was because I wanted to make sure no other woman was gonna be all up in my house. But never did I suspect I had to worry about another man! What do they call it, brothas on the DL?" She shook her head in disgust. "Oh, it's been up and running, taping everything you two did back there. I finally got the heart to look at it after Kelsa told me what Clarke had done right under her own damn nose!"

"Girl, wasn't that some skank shit?" Menesha added.

Antwone was speechless. Clarke looked sorrowful.

"We're not gay," Antwone insisted. And as if to prove his point, Antwone offered, "You've never seen us actually having sex, have you? Think about it. Check all the tapes you want. We were never humping each other." He turned to Clarke. "Were we?"

"I don't hump men!" Clarke insisted.

Kelsa threw her hands into the air and said, "Well, damn, okay. So we're getting technical here. If you only give each other head, you're not really gay? Phhuuuleeeese! Get real!" Kelsa looked at Persha. "He's all yours, girlfriend. And I really hope he's worth it because all three of you," she pointed her finger at Persha, Antwone, and Clarke, "You will be real sorry by the time I'm through taking each of you for every worthless thing you have. I'll make all of you sorry you ever crossed me."

As if on cue, Kelsa and her friends turned and sauntered out of Persha's hospital room.

"Ah, Persha?" Clarke said as he eased up to her bed, which was the closest he'd gotten since arriving at the hospital.

Her eyes narrowed as she looked at him. She didn't feel the urge to cry. The strength she had prayed for to deal with this situation had finally arrived.

Before he could say anything else, she cut him off.

"I don't care whether you're gay," Persha said. "I

don't care what you did or did not do with Antwone or anyone else. I love you."

Paula gasped. Cricket threw her hands up and Kori frowned. Persha briefly looked in their direction and then turned back to address Clarke.

"But loving you has caused me so much pain, misery, and shame I don't know if I'm coming or going," Persha stated. "I don't know who I am anymore. You've sucked up every inch of self-respect, self-confidence, and even self-pride I've had. I'm exausted. I don't have anything else to give you."

"But Persha," Clarke cried.

She shook her head. "No, I need to finish this. The thought of being with you is no longer soothing to my soul. I don't know who or even what I've become. Again, you took me through this once before, and like a fool longing for pain and abuse, I walked right back into your trap. I'm tired. And I have to be strong for that beautiful little boy of ours. I want you—" she put up a finger—"no actually, I need you to leave. Right now!" Clarke stood there for a few minutes. "I mean it, and take him with you!" She nodded toward Antwone.

As they walked toward the door, Kori, Cricket and Paula stood and started clapping.

"You'll be just fine, baby," Paula said.

When Clarke extended his arm to reach for the handle, the door swung open, pushing him back and nearly into Antwone. Clarke Sr. stepped in.

"Sorry, son, I was held up on a business call," Clarke Sr. said.

At the sound of the loud gasp, everyone turned toward Paula. She went still. "Sweet Jesus! Be still my heart," she uttered before collapsing to the floor like a lifeless doll.

* * *

When Clarke saw Persha's mother sprawled out on the floor like that, his first instinct was to break out into laughter. *That's what the old hag gets,* he thought. He tapped his father on his shoulder.

"C'mon, Pops, let's get outta here!" Clarke said as he turned, ready to leave.

"Boy, are you crazy? We're not leaving!" Clarke Sr. said. "This woman could need help." He rushed over to where Paula was lying on the floor.

When he finally was able to look down on the floor, he jumped back. "Shit!" he screamed, clutching his chest as he feverishly tried to make his way to the door.

"Pop! Wait, man, whassup? What's wrong?" Clarke said as he ran to catch up with his father.

Down the hall, near the bank of elevators, Clarke Sr. moved, pacing back and forth. "I've got to get out of here!" he said.

"Whoa! Pop, slow down, man. What's going on? What happened back there?"

Still pacing back and forth, Clarke Sr. took his stare up to the numbers atop the elevator doors. It was like he never heard his son. Unsure of what to do, Clarke stood there trying to figure out what went wrong in the room. He went over it again and again in his mind. By now Antwone caught up with them.

"Is everything okay?" he asked, still holding the papers in his hands. He knew they'd never get to the conversation he and Clarke needed to have.

"Pop! Man, talk to me," Clarke demanded.

Just when the elevator cab pulled up, Clarke Sr. turned to Clarke. He held the door open then said, "You don't understand. That woman back there . . . that's the one I was telling you about earlier. We had an affair years ago. I didn't think I'd ever see her again."

"Yeah, but man, that's water under the bridge. You

even told me yourself. You said you cut things off and you never saw her again."

"Son, I never saw her again, but I didn't tell you that when I met with her that final time to say I was choosing you and your mother, she confessed to me that she was pregnant. Then about a year later, she sends this letter, giving me an update about her daughter. I burned that letter, hoping, thinking it wasn't my problem. Messing around with Paula had caused me much more than I wanted to think about. But the point is, I never tried to find out. When your mother took me back, I just wanted to move on with my life. We moved and I never saw her, nor heard from her again."

Clarke moved back! "Wait man!" His head started pounding and spinning at the same time. "What are you trying to tell me? What are you saying?"

"All I'm saying right now is, I need some air. I need to get out of here and breathe."

With horror plastered across his face, Clarke looked toward the room down the hall, then back at his father standing inside the elevator. *What the fuck! What the hell?* he thought. This made no sense to him. Turning back toward the room, he stood there. When the elevator bell rang, Clarke turned back to see the doors closing. Before the doors closed, he saw tears running down his father's cheeks.

Antwone put his arm on Clarke's shoulder and said, "You all right, man?" he asked Clarke. "Let's get out of here."

Clarke pulled himself away. "Do you know what this means?" he asked Antwone.

Antwone answered by nodding. "That's why I'm saying we need to get out of here. You need some air too."

"You mean to tell me that all this time I've been fucking my own damn sister? And now, now we have this child together?" He slammed his fist into the wall, turning every nearby head.

Consequences

Moments after Paula came to and was helped up off the floor, she was still trying to catch her breath. She knew her day had come. Suddenly the room felt as though it was closing in on her.

"Ma! You had me so scared," Persha said. "What was that all about? One minute you guys are cheering on my courage, the next we're calling a nurse for you."

Paula walked up to Persha's bed. Looking down at her daughter, she struggled to steady her voice. She trembled as she spoke.

"I have so much to tell you. I don't even know where to start," Paula said, swallowing back tears.

Unsure if she really wanted to hear another dark secret, Persha closed her eyes. When she opened them, she looked at her mother and struggled to remember a time when she'd ever seen her so distraught.

"Whatever it is, Ma, can we just make it short and sweet; Do you really think I can handle another thing, considering all I've already been through today?"

"I know, I know, and this is my fault. I needed to tell you this so very long ago, baby. And as God is my witness, the only reason I did what I did was to protect you. I didn't want you to go through what I had been through. I only wanted better for you."

Persha sighed. "What is it, Ma? I'm sure it can't be any worse than what I've already heard."

Paula looked down at the sheet. "Well, that man, Clarke Hudson Sr., he's your father. I know I told you your father was dead, but I lied. I lied, baby. It's just that simple."

With her face twisted and frowning, Persha started to cry. She began clutching toward her stomach and grabbing the sheet and her gown.

"OMIGOD! What?" She felt the bile moving around in the pit of her sore belly.

"When I heard him refer to Clarke as *son*, I don't know what happened, I lost it." Paula started crying. "I'm so sorry. If I had a thousand tongues, I wouldn't be able to say those words enough to you. I've ruined your life," she sobbed.

The cold stare across Persha's face lingered as her mother cried. She didn't know why she was being punished. Of all the gay men, in the city of Houston, with a population of more than four million people to be exact, why did she have to run into her own damn brother? This started way back in Arizona. How could the sickness have followed her here?

Persha shook her head, with snot running from her nose and her eyes burning from the tears that wouldn't stop rolling, she sat defeated and slumping.

Cricket and Kori rushed to her bedside.

"Persha, this is not your fault! How could you have known? You can't blame yourself," Cricket said.

Kori didn't say anything. She stood there hoping her presence showed just how much she really cared. She didn't know what she could possibly say.

Cricket turned to Paula. "It seems like you two have

tons to talk about. We're going to step outside. Maybe we'll see the doctor and ask about the baby."

Putting her hand up to her mouth as the word *baby* spilled from her lips, Cricket quickly left the room. Kori couldn't move. She was so sickened by the mere thought that Persha had slept with her own brother and didn't even know it. Soon, she ducked out too.

Alone in the room with her daughter, Paula didn't know if she should try to explain or allow the horrid mess to sink in.

"What can I do?" Paula mumbled. "You tell me and I'll fix this. What can I do?"

Still . . . nothing from Persha.

Suddenly, Clarke burst back into the room.

"We tried to stop him," Cricket said, standing at the door behind him.

"How could you let some shit like this happen?" Clarke tossed his words toward Paula. "This is some sick and twisted shit!"

"I don't know what to say," Paula countered.

"What else is there for you to say?" Clarke said. "I guess that means it's true. You're the ho who fucked my father and tried to tear up my folks' marriage."

Still crying, Paula barely blinked at his insults. There was nothing he could say to her that she hadn't already said to herself. She was embarrassed, felt like a hypocrite and any other demeaning words she could think of.

"Your verbal abuse isn't helping this situation," Persha finally found her voice to say. She focused in on Clarke. "I don't know what to tell you. I don't know how we're gonna get through this, but attacking my mother isn't helping. Why don't you leave?" She didn't have any more tears left. Her heart felt heavy and tired.

"You're so stupid," he spat at Persha. "I didn't want you to begin with. When you saw my father, why didn't you put two and two together? My pops told me all about your mother. How she couldn't keep her hands off him, she wouldn't leave him alone. First his brother, then when that didn't work, she zeroed in on my pops. Even after he told her that he wanted us! He wanted his family, not you!" He was in Paula's face, pointing at her. "But no! That wasn't good enough for you! You stalked him, even followed him to the city we lived in and still kept calling. What's wrong with women like you? Why can't you just keep your fucking legs closed?"

Paula reached up and slapped Clarke's face. "You have no right," she cried. "You don't know me or anything about me. I didn't put a gun to your father's head!"

"And not only that, but how dare you judge her? You cheated on your wife just like your father," Persha jumped in. "Get out of here! I need to talk to my mother and I really don't want to see you right now."

Looking back as he walked to the door, Clarke's face was wet with tears. He opened the door and walked out and Cricket followed.

Once alone again, Persha sniffled back her tears. She didn't know what to say to her mother, but she knew she didn't need to sit there and hear Clarke cut her down like that.

"I guess the part that bugs me the most is how you never told me what you did," Persha said. "I honestly believed you never had sex until you were married. I can't remember a time when you weren't this super-religious person I've known all my life. There were times you made me feel so dirty, so ashamed of being your daughter because I wasn't good enough; like I wasn't worthy. Now you're telling me that you made the very same mistakes?" Persha shook her head, denying her own words. "You're no better than me! Is that what you're trying to tell me?" She was disappointed with her mother.

"I should've said something sooner," Paula said. "But each time I tried, for some reason, I'd talk myself out of it. I know it was wrong, but I've prayed about it and I am so very sorry."

Persha looked up at her mother through swollen eyes. "Sorry? Where's your God now, Ma? What loving God would allow something like this to happen? So many times you've questioned my faith? But what about yours? Can you use your sanctified imagination and tell me how your precious savior could've allowed something this sickening to happen?"

Clarke

Two months after Clarke and Kelsa's divorce was finalized, Clarke was planning to go back to court to ask for a reduction in his mandatory payments to Kelsa. Those payments weren't alimony, but something similar. He lost heavily during the battle in spite of the attorney Clarke Sr. had secured for him.

He was recently promoted at his job. While he's still not the vice president, in his new position he is responsible for all of the horticultural needs of his company's upscale clients in the River Oaks and Highland village parts of Houston.

With his promotion, he was able to move to North Houston and hasn't seen Persha in more than a year.

He and his father visit regularly but have vowed never to mention the names of the two women who'd forever changed their lives. They'd decided what happened was best left forgotten and agreed to take their unbelievable stories to their graves. Both now take women through a series of carefully crafted questions about family history before progressing to the second date.

Antwone was so upset over all he lost in his divorce, he stopped talking to Clarke immediately afterwards. He cringes when he thinks about how any judge could allow a frivolous lawsuit like Kelsa's to go forward. He's expected to see the entire gang again at the deposition.

Persha

Persha and Clarke's baby survived for three days. He weighed less than three pounds and his lungs never fully developed. After making several unsuccessful attempts to reach him about the baby, she and her mother decided it was best to have the infant cremated.

Persha, Paula, Cricket, and Kori all agreed they'd never speak of the unusual story again. They also made a pact to always thoroughly research any future love interest before making a commitment.

Immediately following her baby's cremation, Persha flew back to California with her mother. Their relationship hasn't fully recovered, but both are praying about it and are looking forward to becoming even closer with all their secrets now out in the open.

When Persha returned, she learned that her insurance company had fixed the mix-up and finally agreed to pay for her condo. At her attorney's urging, she bought her new condo in her mother's name to avoid it being taken away in any pending litigation.

Cricket's aunt passed away, leaving her entire estate to Cricket in appreciation for her continued love and support. Upon finding out the sum of that estate, well over one million dollars, Cricket sprung for an all-inclusive, all-expenses paid, round trip for three to Jamaica.

While packing for that trip, Persha fantasized about possibly staying there until her eye caught a glimpse of the lawsuit. She was dreading the deposition herself, and was hoping the suit would've been thrown out.

An attorney jokingly told her this case was a new trend in new-age divorce and that he only knew of one other similar case. He was still researching to find the outcome in hopes of being able to properly defend her against the charges. To Persha's knowledge, Kelsa never found out about her relation to Clarke and she hoped to keep it that way.